Reviews for *Beneath the Surface*

"The book is mesmerizing! From the very beginning Lenz ensnares the reader with her narrative hook. As a reader, you feel like you are on the edge, trying to make sense of the protagonist's bizarre set of circumstances. Lenz keeps the reader mystified and guessing up to the climatic end. With every word written, Beneath the Surface pulls at your heart and challenges your soul. It takes you into the world of delusion and reality, and keeps you wondering which one is the truth." - Cheryl E. Rodriguez for *Readers' Favorite*

"Beneath the Surface by Heather Nadine Lenz is an intriguing story set in the beautiful city of Zürich, Switzerland, which gives us some wonderful descriptions of the country. Readers will find themselves getting more curious page after page, wondering which reality is truly Natalia's. As the mystery unravels, links appear between characters and strands of the narrative in a satisfying way. Simply put, Beneath the Surface is a solid debut from Lenz and I enjoyed it." -Lit Amri for *Readers' Favorite*

"Lenz's prose is meticulously crafted such that the reader, like the author's main protagonist, is kept off kilter throughout the story. Certainly, Beneath the Surface is an entertaining read but as much as it is entertaining, it also underscores the fact that our subconscious mind is influential in ways that we cannot even begin to fathom." -Marta Tandori for *Readers' Favorite*

Beneath
the Surface

HEATHER NADINE LENZ

Plum Tree Press

UNITED STATES

www.heathernadinelenz.com

Plum Tree Press

Published by Plum Tree Press

First Edition September 2015

Beneath the Surface is a work of fiction. Names, characters and incidents are either the
product of the author's imagination or are used fictitiously. Any resemblance to actual
persons, living, or dead, or events is entirely coincidental.

e Book ISBN-978-0-692-54561-4

Book ISBN-978-0-692-56144-7

Printed in the United States of America

To my daughter Isabelle

Beneath
the Surface

Awaken to Me

Chapter 1

A LIGHT PIERCED NATALIA'S EYES and she closed them against the brightness.

"Wake up, Natalia! Your children are here," called a familiar voice.

Natalia tried to open her eyes; she tried to answer, but she was just so tired. Her entire body heavy with exhaustion, she felt herself drifting away, slipping back into sleep, until she heard her children. They were all crying. She needed to go to them. In a panic she tried to sit up, but someone was holding her back.

"Let me go," she screamed, but no one answered.

The brilliant light was gone and she was in darkness. She couldn't see anything, nor could she hear her children any longer. All at once she felt pain flash through her entire body and explode in her head. She felt her limbs go weak and she fell, slipping and falling, as her scream was swallowed up in the void around her.

With a sharp intake of breath Natalia opened her eyes, sitting straight up in bed, all her senses heightened. She could hear children playing downstairs. She felt the silkiness of her duvet cover. Surveying the way the light hit the blue vase of pink roses next to her bed, Natalia smiled at the smell of freshly baked bread wafting up from the kitchen.

"Good morning, love," said a ruggedly attractive man with tousled dirty-blond hair, green eyes, and an extremely muscular physique while walking into the room.

"I thought I heard you scream, are you okay?" Sitting down next to her on the bed, he placed a cup of coffee on her nightstand and smoothed the hair back from her face. "Were you having a nightmare?" he asked.

"Evan," said Natalia. "What are you doing here so early?"

"It's time for you to get up, love, the kids and I have been awake for hours and we are ready to start the day's agenda. Here's a cup of coffee to get you going," he said, motioning toward the cup. "Drink it while it's hot."

Falling back against the pillows, Natalia asked again, "What are you doing here so early?"

Evan frowned. "It isn't early. We've all been awake for hours. It's time for you to get up too. See you downstairs, dressed and ready to go in fifteen minutes, yeah?" he said on his way out of the room.

Natalia felt she would give anything to fall back asleep, even for a few more minutes. Her entire body ached with exhaustion. But what was Evan doing at her house? Concentrating didn't help. She couldn't remember why he would be at her house so early in the morning and where they were going together.

In fact, she couldn't remember what day it was. Or what she had done yesterday, or the day before that. In fact, she was having trouble recollecting the entire past week. Natalia shook her head. *Coffee will help*, she reasoned. *I'm just not awake yet, and sleep deprivation can cause havoc with memory.*

Natalia counted to three and jumped out of bed all at once, quickly dressing in an aquamarine dress. Twisting her red hair up and pinning it expertly on autopilot, she took three more minutes to efficiently add some makeup to her face, grimacing at the sight of her normally bright blue eyes, now bloodshot. Why did she look and feel so terrible this morning? Where had she been the night before? Natalia, frowning, realized she still couldn't remember.

Wandering barefoot down the stairs and toward the kitchen, Natalia paused when she heard children playing. She didn't recognize the voices. With a knitted brow, she walked into the family room.

Three little faces looked up at her.

"Who are you?" she asked. "Where are my kids?"

"What do you mean, Mommy?" asked the little girl, pausing in her play and tilting her head to one side. "We're right here."

"Very funny, sweetheart," Natalia replied while admiring the pretty little girl's curly blond hair and bright blue eyes.

"Where are my children? Do I know you? Are you new neighbors?"

One of the boys stood up. "Mom, tell Nathan it's my turn to play the game."

"No!" screamed a boy identical to the first, pushing his brother. "Mom, Nick played the game the entire morning. It's my turn!"

Natalia turned and looked behind her. Was their mother here? What were these strangers doing in her house?

"What's going on?" Natalia wondered out loud. "Where are Anna, Allan, and Ben?"

"Who are they, Mom?" asked the girl on the floor, without looking up from the Lego tower she was building.

The breath caught in Natalia's throat. Her heart began hammering louder and louder as the room began to spin faster and faster.

Grabbing onto the nearby cheery wood desk to keep from falling, Natalia asked, "Why are you calling me Mom?"

The two boys, whom she could now see were identical twins, had bright blue eyes and pale blond hair just like their sister. Both came and hugged her around the waist.

"Mom, I don't want to go swimming, I want to go to the zoo," declared one of the twins.

The little girl jumped up from the floor. "The zoo? Me! Me too!"

"I want to go swimming. Dad promised we could go! Don't listen to them, Mom. Mom! Mom?"

"Are you okay, Mom?"

Natalia's hand was still clutching the desk, and looking down, she noticed her fingers turning white from her grip. She was swaying a bit from side to side; the room was beginning to spin.

She heard a voice down the hall say, "Hey, honey, I thought we should go swimming with the kids this morning at La Meer. I know you love that warm salt-water pool and perhaps I could go to the sauna while you take the kids down the slides? We could eat lunch in the café. Natalia? Natalia, where are you?"

Evan entered the room and examined Natalia closely before kissing her lightly on the lips.

"Are you okay, Natalia? Your face looks a little white."

Natalia could hardly believe Evan had just walked into the room and kissed her in front of these kids. What on earth was he doing? And who were these children in her house anyway? Natalia inspected the children more carefully. She noticed the boys had blond hair exactly like the little girl. Three pairs of bright blue eyes looked up at her.

"I need to talk to you alone," said Natalia.

"What, why?" asked Evan.

Natalia didn't answer. She had already gone into the kitchen and was looking out the floor-length windows into the garden.

"Okay, my little bunnies," said Evan, "you are allowed to watch one cartoon and then we are leaving for swimming. No, we are not going to the zoo today, but after the swimming we can go out to lunch in the cafeteria."

As the boys and little girl happily cuddled together onto the couch to watch a DVD, Natalia began searching the entire ground floor, then made her way upstairs and was glancing in each bedroom in search of her children. Evan found her looking into the children's bathroom. Wordlessly he took her by the hand and led her down the hall to the master suite. She felt so bone tired. All she wanted was to find her children and have them climb back into bed with her. They could cuddle up and she would read books to them for the next hour. But where were they?

Suddenly, thoughts of her children swept out of her mind. She stood there, suddenly frozen, watching as Evan relaxed back onto her bed. What was he doing? She could hear the children's voices rise in argument from downstairs, debating which episode to select, and then an irritated boy's voice admonishing his younger sister for taking up too much space on the couch. Then silence fell over the house.

"I can take our kids up swimming alone if you're not feeling well," Evan offered, relaxing back on his elbows and splaying out his legs in front of him.

"Oh. Well, that is really sweet, Evan. But I don't even know where my children are. Let's go find them," answered Natalia as she turned to leave the room.

"What are you talking about?" asked Evan. "We just left our kids watching cartoons downstairs."

Natalia recoiled in surprise. Did he say *our kids*? No, Natalia decided she must have misheard him. And yes, she did think it inappropriate of Evan to be so at ease in her room, lying back on her and James' bed. Even if she did adore Evan and he was her best friend, he was still Eva's husband. She knew James would be less than thrilled to come home and find Evan in their bedroom.

Then again, what was Evan thinking leading her into the master suite instead of back downstairs into the living room in the first place? Natalia imagined James leading Eva into her bedroom. She didn't like that thought at all.

"Did you hear me, Evan?" asked Natalia, stepping up to him.

"Let's go back downstairs. Where is Eva anyway?" she asked. "Where are my kids? Where are your kids, while we're at it?"

"I have no idea where Eva is. Why would I know where Eva is? And our kids are happily engaged for a few moments, so…"

Evan reached forward and pulled Natalia onto his lap. Natalia gave a shout of surprise and clumsily freed herself from Evan's embrace.

"What are you doing, Evan? What on earth are you thinking?"

"What do mean? Oh."

Something seemed to occur to him. He stripped off his shirt, revealing a sharply defined stomach and muscular arms. Taking off his jeans, Evan went to the bedroom door, firmly shutting and locking it behind him. Natalia watched, mouth open in shock.

This is a dream, Natalia, she told herself, *just like the one before. Any moment you are going to wake up and snuggle up next to your husband, feeling just a bit guilty for dreaming about your best friend.*

Evan walked back to her and leaned in again for a kiss. Natalia took at step back, knocking over her vase of flowers.

"Evan, no. What, are you crazy? What has gotten into you?"

Natalia turned and began gathering the flowers back into the vase. "Can you hand me a towel to mop up this mess?" Natalia asked.

"Leave that for now," whispered Evan, reaching out and pulling her to him. "And don't worry about our kids; they are watching something educational for a few minutes."

"Our kids? Are your children and my children down there watching now too? Who are those other children in my family room anyway? When did they get here? Oh, I'm going to go call James," sighed Natalia, heading toward the bedroom door.

Evan blocked her way. Reaching out, he took hold of Natalia by the shoulders and considered her a moment, head cocked to the side. Then, giving a forced laugh, he released Natalia and sat on her bed once again.

"What is this? Are you trying to make me jealous or something? I know you've always had a crush on the almighty James," said Evan. "I didn't think you were in regular contact with each other."

"Of course I am in regular contact with him, and I certainly think we are beyond the crush stage. And why would I try to make you jealous of James? That is ridiculous. Listen, Evan," said Natalia, "let me use your phone, okay?"

Not taking his eyes off her, Evan handed Natalia his cell phone and Natalia dialed James' number.

"Hello?"

Natalia felt her entire body relax at the sound of James' voice. Of course she had been overreacting, she thought. Her children were off somewhere with James. Evan, the eternal prankster, was playing a practical joke on her. He would probably be telling this story at every cocktail party they all went to for the next ten years.

"Hi, love, listen, where are you, Anna, Allan, and Ben?" asked Natalia, smiling. Natalia glanced at Evan while sitting down on the bed beside him. He was glaring at her. Smiling back at him, Natalia punched him playfully on the shoulder.

"Natalia, is that you?" asked James, sounding bewildered.

"Yes. Hello, James. I am here with Evan. Where are you? Are the kids with you?"

"The kids are all out shopping with Eva. Listen, can I talk to you tomorrow? I've got to go. I am meeting Eva, the kids, and my parents for brunch downtown in ten minutes and I still need to jump in the shower; I'm going to be so late. But I am looking forward to seeing you at your office tomorrow. Until then, darling!"

Natalia's heart was racing again. She felt cold, as if she had been standing for hours in a freezing wind. Without thinking she climbed under her duvet and pulled the covers up to her chin. She just couldn't make sense of what was going on. Why were her children shopping with Eva? Why was James meeting Eva, the children, and his parents for brunch? If this was some kind of practical joke James and her friends were playing on her, well, it was going to end now.

"Okay. This isn't funny anymore, Evan. I want to know what is going on," said Natalia.

"Natalia, listen. I agree it isn't funny anymore. Our kids are downstairs. You just saw them. And don't even think about it; Eva's kids are not coming over. I am not up for six kids in my house this weekend," sighed Evan. He started fidgeting with his watch, and then he looked into her eyes as he continued to speak.

"And what is the deal with you calling James 'love'? Are you just trying to start a fight with me this morning or what? That's what we call one another; it's our thing. How would you feel if I called Eva 'love'? I know James has always called you darling. That guy better watch himself. He is continually overstepping." Evan pressed his lips into a thin line, and Natalia could see the muscles in his shoulders and neck tensing.

"Evan, you are not making any sense," began Natalia.

"I got up with the kids early this morning, baked bread, fed them breakfast, cleaned the kitchen, and played three rounds of a racing rabbit board game with them while my wife slept peacefully on in our bed," interrupted Evan.

Frowning, he glanced at his watch. "Look," he said, motioning at his watch, "it's almost nine thirty. I have been up with the kids for over three hours while you lay sleeping. And here you are now, calling James 'love.' It is too much, Natalia. Every day, five days a week, you leave before the kids wake up in the morning and come home after they are in bed. I do all the housework, all the parenting, and spend my evenings preparing for school and correcting tests and homework. But I make an effort to find time to organize romantic nights together on top of everything else. Only, you almost always cancel on me. Why do I keep trying so hard? Nice guys come in last, even after they get married. You don't deserve me as your husband," said Evan, crossing his arms over his chest.

Natalia watched Evan's expression out of the corner of her eye. Her entire body was shaking, ever so slightly, and her eyes were wide while her hands continued to clutch and unclench the top of the duvet. Natalia wondered if Evan was having a mental break.

"You are not my husband Evan," she said.

Evan stood up abruptly and stared at her open-mouthed.

"What?"

"You heard me," said Natalia.

"Well, I mean, I know we have been fighting quite a bit lately," said Evan, running his fingers through his hair and beginning to pace back and forth.

"Really for years now, and all right, yes, I have been very bitter and even mean to you in the past few months," he admitted.

"What are you talking about?" Natalia interrupted. "No, you haven't. You are so good to me, Evan. Really, I couldn't ask for a better friend. I appreciate you so much. I just don't think this joke is funny anymore. Game over. You have totally confounded me; you win."

Evan stared at her. "Natalia, you can't just say 'this isn't funny anymore' and walk away from your husband and children. That isn't what you are really saying, is it? Natalia?"

Evan paused, looking at her intently. "You, you are not really asking for a, for a divorce?" he stammered.

"What?" asked Natalia, sitting up in bed.

"No," breathed out Evan, reaching out and taking her hand. "No, of course not. I know I may sometimes be unhappy and unload all of my stress and bitterness on you and sometimes I have been downright mean. I am sorry. I never want to lose you. Can you forgive me?"

Natalia took Evan by the other hand, looking into his eyes.

"Oh, Evan, you have never been mean to me. On the contrary, you have been a brilliant friend. And I understand that you need to vent sometimes, really. I vent to you too. That is part of being a good friend: listening when someone you love is upset, acknowledging their feelings, telling them they have a right to feel whatever they are feeling, and telling them the truth, no matter how hard it is to hear. You are so good at that, Evan, which is really so rare, I'm telling you. And we also always share our good news and happiness with one another. It isn't all just bitterness and complaining."

Running his arms slowly up and down her bare arms, Evan said, "You must be exhausted from working ten-, twelve-hour days all week. Hey, there have been times when I myself have wanted to disown you and our kids out of sheer exhaustion. Life can get overwhelming. I don't want you burning out, or falling into a depression or something. I'm taking the kids swimming. You can go back to sleep and take a bath, or do some kick boxing to vent. Whatever you want. Even if it would be nice for you to do some of the gardening or housework for a change, though we both know you won't end up doing that."

"What do you mean, our kids? Evan, I mean it. Knock it off. You're going to take my kids swimming?" asked Natalia.

Sighing, Evan nodded and went to reach for his clothes, but then turned back, reached out, and gathered her in his arms and held her for several long moments.

"I spend too much time angry. I would never want to lose you, do you hear? We have shared so much together. I love you," he said softly and kissed her on the forehead.

"What?" asked Natalia. "You love me?"

Natalia felt breathless; her heart was racing. Evan was close enough that she could smell the fresh scent of his shampoo, the clean fragrance of his aftershave. She had hugged Evan more times than she could count. This was different. They weren't giving each other a quick squeeze and letting go. Evan was holding her in his arms, smiling down at her, his strong arms still wrapped around her. It felt electrifying. It felt wrong. Her friend's husband was holding her close to his bare chest.

Evan brought his hands to her face, gently tracing his fingers along her jaw line. He had let her go. She could have taken a step back. But she didn't.

His eyes shining, softening, he smiled. She lifted her chin, gazing up at him, parting her lips. Evan leaned in and kissed her. His lips were so soft, and then his arms were once again encircling her, pulling her even closer to him. Running her fingertips slowly up and down, Natalia felt the muscles in Evan's back.

Warmth flooding through her body, Natalia returned his kiss, her anger and confusion at the strangeness of the morning fading away.

Evan's kiss turned angry, searching, devouring. She felt lightheaded. As she pushed her hands into his hair, the hair on the nape of her neck rose, tingling, as Evan's hands began gliding over her body. Natalia felt the heat rise in her cheeks and wondered at how different a kiss could be. Why didn't James kiss her like this? James! Natalia pushed Evan away, shaking her head.

She hadn't kissed anyone but James in eleven years. But when was the last time James had really kissed her? Had he ever kissed her with hunger like that? She couldn't remember.

"No, Evan. Just go," whispered Natalia. "I need time to think."

The world was spinning. Natalia watched as Evan stood, frozen in surprise for a moment, before he angrily threw on his clothes and left the room. Natalia lay in bed, her thoughts reeling. An image of Evan standing in his underwear in front of her, the remembrance of the heat of his lips on hers, caused Natalia to hide her face, burrowing it under the covers. What had she done? She needed to talk with James and confess everything right away. Or did she? Should she tell him?

More important still, how could Evan take the kids swimming if James was out to brunch with the children, his parents, and Eva? What was going on? Where was James this morning anyway, at the gym? Why had Evan been at her house so early, and on further thought, where were Evan and Eva's kids this morning? Were they at brunch too? And who were those other children in her family room this morning?

Furrowing her brow, Natalia thought back on her conversation with James. Why had he said that he would see her at her office tomorrow? What office and why wouldn't she see him tonight? Sighing, Natalia decided there must be a perfectly reasonable explanation for everything.

She thought about calling her dad but reconsidered; it would be the middle of the night in Oregon.

Evan and the children made a great deal of noise downstairs putting on their shoes and exiting the house. As silence descended Natalia felt her eyes grow heavy and in a few moments, she felt herself slipping into sleep.

Castles of Sand

Chapter 2

A FEW HOURS LATER Natalia opened her eyes and slowly climbed out of bed. She looked down. She was already fully dressed in her aquamarine dress. Her eyes hurt and her hair was askew. Confused, she started to pull one bobby pin after another out of her long red hair while she walked over to the mirror over the sink in her master suite. Quickly she twisted her hair back up and replaced the bobby pins. Looking more carefully at herself in the mirror, she noted many more small lines around her eyes, and much worse, under her eyes, than she remembered. Three kids' worth of sleep deprivation had most definitely been taking a toll.

Wandering down to the kitchen, Natalia noticed the sun sparkling on the lake as she cut herself two slices of Evan's freshly baked bread, spreading butter and homemade strawberry jam on each slice. She made herself a strong Americano and let the smell of coffee wash over her. It had taken years of living in Switzerland to appreciate espresso and she now found her cup of the aromatic caffeine one of the best parts of her day.

Opening the patio door, she stepped out onto her terrace overlooking the lake and wandered aimlessly down the stone steps across the grass, her cup steaming in the chill, examining her garden and wondering when the first frost would come this year. Perhaps she should already put in her winter flowers, but then again, the geraniums and roses still had a bit of color left. Despite it being the first of November the weather remained mild and sunny. Stepping out onto their dock, she turned and looked back up at their house.

They had moved into this house for the huge garden sloping down to Lake Bodensee, with its huge willow and apple trees. It was difficult in Switzerland to find affordable properties with large gardens anymore, let alone one directly on a lake with a dock and a beach. Therefore, James had deemed it worth the hour train ride into Zürich every day to work. Even with James' partnership in the consultancy there would be no way for them to afford a property in the Zürich area even close to what they could attain an hour's train ride away. They were lucky that they had found their dream property after only two years of hunting. The house, however, had been a disaster.

Natalia had found the remodel of the extremely old house very stressful. Of course the work took twice as long as originally planned and for over two years she was living with her family in a half completed house. The entire south-facing and east-facing walls of the house had been rebuilt with floor to ceiling windows, so their home would be filled with light from morning until early evening and they would have views of the Alps in the distance as well as out over the huge lake. They had also installed a modern kitchen, designer bathrooms, and warm wood floors. But now, standing on her dock on the lake and looking back up at the garden and house, she felt it was worth all of the effort and stress they had endured.

"Guten Morgen, Natalia," she heard a cheerful voice call out.

Looking over to the next yard, Natalia saw her neighbor working in the garden.

"Good morning, Andrea," she replied with equal friendliness. Inwardly she swore. She was so tired. The dream she had had about her children disappearing was terribly upsetting. She just wanted to have a morning all to herself with no interaction whatsoever. Even from her favorite neighbor. *Maybe if I just quickly, but naturally, walk back inside.*

"How was Annabelle's first day of kindergarten?" Andrea called out with a bright smile. "Did everything go smoothly for her?"

Natalia looked at Andrea with raised eyebrows. "Excuse me, who are you talking about?" she called back.

Andrea stood up from her vegetable bed and a perplexed expression came over her friendly face. She put down her trowel and took off her gardening gloves while walking over to Natalia's garden.

She opened the fence door while repeating, "Your daughter, Annabelle, how was her first day of kindergarten?"

"You mean Allan, of course? Yes, he was very worried about his first day but he really likes his teacher."

Andrea's smile had left her face and her brow furrowed.

"Natalia, who is Allan?"

"Allan, my son? Andrea, what is wrong with you?"

"I have never heard of an Allan, dear," replied Andrea. "Is he much older than the other three? You've never talked about him before… Where are Nick, Nathan, and Annabelle this morning anyway?"

The two faced each other silently for a moment. Natalia's heart began to race, her head pounding, her hands clenching unknowingly at her side. "Who are Nick, Nathan, and Annabelle?" Natalia asked, speaking very slowly.

She could hear Andrea reiterate that she didn't know anything about a son named Allan, but that she of course did know Natalia's two six-year-old twin boys, Nick and Nathan, and her darling four-year-old little girl named Annabelle. But the voice seemed to come from very far away. She felt the world starting to spin as a wave of dizziness rolled over her. All at once Natalia felt like she was both falling and floating away. The pain in her head lessened. As the tension relaxed from her body she heard her name repeated over and over again from far away.

"Natalia? Natalia? Natalia, I am here. Don't worry, we're going to take good care of you. Natalia?"

WHEN NATALIA WOKE UP she was lying comfortably on a red chaise lounge in her living room. She looked out the floor to ceiling windows that lined the entire length of the living and dining room, giving the room a generous sense of space and filling the room with light. Natalia noted that it must be early evening, the way the sunlight was reflecting off the Alps in the distance, tinting them a bluish gray.

Natalia couldn't remember falling asleep in the living room. Why was it so quiet? Where were the kids?

Then bits and pieces of her morning floated into her awareness. Her kids should be home from their swimming trip with Evan any moment, or were they returning from their brunch with James? Or did James take the kids swimming together with Evan after brunch? Wait a minute. Natalia shook her head, placing her face in her hands, trying to focus.

The last thing she could remember was talking to Andrea down by the lake. Did she faint out in the garden? She couldn't recall making her way into the house and lying down. Just then she heard voices through the open door to the patio.

"Hello, Natalia, how are you feeling? You slept a long time."

A pretty blond-haired woman with bright blue eyes and a warm smile came in through the glass door with a tall dark-haired man. She surveyed Natalia intensely.

"How did I get inside?" asked Natalia

"You fell and hit your head, dear," Andrea replied. "Then you were so disoriented and confused that I made you lay still and went to fetch Mark. I tried to call your in-laws as well as Evan but I could not reach anyone. Mark said that there seemed to be nothing physically wrong with you. He brought over his medical bag and did a full check right after you fell in the garden. You said you were just exhausted and probably low on sugar since you hadn't eaten anything in a long time. So we just helped you into the house, I fed you some toast, and we thought we would let you sleep a bit here on the couch. If I had known you were going to sleep so long I would have helped you upstairs into bed. But Mark did recommend going in to see a doctor as soon as you can, just to be sure you are in perfect health."

Natalia was silent for a moment, trying to recall coming into the house, eating toast, or lying down on the couch. She was sure Andrea wouldn't lie to her, but she couldn't remember any of it.

"Where are Anna, Allan, and Ben? I should call James," said Natalia.

"Oh dear. I had hoped that a good sleep would have alleviated this... whatever this is. We already talked this through while you were eating toast. I don't know Anna, Allan, and Ben. But I am sure your children, Annabelle, Nick, and Nathan, are just fine."

Natalia sat up straight and replied forcefully, "Anna, Allan, and Ben are my children. They are ages eight, four, and two years old. I do not even know anyone named Annabelle, Nick, or Nathan."

"So you said before, dear. Now, Natalia, I do not know what is happening with you, but it seems to be serious. I am going to take you up to the hospital myself. I'll just leave a quick note and a voice message for Evan..." said Andrea, going into the kitchen in search of a paper and pen.

"I think that is a very good idea," agreed Mark, still standing in the living room watching Natalia intently.

"No, no, Andrea, I don't need to go to the hospital. Could you please hand me the phone? I will call my husband and my dad. I'm sure I will be fine. I will call you if I need anything."

"Oh my, no. I am not going to leave you here like this. Absolutely not. I am driving you up to the hospital right now," insisted Andrea.

"Oh, Andrea, you live right next door and your Mark is a very good doctor. If your husband was really worried, don't you think he would have already carried me straight to the car and driven me up to the hospital already?" said Natalia, looking at Mark for confirmation.

Mark tilted his head to one side in concentration.

"Well, just because I couldn't see anything wrong doesn't mean there isn't. It would be a good idea to talk to a psychiatrist."

"What? I'm not crazy. You two are worrying too much," said Natalia. "I promise to call or come over if I need help. In fact, I will call in an hour just to reassure you that I am fine. I have been working too hard and not eating enough. That could make anyone's mind unfocused."

Andrea returned to the living room and sat down.

"Unfocused is putting it mildly! You are downright confused. You don't remember your own children! And I have no idea who the other children are that you have been going on about. You need help, Natalia. We need to go have you examined at the hospital."

Natalia absolutely did not want to go to the hospital. She hated hospitals. She felt a fear rising up inside her, almost as if a hand were starting to squeeze her heart. At all costs she would not go with Andrea to the hospital. Natalia decided she needed to lie.

"Did I say children? No, no, I meant siblings," improvised Natalia. "Anna, Allan, and Ben are my brothers and sister," explained Natalia.

"I thought you said you are an only child," replied Andrea, walking over and sitting down next to Natalia.

"I said I want to be an only child," Natalia answered, forcing a laugh.

"Really?" asked Andrea, turning to her husband. "What do you think, Mark? I just don't feel right leaving her here alone like this."

"Natalia, be honest now. You are feeling clear again? You know your children are Annabelle, Nick, and Nathan, and that you are married to Evan? How long have you been our neighbors?" asked Mark.

"Yes. And a little over three years now," answered Natalia.

"I think she will be fine then," said Mark to Andrea. "Low blood sugar, lack of sleep and stress can cause someone to faint and result in some temporary confusion. Goodness knows Natalia has been working long hours."

"All right. If you promise to call in an hour, I will go start dinner for the family," said Andrea, while kissing Natalia on the cheek goodbye.

"Thank you for everything, Andrea. I am so fortunate to have you as a friend. And thank you too, Mike." Natalia struggled to hide her bewilderment and plastered a huge smile on her face as she watched her friend walk out the patio door with her husband.

NATALIA DIALED HER FATHER'S NUMBER the minute she was alone.

"Hello, Natalia."

"Hi, Mom." Natalia paused. "Why do you have Dad's phone? Is Dad there? I really need to talk to him."

"Your voice sounds tired, honey. Did you have a long week at work? How many evening events did you have?"

"What do you mean? I don't work anymore."

"You quit? Well, that is big news. I am shocked really. I thought you loved your work. Or did your business fail? Oh, Natalia, how am I not surprised? How will you pay your mortgage?" sighed Bren.

Natalia's end of the line went silent. James made plenty of money as a partner in a consulting company in Zürich. Of course they would be able to pay their mortgage. And why did her mom think she had her own business? She had not worked for almost three years now. Just before the birth of Ben she had quit her job to be a full-time mother.

When she worked she had felt utterly exhausted all the time. At the end of a long day in the office she had a hard time summoning the energy or patience to enjoy her children. She had felt herself rushing through the bath time and story time ritual so she could at last shower herself, complete a few last chores, and fall into bed.

Then there were the nights when Natalia had just slipped into the sweet oblivion of sleep to be awakened a few moments later by a crying child. Caring for the ill child and begging her boss to let her work from home for the day always fell on her, despite the fact that James was a partner in his firm. No one would question him if he stayed home a few days with a sick child; he was a partner. Yet he never, not once, had even considered being the one to stay home from work and take care of a sick child.

Quitting her job looked like the only answer. She felt like she was drowning in despair and failing both at being a mother and at her job. It wasn't as if James would ease the childcare or household pressure; he worked seventy- to eighty-hour weeks. When she told him it was more than she could handle alone he just suggested the housekeeper come in a few more mornings or that they find a nanny instead of taking the kids to daycare.

She didn't want a nanny; she longed to spend more time with her children. Reading to them. Going for hikes. Working together in the garden. Taking them swimming. Cuddling. She had wanted a perfectly clean and organized house for a change. She had wanted a stress-free family life and time at last to devour piles of books and exercise every day in the fresh air. She had wished for the energy and time to throw more parties for friends and family and become a better cook. And that was what she had.

Okay, she was bored. But she was no longer exhausted. And every morning it brought a smile to Natalia's face to see how happy her children were that she was at home. She wasn't missing any of their childhood; she was always there when they needed her. She would never admit to her critical mother that she felt like her mind was going numb from disuse and she longed desperately to sit in total concentration at work for an entire day. She even missed the lunches with the arrogant people from her consulting team.

"Natalia? Natalia!" her mother yelled over the line. "Are you listening to me? Why are you not answering my question? What has happened to your business?"

"What business?" asked Natalia.

"Your event planning firm in Zürich?"

"My event planning firm in Zürich?" parroted Natalia.

"You gave it up?"

"What, no, I mean, I don't work anymore..." Natalia began, her voice quiet with confusion.

"But it isn't as if your job is very intense," interrupted Bren. "You just plan parties, for goodness' sake. How can you get a burnout from working too hard at that? I still can't believe you left consulting. What a waste. All those years of studying, and for what?"

"Mom, you know I quit about three years ago, before Ben was born, to become a full-time mom. And yes, I know you do not approve."

"Who is Ben?"

"What do you mean who is Ben, he is your two-year-old grandson," Natalia replied, exasperated. She started to clench her fists again. She could feel her foot start to rhythmically shake back and forth. She wished her dad would take the phone from her mom.

"Natalia. This is not humorous. You do not have a two-year-old son that I do not know about. And you are being a stay-at-home mom? You must be joking. Why on earth would I have invested all of that time and money in your education for you to stay home like some subservient fool? Now clearly something is very, very wrong. You are not making any kind of sense at all. If I could get in the car and drive there right now I would. But as you live halfway around the world it will certainly take me two to three days to get time off from work, pack, and fly all the way to Switzerland."

Letting out a huge sigh, Natalia asked, "Can I talk to Dad?"

Bren continued, "If I had known spending six years living in Zürich while I worked abroad would mean you would stay and spend the rest of your life there, why, I would have told the CEO to find a new director of operations. Why on earth you chose to stay and go to college in Switzerland instead of coming back home to the USA with us, I will never fathom. We have the top universities in the world and you should have attended one of them. Where is Evan? I need to talk to him. You have me very worried, Natalia."

"Mom."

"Yes, dear."

"Why would you want to talk to Evan? Why would you want to talk to Eva's husband?"

"What! Natalia, that is not funny. Is that supposed to be some kind of a joke? Wait, or do you mean that Eva and Evan are having an affair? Well, she is very sexy."

Natalia was getting more and more confused. Evan and Eva had been married almost a decade. Did her mother think that Eva or Evan or both of them were having an affair? Natalia considered this for a moment. Yes. Natalia decided it could be possible. Evan had been irritated on and off with Eva for years for her ten- to twelve-hour workdays while he worked part time as a high school teacher and took full responsibility for the housework and the children. But would Eva have an affair? No. Natalia didn't think that this was likely.

Then again, Natalia wondered what it would be like to own and manage a fancy restaurant in Zürich. Certainly Eva met very interesting and charming men all the time. Perhaps if one day Evan was a bit short with Eva and she happened to be charmed by some restaurant guest, then something could happen.

Natalia had a devastating realization. She herself was continually angry and resentful of James for his time away from the family. Far angrier than Evan ever seemed to be with Eva. In fact, it didn't seem to take much effort from Eva for her to put Evan in a really good mood again; she noticed they spent a lot of time laughing when they were together.

If she thought Eva capable of an affair in such a situation, then James could also be tempted. Natalia felt a weight settle on her heart. James worked with some very interesting, beautiful women. She adored James; even after eleven years together she hungered for time with him, for his arms around her, though she couldn't remember the last time James had hugged her. If James had an affair she didn't know what she would do. Who would she be without him?

"Natalia! Natalia, ANSWER me. I need to talk to your husband, you are scaring me."

"James isn't here. He took the kids to brunch and swimming with Evan and Eva."

"Why would James be there, Natalia?" Bren inhaled sharply. "Natalia, are you having an affair with James?"

"I don't think they call it an affair when it is your own husband, Mom."

"Natalia. You are talking just craziness. James isn't your husband."

"Yes he is!"

"No he isn't! Evan is your husband."

"What? When I woke up this morning, I went out expecting to see my kids and James. Instead there was Evan, and these children in the family room I had never seen before calling me Mom. It was so crazy that I thought I must have dreamt it. Maybe I did."

"Natalia, you think James is your husband? He isn't, dear. He is Eva's husband. Are you trying to be funny? Now, Natalia, you know you have never been very amusing. Just as you have never been the life of a party."

"What! Mom, I am sure I know who my own husband is. We have been married for eleven years. Listen, I want to talk to Dad. Where is he?"

"No. You haven't. You have been married to Evan for eleven years. Eva has been married to James for ten years. Oh, Natalia! What has happened? Did you get in an accident?"

"No, Mom, I don't remember an accident," answered Natalia.

"But you do not remember that you have a business in Zürich, or your husband, and not even *your own children.*"

"No. I mean yes. I do not have a business and I DO remember my children and husband. They just are not here and I am desperately worried about them. Where are they? What is going on? I want to talk to Dad. Put him on the phone."

Natalia could feel the world start to spin again. Luckily, she was already lying down. Her heart was thudding so loudly in her chest she thought her mother might be able to hear it over the phone. Suddenly, she was having trouble breathing.

"Mom. I think I am dying. But Mark was over here and already checked me and he said I was fine."

"Natalia, I'll hang up and dial an ambulance right away," replied Bren.

"No! No, that isn't necessary, Mom, don't call anyone," Natalia yelled over the phone.

"Well, dear, I really think I should. You could be having a stroke or something serious!" insisted Bren.

"I am not having a stroke. Didn't you hear me? Mark, my neighbor who is a doctor, was just here and he checked me, so it can't be serious. But then again, why do I feel like I am dying…."

"I think you are having an anxiety attack on top of whatever else is happening to you then. Please try to breathe in long and slow from your tummy and exhale twice as slowly. Relax your body. Then, once you are able to, you have to call that lovely neighbor of yours to come over with her doctor husband and drive you to the hospital straightaway. You belong in the hospital, Natalia. Do you hear me? Tell me you will do as I say."

"I will call Andrea as soon as I get off the phone with you, Mom."

"Good. I will get on the first plane over there. I am coming for you, darling. Don't worry."

"But what about your important job, Mom, you can't just leave. Please send Dad instead. I want Dad to come."

"You are right that my job is important. But nothing is more important than my child. Now you just lay quiet and relax. Remember: take a deep breath in and breathe out as slowly as you can to the count of ten or twenty. You are not dying. It just feels like you are, that is what an anxiety attack feels like. I will call Evan and tell him what is going on and send him to his parents' with the children for the next two nights. It would be terrible for the children to see their mother unraveling like this. I don't want them to realize that you don't remember them. I will also tell him to call your work and let them know you are ill tomorrow. If they allow you to go home from the hospital tonight then eat something, take a bath, and go to bed early. I love you, sweetheart."

"I love you too, Mom."

Suddenly, it was all just too much for Natalia to work through. The anxiety attack was subsiding, fatigue rolling in to take its place. All Natalia wanted to do was eat something, crawl under her duvet, and fall asleep.

"See you soon, sweetie. Now you call those neighbors and go straight into the hospital to find out why you are so confused. Then call me when you find out what is wrong. Promise."

"Yes, I promise. Goodbye."

Natalia quickly dialed Andrea.

"Andrea? This is Natalia. I will be fine. My dad and mom are coming to help me. I am just going to take a hot lavender scented salt bath and climb into bed."

"Are you sure? I can come straight over and help any time you need me. I can drive you up to the hospital if Evan is still not home. Mark would like you to get a full checkup at the hospital to find out why you were so confused today."

"Thank you so much, Andrea. Your concern is so touching. But I am going to go up first thing in the morning. Don't worry. I am sure my husband will be home any moment. Goodbye."

Ephemeral

Chapter 3

Natalia woke in darkness to an alarm clock. What time was it? She glanced at the clock on the modern bedside table and registered that it was five a.m. She got up and went to her wardrobe and slid it open. Still half asleep, she reached for a gray textured dress and noticed as she slipped it on that it was fully lined and fit her perfectly. She tied the silk belt at the waist and pulled on nylons. One minute later she stepped into the bathroom and in five minutes had washed her face, applied makeup, and twisted up her hair. Grabbing her jacket and throwing a pair of red-soled heels into her purse, she pulled on some flat boots and tied a red and sky-blue printed scarf around her neck. Exactly fifteen minutes later she was making her way down the path along the lake to the train station. Halfway to the station she stopped in mid stride and stood looking out over the boats in the harbor.

"Where am I going?" Natalia wondered aloud.

She gazed up the hill at the church tower's large clock and something in her noted that if she did not walk quickly, she would miss her train. Deciding to trust her instincts, Natalia quickened her pace. Beginning to run, she felt the cold morning air rush against her face and heard the first leaves of fall crunch beneath her boots. Managing to step into the train a few seconds before it departed for Zürich, Natalia unwound her scarf and took off her jacket. She made her way through the wagons to the restaurant car and sat down. A few minutes later she sat watching the rolling green hills and small towns outside the window glide past as she drank a cappuccino.

"Where am I going?" asked Natalia.

"Excuse me, what was that?" A man in an expensive suit sitting at the neighboring table looked up over his newspaper at her with raised eyebrows. "This train is going to Zürich."

"Oh." Natalia felt her cheeks warm. "Thank you."

Why was she going to Zürich? Natalia racked her brain. She couldn't remember. In fact, she was having trouble remembering the day before; well, the entire last week really. In fact, she couldn't remember a single day from the last month. What was going on?

Feeling her entire body start to stiffen with stress Natalia suddenly realized she did not want to struggle anymore. She did remember awhile back; how long ago was it? Her life in the summer had been a constant struggle with the children, with her husband, and most of all with herself.

Looking out the window, Natalia noted a tree in autumn splendor. So it was no longer summer then. How could she just forget a few months of her life? Natalia decided to stay calm, to just go into Zürich anyway. She began searching in her purse for her phone; she wanted to check her agenda. Surely there would be an entry as to what she would be doing in Zürich today.

Yet then Natalia saw a book stashed in her bag about body language she had been longing to read for some time, but the children and activities had kept getting in the way. Smiling, Natalia took out the book and began to read.

Just then the waiter came by to pick up her cup. He gave her a tentative smile and asked, "Going on holiday, Natalia?"

"Excuse me, why is that?" asked Natalia. Alarmed, Natalia wondered how this waiter knew her name. She certainly didn't recognize him.

"Oh, I have never seen you reading a book before. You are always typing away furiously on your laptop, or you are on the phone the entire way to Zürich," answered the waiter, smiling at her.

"You have never seen me reading a book?" asked Natalia, looking down at the book in her hands.

"No. Are you feeling well today, Natalia? You always ask after my health and if my family is doing well. Today you said nothing when I brought you your coffee."

"Oh, I am sorry, yes, I am not feeling well this morning," replied Natalia, averting her gaze.

"I hope you feel better soon."

"Thank you." Natalia stared out the window. When had she turned into a woman who worked at every moment in the train, had no time to read a book, but took the time to chat with the waiter? Natalia did not know what to think. So instead, she returned to reading her book.

NATALIA LOOKED UP FROM HER BOOK as the train approached the Zürich main train station. She gathered her purse and scarf and descended the steps to disembark the train. As she stood just outside the doors of the train, people flowed past her quickly on both sides. Natalia stood contemplating where she should go. She took out her phone and started to look at her agenda. But twice she was pushed as people hurried by her and she didn't like standing in a crowd.

After a few moments of hesitation she put the phone away and started walking quickly out of the train station and into the sunlight down along Zürich's glamorous high street, the Bahnhofstrasse.

Strolling down the street, she had no idea where she was going and she no longer cared about any appointments she had made. It just felt good to be out in the fresh morning air, walking down a beautiful street. Around her, elegantly dressed women and men walked with steely determination toward work. In contrast, at this hour, there were only a few tourists slowly meandering along, pausing to look in each luxury store window. Although the street was not thronged with people, the cafés were very busy.

Reading on the train had made Natalia a bit dizzy. *It would be so lovely,* she thought, *to settle into one of the chairs of that cute little café, to sit with the early morning sunshine on my face, watching the people walking by and reading a newspaper, while drinking a strong black coffee.*

Just as she was about to sit down her phone rang. Taking it out of her purse she smiled as she answered, "Hello, Mary."

"Where are you?" answered Mary.

"I am on the Bahnhofstrasse in Zürich. I have just decided to go for a coffee in this charming café," replied Natalia.

"What? You don't have time for that. Drink your coffee in the office. You are already late. I'll see you in ten minutes," finished Mary, hanging up the phone.

Natalia shrugged back her shoulders, loosening the tension. She didn't remember an appointment with Mary. Finally opening the agenda on her phone, she did a double take. Her morning was filled with appointments, as was her afternoon and even evening. What was going on? Was this someone else's phone? And what in the world was she doing in Zürich again? Who was with the kids?

Panicking, Natalia took out her phone and dialed home. Evan answered on the first ring. "Hello?"

"Evan?" asked Natalia incredulously. "What are you doing there?"

"What do you mean?" he answered, his voice irritated.

"I mean, are my kids all right? Are they there?"

"Of course they're here," answered Evan. "But we're late, I've got to run. So see you tonight, love," and he ended the call.

Shaking her head as to why Evan was once again at her house, Natalia opened her agenda. Had she asked Evan to come and watch her kids because she had an appointment in Zürich today? What time did she need to be back home?

She needed to find out where she was supposed to meet Mary. Then it occurred to her. Of course, it would be at Mary's own office! She even had Mary's business card. Natalia began hurrying down the street, no longer glancing in luxury store windows or noticing the people hurrying to work around her.

In front of a massive gray stone building she came to a stop. Looking up, she looked for the building's number. Pulling out her purse, she took out the business card once again. She saw that she was indeed in the right place.

She ascended the steps. *This feels right.* She had visited Mary at work many times before. In the marble-stone lobby she waited impatiently for the elevator. A dark-haired man waited beside her.

Once inside the elevator he turned to her and asked, "What floor?"

Natalia panicked. She knew this man. What was his name? And what floor was it? Oh, there was a sign listing the businesses and their floor number right there on the wall of the elevator. Elegant Events was on the fourth floor. Before she could respond the tall man was already reaching toward the buttons.

"Okay, not the cleverest joke in the world, I know," laughed the man, pushing the number four. "Do you think we have everything under control with catering for the event tonight?"

"Um, why would I know that?" asked Natalia.

"Just like you, Natalia. I know that you have handed complete responsibility over to me for the catering. I will have that for you by the coffee break. I just got behind with some other work and hoped you had done it for me," replied the man honestly, his brow furrowing.

Natalia watched him move with purpose into the office. With a long, lean build, dark brown hair, and startling blue eyes, one could almost overlook his unfortunate choice of tie, bright orange, which clashed alarmingly with his bright-red-framed glasses.

At first impression she thought the office was an open loft due to the bright and airy feel. But now she could see that a series of offices along one side were made completely of frosted glass. She could not see into the offices, but the glass let the natural light in through to the central space, which contained a beautiful long wood table with a huge bouquet of roses, ferns, and hydrangea. She noticed a sidebar with an expensive coffee machine, porcelain cups, two teapots, and a Vitamix juicer placed next to the sink.

Who was that man in the elevator? She waited for a name to rise to the surface, but nothing came. Did Mary work for him? But then why was he delivering work to her by the coffee break?

Natalia felt a hand settle firmly on her lower back as a man stepped in close beside her and whispered in a charming British accent, "Nine fifteen at the café, darling."

Before Natalia could call out, the man was striding away from her and into the elevator. But Natalia managed to catch a glimpse of the man's reflection in the mirrors within the elevator before he vanished behind the closing doors. Tall, with soft brown eyes and brown hair—Natalia had recognized her husband's voice at once.

Where was he going?

Chapter 4

"GOOD MORNING, NATALIA."

Natalia turned to see a tall, striking woman walking toward her. Natalia felt the confusion and stress fall away at the sight of her. Her long blond hair fell in waves almost to her waist and the deep blue of her eyes were brought out by the bright blue hue of her dress. She looked like a beautiful porcelain doll.

But although Mary looked like a doll, she sure didn't act like one; she acted more like a tiger. Natalia loved her completely anyway. Mary could be devastatingly charming and coolly self-assured when she put up her facade, and this was the normal mask she presented to the world, but not to Natalia. Every once in a while, when Mary was either very tired or distraught, her cover slipped even around everyone else.

Natalia had on more than one occasion suffered Mary's biting tongue, clever wit, bossiness, and perfectionism. But she had also felt Mary melt just a bit into revealing her tender side. Natalia knew Mary loved her like a sister.

For Mary love was a verb, not something you would ever say aloud. Mary's attentive gestures of care bore testament to how much she loved the few people close to her heart. Natalia remembered in college when Mary had suffered severe jealously because Natalia was first in all her business classes at the HSG, with Mary a close second. Mary's biting tongue and grumpiness almost led Natalia to want to strangle her. But Mary would bring her a tea when she was up all alone studying into the night. Or leave chocolates on her open notebook when she went for a small walk around the library.

Natalia had a way of concentrating on her goals in a way that left no room for laughter, wonder, people, or even exercise. Mary would insist on Natalia taking study breaks to go walking with her in the newly frozen snow, to visit a yoga class, or get away for a day of skiing. A fan of culture, Mary would drag Natalia to the Zürich Art Museum exhibitions, or talk her into saving up money for the ballet. Natalia always pretended to be reluctant to take the study breaks, but secretly she knew they were her lifelines to a full life. In turn, Natalia had offered Mary loyalty, praise, encouragement, compliments, and affection, regardless of Mary's mood.

Mary was staring at Natalia strangely. Natalia realized she must have been standing there thinking for much too long. She was relieved to find that her memory of Mary and her high school and college years was intact. Maybe it was just a matter of time before the rest of her memory came sliding back into place.

"I said good morning, Natalia," snapped the woman. "Still dreaming? Why are you late, you should have been here five minutes ago."

Natalia was confused. Was she late for her appointment? It was, after all, very early in the morning. Natalia's mind wandered. Did all the Swiss start their workdays at seven in the morning? If they started at seven a.m., did they all work such long hours? She had thought that it was just in certain businesses, like consulting or law, that they worked such crazy hours.

"Mary! I am so sorry I'm late. Can you forgive me? It is so good to see you! Um, I forgot. What is our appointment for?" Natalia beamed at her dearest friend from high school and university. *She's like the sister I never had*, thought Natalia.

"Can I forgive you? It is so good to see me? Okay, the message is loud and clear. You are the boss and you can come in whenever you want," Mary replied.

Natalia felt her heart racing and unknowingly she hunched her shoulders forward, making herself smaller. She didn't want Mary mad at her.

Forcing a laugh she asked, "What do you mean, 'you are the boss'? Do you mean I am your client? Are you putting on an event for me I don't remember?"

Looking at her strangely, Mary frowned. "Natalia, are you trying to make some kind of point? Because I don't get it. And we really don't have time for games this morning; we have so much left to arrange for the event tonight. So grab a coffee, boss, it's go time." Mary motioned to the Jura Swiss espresso machine.

"So," began Natalia, pausing to think of how to respond. What in the world was going on? Was this some kind of joke? What did Mary mean, calling her "boss"?

"Why do you start your workday so early? Does this mean you can all pack up and go home at sixteen thirty?" asked Natalia.

Mary stared at her and snapped, "Funny. I can't imagine how you would work the event tonight all on your own. Now get to work or we will be working together in stress come this afternoon."

Natalia wondered how she could forget that she was now working at Elegant Events with Mary. This couldn't be right. In despair, Natalia massaged her forehead with both hands. When had she accepted a job working for Mary?

Mary stopped in mid stride on her way to get a cup of coffee and turned to gawk at Natalia. Noticing, Natalia dropped her hands and quickly moved to follow Mary toward the espresso machine.

Didn't her Mom insist yesterday on the phone that she owned an event planning business? But Mary owned Elegant Events! Natalia was sure of it.

First the confusion at home yesterday and now this was happening. Should she go in to the hospital, like she promised her mother she would do? She felt fine. There must be a logical explanation for her confusion and memory loss, she thought. No, she would just play along and hopefully her head would clear and everything would be fine again.

Yet how should she play along when she couldn't remember anything about this business? She didn't even know which office was hers. She'd never been a good actress. How was she going to pull this off?

Mary placed a porcelain cup on the espresso machine and pressed the button for a cappuccino. Seconds later the smell of coffee filled the room.

"Mary, you have a client on line one," called a male voice.

Natalia turned to see a man stepping out of an office and realized it was the man from the elevator.

"Of course there is, Mike. Of course, it being only seven in the morning, there is already a client on the phone and I cannot have just a few minutes in peace to drink my coffee hot for a change."

Slamming the door to the fridge, Mary made her way to her office, her heels clicking rapidly across the hardwood floor.

Wow, I can't believe Mary has dropped her facade around this guy, Natalia thought in wonder. *I hope she's not always this grumpy at work though.*

Mike saw her expression from across the room and winked at her, a smile spreading across his face.

"I think everything is on track for tonight boss, " said Mike, while walking to the fridge and pouring himself some green smoothie.

"Can't she talk on the phone and drink coffee at the same time, Mike? I am counting on you doing something later this morning for Mary to put her in a better mood," Natalia said quietly as she approached Mike at the sidebar. He was searching through the cupboards for a straw.

"Like what?" asked Mike, distracted.

"Use your imagination, Mike," Natalia parried.

Mike laughed out loud. "Hey boss, I'm not accustomed to you making jokes!" Still laughing, he pointed to the largest office in the corner. "I already rechecked the catering and put the bill from the company on your desk."

"Well, at least I know where my office is now," said Natalia, smiling. "And I wasn't making a joke. It would really be great if you could do something to snap Mary out of her bad mood."

"Funny, Natalia. Wow. You are in a good mood this morning."

Natalia walked to her office and paused a moment at the door, taking in the view of the cobblestone streets below her and the church tower in the distance across the river. Then she settled into her chair and surveyed her desk for clues. There was a vase with roses, a beautiful clock, a container of multicolored pens, and the bill. Nothing else.

Searching the desk drawers she found a gorgeous pair of designer shoes, with even higher heels than the ones she had stashed in her handbag earlier that morning. Pulling her boots off, Natalia slipped into the high heels. Standing up straight, she walked shakily across her office and back to her desk. She couldn't remember the last time she had worn a pair of high heels and she certainly didn't own any as expensive as these. Maybe the shoes were on loan from Mary, Natalia reasoned. Natalia had to admit, after all the days she had spent in jeans and ballet flats, it was fun to be all dressed up in designer clothes and wearing pretty heels.

Smiling, Natalia turned on her computer and opened her calendar. Her pulse quickened and she could feel her face flush. There was a meeting or work scheduled for every half hour from nine thirty in the morning until ten o'clock at night. Surely that could not be right. Who worked until ten o'clock at night? Natalia glanced at her watch and noted that it was almost seven thirty. She had time to prepare herself. She started clicking to open the details of each individual appointment.

Ten o'clock meeting at the florist Fleur au Lac. Mmmm, she loved their Italian coffee. Did she have ten minutes in her schedule to stop for a coffee break there after the flower arrangements were completed for the event tonight? Maybe she should cancel the hot yoga session over lunch with such a full schedule. But then again, she could use the stress reduction given the long day ahead of her, and she did love yoga.

Natalia paused. She was suddenly aware of her thought flow. Italian coffee? How did she know the florist also served coffee? Yoga session? She clicked on the lunch box and up sprung the yoga session from noon until half past one. Going through the rest of her appointments for the afternoon, she felt a smile spread across her face, the knots in her stomach loosening. This all looked easy and, well, fun. Except for the party that night. Natalia was not looking forward to having to talk to all of those people; how would she manage that?

I can fake it in this job until I fall back into the sway of my things. After all, I do have a master's in business administration, I should be able to plan and execute an event. My memory will come back a bit at a time, surely, thought Natalia.

She wouldn't think about her kids or husband. Today she would just focus on one appointment at a time and perhaps, she prayed, everything would fall back into place.

Natalia turned back to the screen and her detailed schedule. Thank god she was so organized. If she just followed the appointments she could complete her job for today somewhat with ease.

"Natalia! Natalia!"

Hearing her name being called, Natalia went to stand up and turn at the same time in her ridiculously high heels. She felt her legs give out from under her and she was falling toward the floor in what felt like very slow motion. She tried to reach for the desk on her way down, but it was just out of reach. Natalia waited for her body to feel the jolting impact of the floor but instead, everything just went black.

JUST AS NATALIA WAS STARTING TO AWAKEN, just before she opened her eyes, she could sense people standing over her.

She heard James say, "Natalia, everything is going to be all right. Natalia? Can you hear me, Natalia?"

Natalia wanted to respond. She strained to open her eyes as she answered, "Yes, thank you, I'm fine now. So silly of me to fall over my own heels!"

Suddenly a wave of fatigue washed over her. *Perhaps just a few minutes of sleep wouldn't be such a bad idea.* Natalia let herself fall into the sweet oblivion of unconsciousness.

Chapter 5

Natalia opened her eyes and sat up quickly.

"Not so fast, darling! Take it slow. Mary and Mike here told me that you hit your head quite hard when you fell," said a deep voice with a British accent.

Natalia sat on the floor of her office, looking a little dazedly into the soft brown eyes of the man kneeling next to her. *He has startling white, perfectly straight teeth for a British man,* thought Natalia. *Or is that wrong? Perhaps the British now all have dazzlingly white teeth like the LA crowd?*

"Are you feeling better, my dear, do you require medical assistance?"

James! Natalia placed her face in her hands. Perhaps she would not have to pretend her way through this life after all. Her husband and Mary were here. They would help her sort everything out.

"Natalia, darling, I am going to hold your hands. Please try to get up, darling. I think we shall take you to the hospital," said James.

Natalia felt strong hands wrap around hers and she looked up at the handsome man towering above her. He pulled her gently to her feet and they remained there, her hands enfolded in his, looking at each other in silence for a moment. Natalia couldn't remember the last time they had stood together like this, just staring into one another's eyes. It felt wonderful.

"What are you doing here, James?" asked Natalia.

"I am here to meet you," he answered. "We are going over the details of my event tonight, remember?"

"Natalia! You look like you are doing much better! Thank goodness. You really gave us all a scare," said Mary as she entered the room with an ice pack in her hands. She continued, "Is there anything I should bring her, James, anything that she needs?"

"Hello, I am right here," exclaimed Natalia. "And I know what I need. I need a cup of strong coffee. I don't need to go to the hospital, James. I will be fine. I fell over my own feet. I am going to just get right back to my schedule for the day. I have a florist appointment at ten and they have deliciously strong coffee. I will head there already and enjoy a few moments to steady myself before continuing with my day."

"Brilliant idea, beautiful," exclaimed James. "Of course I will accompany you. We can have our meeting on location. Here, let me help you until we are sure your dizziness has passed."

Natalia's thoughts started to circle too quickly. Should she tell Mary and James that she had lost her memory? Confide in them about the curious day she had yesterday?

But then James' strong arm encircled her waist and she felt herself gliding toward the elevator. Just before they entered the elevator James turned and called out, "Mary, love, please be a dear and bring me Natalia's purse and phone."

"Oh! I should have thought of that," replied Mary.

She turned back toward Natalia's office and her heels made a rapid staccato across the floor to retrieve Natalia's red Chanel purse. As she returned and walked toward them Natalia noticed Mary looking at her strangely.

As the elevator descended toward the lobby she let her eyes close and her entire body relax. She rested her head on James' shoulder. She could smell his spicy citrus cologne and feel his arm still wrapped around her waist. It felt like home. Natalia missed this; when had James stopped putting his arm around her? Natalia couldn't remember. When the elevator doors opened Natalia stood up straight and walked out into the lobby unassisted. James caught her hand before she reached the front door and pulled her gently around to face him.

Reaching up and smoothing her hair back from her face, he said, "There, almost picture perfect once again. Of course you could use some lipstick; you look a bit pale. Are you sure you are okay, love?"

Natalia found that her lips were slightly parted but no words would come. Thoughts of Evan kissing her came swirling into her head. Flushing, she merely nodded. As they exited the lobby and moved out into the fresh, crisp air Natalia felt herself snap back awake. She still felt a bit wobbly in her high-heeled shoes though. She contemplated the shoe store right across the street.

In theory I could go back upstairs and put my boots back on, she mused. Instead, she looked up into the eyes of the tall man steadying her with a hand on the small of her back.

"I am very sorry, James, but I need just ten minutes to buy a pair of ballerinas for the rest of today. There is no way I can make it through until the event this evening in heels."

"If you must, Natalia," sighed James. "But make it five minutes. I do want time for a leisurely coffee and we are running behind schedule."

NATALIA ENTERED the shoe store while applying pink lipstick and requested a pair of black ballerinas in a size 37. The attendant brought out a beautiful pair of red shoes instead.

"These will go beautifully with your handbag and scarf," urged the woman. "They are very comfortable too," she added.

Natalia tried on the shoes. She didn't want red shoes. They were too flashy in her opinion and she wanted the black ones. But the saleswoman was so nice and said, "Oh, you look so chic in those shoes with that dress and scarf! You must buy them."

So Natalia did just that, wincing as she saw the price tag.

"This is rather an emergency," Natalia rationalized to the saleswoman as she packed up Natalia's heels and gave her the flats to wear. "I don't generally go and spend so much on shoes for myself."

Looking Natalia over from head to toe, the saleswoman noted the designer dress, the jacket, the outrageously expensive handbag, jewelry and scarf.

"Then who buys your wardrobe then?" replied the woman, smiling. "Do you have a stylist?"

BACK OUT ON THE STREET, Natalia could see James reading something on his phone.

"What are you reading, James?" asked Natalia.

James began to walk down the street with large strides as he answered. Natalia could hardly keep up with his pace.

"The latest McKinsey issue. This article on the gap between academically created strategic models and the reality of their application in a real world setting is very interesting."

"Hmmmm. Yes, it would be interesting to put together a symposium of CEOs and the top management tier together with the leading academic strategists to determine which strategic models actually result in higher returns on investment when applied across a range of industries. But there is so much grandstanding at those events. First you should execute an anonymous survey of top management on which strategy frameworks, in practice, they believe to increase a company's long-term profitability. You could also interview top academics and solicit their opinion on…"

Natalia hesitated before continuing, looking over and noticing the look on James' face.

"Are you sure you have put consulting behind you, Natalia?"

"What do you mean? I am sorry, James. I'm sure I was boring you." Natalia suddenly became very intent on watching the cobblestone walkway in front of her.

"Listen, you have built up an impressively reputable event management firm; that is why we have booked you for the event tonight. But you could always come back to consulting. Reconsider my offer yet again for junior partner."

Natalia stopped walking and turned to look at James, searching his face to make sure he was serious. "Sure. I mean, I'll think about it," replied Natalia, smiling

"Really? I am stunned," answered James, lifting his palms upward.

"Is that so surprising that I would consider your offer?" asked Natalia, furrowing her brow.

"Well, it is rather a game we play since you left us," said James. He took a step closer to Natalia and placed a hand on her upper arm, looking into her eyes.

"I say 'please come back to work with us' and you always answer that you would rather serve people wine than strategy."

"I do? Since when have you ever wanted me to work with you again?" asked Natalia as she unconsciously reached forward and straightened James' tie and smoothed down the lapels of his suit.

"I would love to go back to work in consulting. I miss it actually. I miss it very much. But what shall we do with our children, James? We can't both work such long hours. I don't want that for them again."

James didn't answer. He slipped his hand down her arm and taking her hand, tucked it under his arm and continued walking.

"I miss working with you," said Natalia, more to herself than to James, admiring the sun sparkling on the water of the stone fountain in front of them.

"Well, that is astounding," replied James, his eyebrows lifting, his jaw dropping open. "Look, here we are…"

Natalia and James knocked on the door of the floral boutique and café. The café was strangely empty.

"Hello!" called Natalia.

A man with soft brown eyes and dark hair tinged with gray stepped out from the back room, opening the door with irritation. But a smile spread across his face as he recognized Natalia. "Good morning, Bella! You are here early for your appointment," he said, as he kissed Natalia on each cheek.

"Yes, we thought we would enjoy one of your Italian coffees before our meeting, Antonio," replied Natalia.

"Well, we have the café closed today, as it is reserved for a private tea this afternoon, and we are quite frantic in the back in preparation for various event orders. But if you can work the espresso machine on your own, you are welcome to as many of them as you would like on the house," called Antonio, already heading to the back room. "I will be out for our meeting in twenty minutes!"

"Allow me," said James as he stepped behind the counter.

A moment later he brought two espressos to a table in the sunshine and she contentedly admired the exotic flowers while sipping the aromatic coffee. She felt the caffeine immediately hit her system. Instead of feeling keyed up she felt all at once completely relaxed. Her breathing was slow and even, her eyes registering the textures and tiny details of each flower. She sensed the silkiness of her dress lining, the moisture in the air on her skin. Natalia closed her eyes for a moment. The smell of robust coffee and roses engulfed her. Totally relaxing, Natalia cleared her mind of all fear and uncertainty. *When was the last time I sat in a cafe in Zürich?*

"Natalia. Natalia, my dear, do at least pretend you are paying attention," said James, smiling at her.

"What? Oh, I'm sorry. I was just enjoying the moment. Could you repeat that, please?"

Natalia turned her attention to the man sitting across from her. She watched the way the sunlight hit his brown hair and cast shadows over his face and strong jaw. *Focus, Natalia*, she told herself.

"I just said, Natalia, that if you really would like to come back to work for us you must give me a serious answer by the end of the day. We have a junior partnership open but we are of course considering promoting from within. The position, as you know, is quite coveted. Don't waste my time."

"So serious, James, love, loosen up," answered Natalia, surprising herself. Where had that come from? Natalia smiled. She had always felt a bit intimidated by James; she had never teased him before. It felt good. Natalia smiling, sat up straighter in her chair.

Looking up from his phone, James answered, "Yes, of course, my darling. How inconsiderate of me. You did have quite the tumble today. Agreed. I will call you bright and early the morning after next."

James returned his attention to his phone and quickly entered the note into his calendar. Natalia watched him, bewildered. She did not understand why on earth he would need to make an appointment in his calendar to call her when he could just as easily ask her in person at home on any evening.

"Alas, I must be off, darling. I have a meeting with a CEO to prepare for and then my top team and I have a conference to attend this afternoon," said James, his gaze still fixed downward as he rapidly checked his messages on his phone.

"Of course, James, you are such an important person," she answered mockingly, smiling up at him. She rose to hug him and kiss him on the cheek, just as he leaned down to kiss her goodbye on the other cheek. Somehow they met in the middle. She had stood up into the most deliciously soft kiss.

James' hands slid around her, slowly, up her back, pulling her into an embrace. He kissed her tentatively at first, gently. Natalia felt the sun through the window warm on her face, felt the color rise to her cheeks, her heart beating wildly. The smell of expensive citrus cologne, the taste of his lips on hers, and the feel of his strong arms holding her to him gave her a rush of adrenaline. At the same time it was all so familiar, so reassuring. The kiss grew more passionate and Natalia sensed a hunger to the kiss she hadn't felt from James in a long time, and possessiveness. Reluctantly, slowly, Natalia pulled away. Like waking from a beautiful dream.

"You are late for a meeting."

She smiled up at him with her eyes twinkling, her cheeks pink, as she stepped slightly backwards. She couldn't remember the last time James had kissed her like that. James took her face gently in his hands, a smile spreading across his face and lighting up his eyes.

"I've always loved you, Natalia. I think you've always known that."

"Yes. Of course I know. I love you too."

"You do?"

"What do you mean?" Uncertainty crept into Natalia's voice as she felt her face flush. Natalia recalled the morning before when Evan was kissing her, could feel his hands moving over her. "Of course I love you. You know that."

"What about Evan?"

Startled, Natalia looked James over carefully. Noticing his expression, she avoided the question.

"What is wrong, James? We're happily married, aren't we?"

Natalia felt panicked. Did James already know of her kiss with Evan? Perhaps Evan had already admitted the kiss to Eva and Eva had called James, enraged. What would James say? What would he do? James reached out for her once more, and sliding his hands around her waist, he stepped in close and looked into her eyes.

"Yes, quite tragically, we are more or less happily committed."

"What do you mean, 'tragically' and 'more or less'?"

"Oh, darling. You know Eva. You know just as well as I do how marvelous she is and how lucky I should feel to be with her. But…" Hesitating, he stepped back, running his hands through his hair and looking down at the floor.

"I love you. I have for a long time. Actually, I fell in love with you the first time I saw you entering the building on your first day of work at the consultancy. All the women were hurrying with steely determination into the building in dark blue or black suits. And then there you were. You came gliding into the lobby in a sleeveless red sheath dress with a business jacket over your arm. Your head was up and a smile lit up your face. You glowed. All of a sudden time seemed to move in slow motion. I felt certain I had met you somewhere before. I felt I knew you before we introduced ourselves. I loved you long before we all went out for drinks after finishing our first project together and you brought Eva with you."

"Yes," answered Natalia, hardly daring to breathe. "And then we got married and had three beautiful children."

Natalia gave a sigh of relief. Everything was okay; in fact, better than before. James was falling in love with her all over again. Their life together would be happy again. Perhaps he would even come home most evenings and they would enjoy a glass of wine together while talking over the day, like they used to years before.

James slid his hands through his thick hair. Shaking his head he muttered, "You are right. I had my chance then. It's too late. I shouldn't be doing this to Eva. Not in this way. We have been together for too many years."

Natalia was silent, a sense of horror shattering her out of her shame, erasing her few moments of previous bliss from their embrace, fracturing it.

"But Natalia, darling, I meant what I said about you coming back to work with me," said James, his voice once again all business.

"As for your children, well, Eva and I both work long hours. Our children love their nanny; they are thriving in school. If Evan is planning to start working full time again instead of being there for your kids in the afternoons, then you could hire a nanny too. I think your children would be fine too. And as for the hours, I seriously can't imagine you working in consulting would require more hours than you put into your business right now."

Natalia's face was still frozen in a smile, while her mind was swirling in confusion and resistance. Evan, her own mother, and now even James believed that she was married to Evan, that she had children with Evan, that her life was with Evan. It just couldn't be true. James, her James, was married to Eva? Did that mean Eva had her children too? Wait. *That didn't make any sense*, she reasoned.

If she really hadn't married James, then they never had had their children. Natalia shook her head. She refused to consider a world in which her children didn't exist.

Once again staring at his phone, and without looking up into her eyes, James continued, "See you tonight at the event, Natalia."

Gathering his briefcase, James strode quickly out of the floral boutique.

"So, so, so, here I am, Natalia," called Antonio as he came out of the back room. "Time to go over the flowers for the evening!"

Antonio found Natalia standing still as a statue, staring at the front door of the shop. She was so overwhelmed with confusion her mind had gone blank.

"Natalia? Natalia!"

Natalia turned, trying to recollect herself. "Hello, Antonio?"

"Where is James? I thought he wanted to review the order with you."

"He had a meeting. You can review the order for tonight with me."

"Everything all right?" asked Antonio as he placed a folder on the table and started showing her the arrangements.

"Fine," said Natalia, smiling. "These are an elegant design. Vibrant colors. Brilliant, Antonio, they are perfect for..." Natalia couldn't remember what the event that evening was, or where it was. She tried to hide her confusion by admiring the photos a moment or two longer, wondering at the price of the exotic flowers but certain she should already know such information.

"I shall deliver the flowers to the venue this evening. You will need to of course help me with where exactly you would like them to be placed. Have you decided on using the terrace or the bar?" asked Antonio.

"Both, I think. The weather is still mild. We will serve the Apero on the terrace so that these professionals will have some fresh air after being at their desks all day. Then we will move into the restaurant," Natalia improvised.

Natalia considered the flowers around her for a moment. "Do you think they even notice the flowers at these events, Antonio?"

"Yes, they add a distinct ambiance to an evening. Even men who do not appreciate the beauty of flowers sense the change in energy when a room is filled with flowers and candles."

Natalia rose and gathered her purse. She kissed Antonio on each cheek and began slowly walking back toward her office.

Chapter 6

Natalia had spent the remainder of the morning working together with Mike and Mary on the event for the evening. It was a customer event for James' consultancy company at the Hotel Storchen's beautiful riverside restaurant. Over the course of the morning Natalia could feel knots in her shoulders starting to form and she found herself holding her breath while concentrating. The program, appetizers, welcome cocktails, menu, dinner wine, entertainment, and lighting concept were all reconfirmed before lunch.

Natalia sat in her office and regarded the new bouquet of flowers on her desk that Antonio had given her before she left. Apparently, she was meant to be leaving for yoga, but she had no idea where it was and her agenda gave no details.

Just then Mary knocked on her door. "Ready to go?"

"I didn't bring any yoga clothes with me today, Mary."

"No problem. Grab your mat and you can borrow some of mine. But don't you keep reserve clothes here?"

Mary made her way out to the common area and opened the top cupboard above the coat rack. There, stacked neatly, were at least ten different sets of workout outfits next to a stack of clean towels. Natalia selected an outfit and some towels and looked for a bag.

"Now, Natalia. I know you hate these yoga sessions, but I will not give you an excuse not to go. Hurry now, lady, or we will be late!"

"But I love yoga," answered Natalia.

Mary just snorted in response. "Sure you do."

Natalia quickly slung her mat over her shoulder, took out an outfit and a towel, and followed Mary to the elevator. They made their way rapidly down the street and into a building overlooking the lake. On the top floor the elevator doors opened and a waft of lavender hit her senses as she stepped out onto dark hardwood floors.

"Natalia, move it, lady, move it! We do not want to go into class late. What are you, eighty?"

Natalia turned and followed Mary into a changing room with soft lighting, a water fountain, and candles. After quickly changing and hanging up their clothes and bags in wooden lockers, they made their way back across the entry area and into a large bare room of sparkling white floors and huge windows looking out over the lake and the Alps in the distance. Both women unrolled their mats as the instructor closed the door to the room and flipped a switch. Lavender-scented steam started filling the room.

In a few minutes the temperature began to rise. Natalia felt herself smoothly following the instructor through the poses, her face flushing from her effort and the warmth of the room. Soon she was absolutely drenched in sweat and wondering exactly how much longer the class would continue. She glanced at her watch.

Out of the corner of her eye she noticed Mary smiling.

"Nice view, right, Natalia?" whispered Mary.

Natalia looked out the windows at the sun sparkling on the lake water and the sailboats gliding in the distance. She could see the rolling green hills and the snow covered alps in the distance.

"Not that view," laughed Mary, motioning with her head as she transitioned to downward facing dog. "That one up front."

Natalia examined the instructor as he effortlessly held himself in a handstand before gliding back into downward dog. Shirtless, the dark-haired man with brown eyes was pressing his hands into the ground and his hips back as he reached his heels effortlessly to the ground. Muscles rippled along his arms and back.

"Sexy," whispered Natalia. Mary grinned.

All at once Natalia started to feel dizzy. *I really should have eaten something before this class.* She was standing on one leg with her arms reached overhead in tree pose when she started wobbling dramatically. The instructor told them to transition to an arm balancing pose, but as Natalia tried to balance her weight on her arms and hug her knees onto her elbows up off the ground, she felt her entire body start to tremble and was suddenly certain she was going to fall flat onto her face. The gorgeous instructor was immediately by her side, placing his hands on her waist to keep her from falling.

"That is enough for you for today, Natalia," he said, helping her safely out of the pose. "You need to take child pose for the remainder of the session. Just relax."

Natalia slowly sat down on her heels and then bent forward, placing her forehead on the floor. A few minutes later everyone moved onto his or her back to rest. Natalia rolled over and joined them. Her body felt so heavy and relaxed. She let go of her deep yoga breathing and let her body breathe naturally.

"NATALIA! NATALIA, WAKE UP! Natalia, my dear, you need to open your eyes for me."

Natalia realized Mary was standing over her; she wanted her to wake up. She struggled to open her eyes and then gave up. Natalia reasoned that it was okay to fall asleep for a few moments after a yoga class. She fell back down deep.

NATALIA WAS VERY COLD. She opened her eyes and looked around at the large yoga studio. The room was cool again and the instructor was quietly cleaning the floor.

When he saw that she had opened her eyes he called out with amusement, "Good afternoon. You must have been exhausted to sleep so long on a hard floor!"

Natalia sat up sheepishly. How long had she been lying here?

"Why didn't you try to wake me up? Or Mary? I am so sorry."

A face peeked around the corner. "Here I am!" called Mary, smiling. She was showered and dressed with her hair and makeup perfectly done. Natalia felt a bit jealous of how radiant Mary looked with her glowing skin and thick flowing blond hair. Whereas she decided she must look as gross as she felt. Her red hair was a wet mat and she felt certain her mascara must have run down under her eyes.

"I tried to wake you but you were out cold. Listen, thanks for coming to yoga with me, I know this means I need to go with you to kick boxing tomorrow."

Natalia looked up at Mary, confused.

"You know? We agreed I could use some serenity?"

Natalia sat up. "Serenity?"

Mary laughed. "Okay. I need to learn to 'chill the hell out,' is how I think you put it. Well, I'm heading back to the office. I will pick you up a sandwich on the way. I know what you like. Would you also like a smoothie? How does strawberry mango sound today? I'll leave yours in the blender for you."

Natalia regarded Mary a little dazedly. "That is so sweet of you, Mary, thank you," she replied. Had she really had the nerve to tell Mary to 'chill the hell out'?

"Sure thing. Now snap to it, lady! We have work to do!"

Natalia heard the instructor laughing. "That Mary is a firecracker. Does it ever upset you how she talks to you? You are *her* boss, right?"

Natalia slowly stood up with a wry smile. "Maybe a little? But I think she talks to everyone like that. And apparently I tell her to 'chill the hell out.' I'm so sorry for falling asleep. I am so embarrassed."

"Think of this as an oasis. You can fall asleep like that every time if you need to, Natalia," said the yoga instructor.

"Thank you!" called Natalia as she hurried out of the room and toward a hot shower.

WALKING BACK TO WORK, Natalia felt like her every muscle had been massaged. She started thinking about her children. Guiltily she realized that she had not given a thought to them all morning. Then she remembered why. The children at home were not her own. Or so she had thought yesterday. Perhaps that had just been a strange dream. She would just call James and find out once and for all. She took out her phone and said, "Call James."

"Hello, Natalia."

"How are the kids, James?"

"Which kids?" asked James.

"Our kids!" answered Natalia.

Panic slowly filled Natalia. She couldn't remember who was watching her own children. Who was taking care of their children if James was still working crazy hours and she was now working sixty- to eighty-hour weeks?

"Who is taking care of them?" asked Natalia, panic in her voice.

"The kids are at school," answered James.

"And afterwards?"

"Afterwards they will be at home with the nanny."

Natalia considered this.

"A nanny is taking care of Anna, Allan, and Ben?"

"Who are they? Are they friends of my kids or something? Natalia, you are confusing me, darling. How can I help you? I am really busy; you need to be clear. Or you can still call Eva. I am sure she will help you in any way she can."

"I want to know where Anna, Allan, and Ben are. Do you know?"

Through the phone Natalia could hear James drumming his fingers on the desk.

"Natalia, I just told you that I have no idea who those kids are. See you this evening. Wait," said James, clearing his throat. "Please listen to me, Natalia. I never intended to hurt my kids or my wife by having an affair. I am so sorry. I hope you can forgive me."

Natalia saw a park bench in front of her and slowly sat down. The metal bars were very cold through her dress. She felt the cold seep in and move through her entire body. She was finding it difficult to breathe and her heat felt tight, aching in her chest.

What was James talking about? How could he not know Anna, Allan, and Ben? Natalia couldn't fathom a world without her children in it. The world began to spin.

Natalia decided to lie down on the park bench. She noticed people looking at her strangely, but she didn't care. The world was still twisting, her head felt light, and she needed to lie down to stop the spinning.

"Have a good day, James," she managed to say and ended the call.

Natalia lay looking up at the blue sky on the park bench. Three times a stranger approached her and asked if she required assistance. She told them all no, although she was beginning to think that she should go to the hospital. She decided to call Evan first.

"Hello, Evan, how are you? How are my kids?" ventured Natalia weakly when Evan answered the phone.

"Things are going smoothly today. Annabelle is fast asleep and I am reading to the twins."

Natalia paused. So this warped reality still remained. James had confirmed it and now Evan. She could not remember the children everyone insisted were her own. She struggled not to panic as memories of Anna, Allan, and Ben crowded into her mind. She longed to hold them in her arms. She missed them terribly. How could they not exist? That just was not possible.

"Hello? Natalia, are you still there?"

"Yes, yes, Evan, I am here. I still do not remember our children." Natalia could hear a door shut and her husband swearing.

"Evan? Are you there?"

"Yes, Natalia, I am here. I just needed a moment. What is going on with you? If you cannot remember your own children, don't you think you should be at the doctor's office instead of at work? I mean, who just wakes up and forgets their own children's existence! But then again, you are here so rarely, no wonder you have forgotten them. They almost do not remember you."

Natalia felt cornered. She didn't know how to respond to such animosity from her, her what? It was almost impossible to believe Evan was her husband. Then again, it also didn't sound like her best friend, like the Evan she knew and loved. What was going on? Where was the animosity coming from?

"Listen, Evan, I feel, I mean, we aren't really married, are we?"

"Are you crazy?"

Natalia hesitated. She did feel crazy. But she didn't want Evan to be angry with her either.

"I just, well, I mean, we certainly are not so happily married?"

"We are not so happily married? Is that some kind of joke, Natalia? How can we be happily married? When. You. Are. Never. Here!"

Natalia hated to have anyone, let alone Evan, angry with her. He had always been such a dear friend. He had never once raised his voice to her in all their years of friendship. He was her rock. She called him every day. They spent at least two afternoons a week together with the children swimming, skiing, going hiking and on picnics. There had been countless trips to the zoo, to the art museums, even holidays in hostels where they had shared the cooking and afterwards a bottle of wine. How could Evan be so mean to her now? It wasn't like him at all.

She lay there on the bench, tears stinging her eyes, her heart aching.

"You are a terrible wife and a terrible mother," Evan continued.

It was too much. Evan sounded just like James. Maybe everything James had said about her being a terrible wife and mother was true, because now Evan was saying the same things. Natalia shook her head. That didn't make sense. If she had never been married to James, then he had never said those things.

Natalia took the phone away from her ear and looked at it in shock. *There is no way this belligerent jerk is Evan.* Natalia knew Evan as a kind man, a generous, thoughtful, loving friend she could always turn to for support, help, laughter. Who was this stranger being so cruel to her?

Evan was still ranting when she put her phone back to her ear. "Natalia, you have an event every other night four nights a week! It is always the same. You always say after this event, life will settle down. But it NEVER does. I am like a single parent. I wake the children up in the morning, get them ready for school, see them off, drive to school, teach all morning, and then rush home to make the kids lunch. I play with them, discipline them, fill up their individual needs for recognition, love, and attention, and make sure they get plenty of exercise, fresh air, and healthy food before I shovel them into their beds every night. Repeat. Then I do all the washing and cleaning, work some more, and fall asleep before you come in the door."

Natalia felt like she must be dreaming. These were her complaints, the resentments about James she had buried beneath the surface of her friendly, accommodating exterior.

This phone call feels so surreal, thought Natalia.

"Natalia? Are you even listening to me?"

"Am I never home?" asked Natalia.

"Is that a joke? Why did you quit your last job? You promised us that owning your own business would enable you to spend more time with us. But it is just the same as before. Correction. It is worse than it was before. You should think about selling out of this new business and working for someone else again. At least you took your holiday and were home on the weekends during the day."

"Isn't my business profitable?" answered Natalia. She felt disconnected with the conversation, with the world even. It felt like she was looking down on herself from above. She looked so small, so powerless there on the park bench.

"Nice try, Natalia. Yes. You and I both know how much money you make. But you also know that money past a certain level of comfort is just not that important to me. It is you with the designer handbags, clothes, and shoes. You crave the wealth and the fancy four-star holidays. Not me."

Lying on her back on the icy bench, the cold seeping into her, Natalia began watching the clouds drift slowly across the sun. A burst of wind caused a shower of bright yellow leaves edged in crimson to flutter down from the tree in front of her. One landed in her lap.

Evan's words didn't hurt her at all. It felt like this man on the phone wasn't real. Natalia remembered all the conversations with Evan about his marriage to a completely different person, to Eva. Wait. Natalia sat up, the red and yellow leaves drifting down from her lap to the street.

Natalia knew how Evan felt and he knew how she felt. How many times had she told Evan that she was also married to a workaholic? James was never home, he was always aspiring toward ever more wealth and success at the cost of time with his children, with her. Natalia began strolling down the street.

"But you love me. We have children together, years of memories together," said Natalia softly, thinking of how she felt about her life with James.

"Love is a verb, Natalia," replied Evan.

Natalia paused and looked in the window of Louis Vuitton. She was tempted to go in and buy a new handbag. Evan said she was a spoiled, wealth-obsessed woman, and apparently she earned enough to afford one. Why not go with it? But then she turned away. She had a designer handbag on her arm; why should she buy another?

"Hello, Evan? I will not be home tonight. I think you know that I have an important customer event. I have some things to think about and yes, I think I should go and talk to a professional. I do not remember marrying you and I do not remember those children. Goodbye."

Natalia placed her phone in her purse. It immediately began to ring. Taking it out, she went to turn it off and then remembered that clients might need to reach her on her phone. She decided she didn't care.

Play the Game

Chapter 7

Natalia climbed the stairs to her office slowly, brushing tears from her cheeks. Nothing was making any sense. Evan was such a laid-back, funny guy. She had never heard him so bitter. He had never voiced his resentments so clearly. Generally he was quite easygoing and quick to forgive and make a joke out of an upsetting incident. True, he could be a little passive aggressive. But generally that was all to the good because most minor everyday irritations just did not need to be argued over. This was something different.

Clearly being married to Eva had made Evan happier than being married to her, Natalia thought. But even as the thought crossed her mind, Natalia realized how crazy it was. Either Evan had married her, which by all evidence was pointing to being the reality, or he had married Eva. One was true. The other was not.

And yet, Natalia remembered Evan being married to Eva. She could recall their wedding day, the birth of their babies. She remembered the way Eva had of showering Evan with admiration, appreciation, gifts, and special romantic weekend trips for the two of them alone over the years. Natalia admitted to herself that she had been a bit jealous.

Perhaps I should treat Evan more like Eva did, thought Natalia. Shaking her head, Natalia immediately realized what a crazy statement that was as well. Either Evan had always been married to her, or he had always been married to Eva. Unless he had divorced Eva to marry her, and James had divorced her to be with Eva? No. That really was highly unlikely, because what about the children? She would still have her children. Tired of going in circles, she decided to push all of it out of her head for a while.

Natalia walked into her office and Mike came running by her toward the stairs. Mary was close behind him.

"Natalia! Thank heavens you are here! We are late. I thought that perhaps you had fallen back asleep on the floor of the yoga studio. Here is your sandwich and your smoothie," said Mary, thrusting a wrapped sandwich into one hand and a drink into the other.

"Now you will just have to eat in the car on the way to the location. I do not know what has gotten into you. Punctuality is woven into the very fabric of your being...."

Mary was already on her way into the elevator. Natalia turned on her heel and walked in after her.

"Natalia! Your bag! Go grab it from your desk."

Natalia ran back into the office and grabbed the bag next to her desk. She ran back again.

"Off we go," said Mary happily as she pushed the button for the lobby. "Mike will pull around the office car."

Natalia decided she needed to establish the truth once again from yet another source. "Will my husband be at the event tonight?"

Mary turned around in her seat and giving Natalia a strange look said, "You tell me. Will he?"

Natalia sighed. She gave up on being subtle. "Do you remember the names of my husband and kids, Mary?"

"Of course I do. Evan, Nathan, Nick, and Annabelle. Really, Natalia, what has gotten into you today?" said Mary, applying lipstick while examining her reflection carefully in the elevator mirror.

"I think it was that bump on the head this morning. I am feeling a bit out of sorts."

"Oh, how thoughtless of me. I am sorry, Natalia, of course. Perhaps that hot yoga was not such a good idea after all?"

"I think I will be fine. I am just not myself today. I am so sorry I was late. I hope I didn't cause you undue stress? Perhaps you could be sure to help me through the event tonight? I have a feeling I could forget some names I should know."

"Of course I will help you," Mary beamed. "You are so self-sufficient and disciplined, it is like you pride yourself on not needing to ask anyone for additional help," said Mary. Pausing on the steps outside the building, Mary reached out for Natalia's hand and looked directly into her eyes. "You know you are important to me, Natalia. I want to be good to you, to help you in any way I can."

Natalia felt tears rise to the surface and looked quickly away. She could not remember Mary ever being able to voice her affection before, not in all their years of friendship. Why now? "That means so much. Thank you," Natalia breathed out, giving Mary's hand a squeeze and letting go.

Smiling, Mary stepped out onto the street and hurried down the steps and into the front seat of the car Mike already had waiting at the curb.

"What has gotten into you?" Mike asked.

"Can't a girl just smile for no reason?" replied Mary, winking at Mike.

"Sure, Beauty." Mike took her hand and kissed her fingertips.

Natalia took in the scene from the back of the car. What was going on here?

Mary looked back at Natalia.

"Eat your sandwich, lady, the drive isn't that long! And really, Mike, when was the last time you washed this car?"

"There she is again," laughed Mike. Mike looked in the rear view mirror and winked at Natalia. Natalia smiled back.

"What do you mean?" asked Mary in a sharp voice.

"Forget it, Mary," responded Mike.

NATALIA STARED OUT THE WINDOW. She reasoned that she had two options. One, she could admit that she believed she was married to James and her children were Anna, Allan, and Ben and possibly end up hospitalized. Two, she could try to accept this new reality, even if it seemed impossible to her to believe. Natalia began to eat her sandwich and consciously decided to put her worries about her children, her husband, and her very sanity away for the rest of the day. Focusing on work would be a welcome escape from the fear that she most likely was suffering a severe mental psychosis of some kind.

"So what are you wearing tonight, Natalia?" asked Mary.

"Um, this?" said Natalia.

"Really? Wow. You always wear some stunning dress," said Mary, turning in her seat to look back at Natalia.

"Yes, but I was wondering how appropriate that is," responded Natalia, improvising. "I mean, it is a customer event, right? Won't all the guests be coming direct from work in their suits?"

"Sure. But that never stopped you before," countered Mary.

"Well, what do you think?" asked Natalia.

Mary paused before answering. She turned and looked at Mike.

Mike answered, "I think you generate new business by looking different from the guests. That way they can easily see that you are not one of them. Or not anymore, anyway."

"I agree," said Mary.

"What shall I do then?" Natalia wondered aloud.

"I didn't bring a dress with me for the event."

"We will make a quick stop at Prada. I like their collection this season. They had a gray dress just your style."

"Prada, Mary? That's a bit pricey, isn't it? We could stop in somewhere else. Look, there is a pretty blue dress in the window of Esprit."

"You can't wear blue."

"Why ever not?"

"Because I am," retorted Mary. "And you are certainly not shopping at Esprit. Come on."

Mike dropped the women off in front of the Prada store and continued on to the location to set up the sound system and check the lighting on the small stage being set up.

Natalia followed Mary into the store. A clerk noticed them enter and then turned away, continuing to straighten handbags on the shelf. Natalia was surprised. In such an exclusive store she thought they would have better service. Instead, the woman was acting like they may not have a right to be in the store. Then a tall man with blue eyes and red hair saw them and immediately approached, breaking into a smile as he kissed Mary and Natalia on both cheeks.

"Mary! Natalia! Welcome. What shall we find for you today?"

"Hello, Hans! Natalia here needs a dress for this evening. The gray one in the window, I think."

"Of course! Right this way."

Hans led Natalia into a dressing room and brought her the gray dress, as well as one in a vivid red. "This lovely red would suit you better," Hans whispered and disappeared out of the dressing room. Natalia carefully tried on the red dress. The red was startling, but she had to admit it was beautiful against her pale skin and it complemented, instead of clashed with, her red hair.

"What do you think?" asked Natalia, turning to model the dress from every angle as she came out of the dressing room.

"Exactly! Sold. That dress looks amazing on you," enthused Hans.

"You don't think the color is too bright?" asked Mary. "Gray would be better, wouldn't it?"

"Now, Mary, don't be one of *those* friends. Natalia, don't listen to her on this one. You look gorgeous. Now off we go to select some matching red shoes," insisted Hans.

Natalia paid for the dress and shoes and followed Mary down the steps into the fresh air. Mary took her arm and they walked toward the lake.

"Sorry," mumbled Mary.

"What?"

"I said sorry! Don't make me shout it. The red dress looks great on you. I shouldn't have gotten all jealous."

Natalia looked over at her friend. Mary was staring straight ahead, her cheeks flushed pink from the frosty air.

"But why would you be jealous of me?" asked Natalia, surprised. "You are the beautiful one. You're so confident and strong. I am the one who envies you."

"Oh, Natalia," Mary said, resting her head on her friend's shoulder, "you don't know how much I needed to hear that today."

THE NEXT THREE HOURS went by in a frenzied blur. There were tables to reposition, seating cards to place on every table, flower arrangements to organize, candles to distribute and light, waiters to be briefed, menus to be placed at each setting. On the terrace hanging out over the river and in the lounge they made sure the appetizers were ready to go, that chilled glasses of champagne, white wine, and beer were ready, and flickering candles were everywhere. Inside, Natalia surveyed the space for the dinner.

The ambiance was perfect. Warm colors combined with the modern furniture and the historical building to dramatic effect in the candlelight.

The entertainment was completing a sound check and the ballerinas were warming up. Some dancers from the Zürich ballet were going to complete a thirty-minute selection from *Romeo and Juliet,* which was currently in rehearsal for the winter season. The small orchestra would accompany the dancing and then add soft background music to the meal. There were a few sword fights, so Natalia thought that even men not enthralled with ballet would be entertained. After the meal the head of the consultancy, James, would make his speech before coffee and dessert were served.

Natalia surveyed the cuisine on the menu card. It was a compromise of extremely gourmet with the familiar. To start there would be a dish of green and white asparagus with sautéed strawberries and prosciutto in a lime ginger dressing, followed by a pumpkin coconut foam soup with chutney. The main dish would be the completely traditional Swiss classic Zueri Geschnetzeltes, with butter roesti. This consisted of pieces of veal in a cream mushroom sauce with crisp hash browns. Dessert would be comprised of a variety of miniature pastries such as mini chocolate mousse cream cakes, crème brûlée macaroons, raspberry tarts, and strawberries in a chili lime reduction. Natalia was getting hungry just reading the menu. She was particularly looking forward to trying all of the miniature desserts.

Evan would appreciate this menu, Natalia thought. *Too bad he can't be here tonight with me to enjoy the meal.*

She knew he would enjoy the novelty of a few gourmet starters followed by a traditional "solid" meal he was sure to like. And she knew he would have everyone at his table laughing as they enjoyed their wine and food.

"NATALIA, LET'S GO CHANGE," Mary said. Natalia followed her upstairs to a room.

"We rented a room just to change our clothes in?" asked Natalia in disbelief.

"Oh, did you change your mind about staying the night then?" asked Mary as she pulled on her silk dress and carefully pulled on new nylons.

"I think Evan and the kids are really missing me tonight."

"No doubt they are; however, the event starts at seven and goes until at least ten. By the time you arrived home they would have been asleep for hours." Mary's voice softened and she looked into Natalia's eyes. "You are starting to look really worn, Natalia. I know I am overstepping my bounds but I care about you and you need the sleep. Mike and I can carry more of the responsibility. I know what a perfectionist you are and that you don't want to overwork us. But you are really good to us and we care about you. You could ease off a bit, go home early once or twice a week, and let us pick up the slack."

Natalia felt tears coming to her eyes. "Thanks, Mary. I will think that over."

Mary switched back to her usual bossy mode. "We have ten more minutes before we need to be out at the venue. Just enough time to freshen our makeup and hair."

But Natalia took just five minutes to get ready and then lay down on the bed to rest. She watched Mary combing out her long blond hair.

"You do look like Sleeping Beauty," Natalia remarked.

"Thank you. Listen, don't tell Mike this, but I love it when he calls me Beauty."

"What is the deal between you anyway?"

"What do you mean? Did he say something?"

"No. No."

"Don't scare me like that, Natalia. I really think he has been acting strange lately. I am seriously worried that he has met someone else and maybe he even has started having an affair."

"Mary!" interrupted Natalia. "Don't let your imagination run away with you."

"You are right. We don't have time for nonsense. Out we go."

NATALIA ENTERED THE BAR and surveyed the ambiance, food, wine, and waiters. Everything was in place. She turned to the railing and looked out at the view. When she turned James was standing in the doorway and took a beer offered him by a waiter. Their eyes met across the room.

Natalia noticed that James suddenly looked uncertain. Or at least she thought he looked less self assured than usual. Generally he was always at perfect ease in any company. Flirting with women of all ages came naturally and talking with men always flowed smoothly. He could joke with his plumber just as easily as he could discuss high-level philosophy and economics with some of his extremely educated customers.

But now he was at a loss for what to say or how to act. He was looking at her dress. Natalia smiled. She knew that James had always found red particularly alluring. She walked over to him.

"Are you looking forward to the evening?"

James smiled at her. "This customer event is essential to retaining customer loyalty and generating new business for my consultancy. It is one of my favorite nights of the year, Natalia."

"Of course it is, James, you workaholic. Other people would think an evening on holiday with their family would fall into that category. But then you wouldn't get to stand on stage and be the center of attention, would you?" said Natalia.

A hand with a huge diamond glittering on the ring finger slipped around James' waist.

"I agree with Natalia, love. Your favorite night of the year should be with me."

James put his arm around Eva. "But you are with me tonight."

"Yes, but at a work event, it's not the same," teased Eva.

"Eva, you and I both know how much you love a party. You like to be admired from all sides."

Eva laughed. "Well, that is true. But what woman doesn't, I ask of you?"

Natalia subtly examined her friend from head to toe. She was wearing a sleeveless black designer dress that hugged her voluptuous figure in exactly the right places. The woman seemed to radiate sexiness. With dark raven hair, creamy, caramel-colored skin, and brown eyes, she had a glow to her that Natalia and any other woman would envy. Natalia had felt beautiful a few moments before. Now standing next to Eva she was aware of her slender, nearly straight figure. She envied the other woman's voluptuousness.

Natalia could not understand why James would be kissing any other woman when he had this gorgeous woman to come home to. Suddenly shame washed over her as she remembered the morning kiss. She could not imagine what she had been thinking to kiss someone's husband, let alone her friend's. If someone kissed her husband she would react with outrage. Natalia sighed. She decided she could always plead insanity. She imagined herself in front of a stern judge.

"Honestly, Judge, I thought he was *my husband*, or I would have never kissed him."

"Oh, Natalia, but you look exhausted! Look at those rings under your eyes. You must have worked so hard to organize this event." Eva took both of Natalia's hands in her own. "It looks simply chic! Everything is so elegant and modern. Now lead me to the champagne."

Natalia led Eva to the bar and handed her a glass of champagne. A handsome man ten years younger than Eva immediately engaged her in conversation and within moments men surrounded her. Natalia heard Eva laughing. Clearly she was in her element.

Natalia began networking. She concluded that if this really was her life, then she wanted her business to be a success. She better manage existing relationships and use this as a platform to generate new business as well. It was quite the undertaking. She quickly realized that just about everyone either knew her well or knew of her. Smiling, charming, and sometimes flirting her way through the crowd, she worked diligently to hide the fact that she could not recall one face or name in the room.

Natalia promised herself to sit at the computer before her next event and look up each and every person on the guest list on the Internet and find out their professional background and perhaps even personal interests. Hopefully she could also even find photographs to match names with faces; with LinkedIn it was likely she would succeed.

She checked with Mary briefly in the lobby to find out if any unexpected guests had arrived. She answered that yes, all of the guests who had sent in their reservation had arrived, and nine more besides.

Natalia made her way to the kitchen and informed the cook that they needed nine more meals prepared. Then she quickly set to work with the serving staff to set up an additional table and put out place cards. She needed a flower setting. Natalia discreetly entered the bar and took a vase of flowers.

"And what do we have here? A flower thief?" declared a man in a deep, gruff voice. While he looked tanned and fit, with sparkling blue eyes, his hair was white and he had lines around his eyes as he smiled.

Natalia leaned in. "You caught me red-handed."

"You are taking those home with you, are you?"

"Yes, exactly, I always crash events like these on my way home from work to collect flowers for my apartment."

"And you get away with it on a regular basis without getting caught?"

"Of course. You would be surprised what you can get away with if you act like you have a right to do what you are doing."

The gentleman laughed. "Natalia, it is good to see you. When are you going to get tired of carrying around flowers and come back and do some real work for me?"

Natalia swore internally. Who was this man? Apparently he was quite fond of her, so it was important to remember him. Her mind was blank. She deduced that he must work at the consultancy, if he wanted her to come back and work for him. Perhaps he was James' boss?

"James is not enough for you then?" Natalia responded, smiling. "I can't imagine you miss me when you still have him to work for you."

"Now, Natalia, you know I continue to hire James to come and work for my company. But just between you and me: the work is not nearly at the same level since your departure. It is now obvious whose brains were behind the real work. I must say I preferred your approach. You have a keen mind, my dear. A keen mind. Shame to waste it on flowers."

"Arthur! So good to see you." Another man interrupted them without a sideways glance at Natalia. "How is your business doing?"

Natalia placed her hand on Arthur's arm and leaning in, looked him directly in his intelligent, amused eyes. "Thank you, Arthur, I needed that. And who knows? Maybe I really will return to strategic consulting soon."

"Good for you, Natalia," answered Arthur, patting her on the arm, ignoring the man at his side.

Natalia smiled brightly and disappeared into the restaurant, sending a furtive glare over her shoulder at the man who had so rudely interrupted them.

NATALIA LOOKED AT HER WATCH. It was seven fifteen. In ten minutes she needed to announce dinner and usher all the guests from the bar to their tables. Natalia quickly made her way to the lobby and took the elevator to her hotel room. On the way she dialed home. Natalia almost thought she must have dreamed her last telephone call with Evan. If she was married to him, was he really so antagonistic toward her all the time? Did he always talk to her like that on the phone? Natalia wanted to find out. She also thought it might bring her memory back if she heard her children's voices over the telephone.

"Mommy!" answered a little girl. Natalia was taken aback anew. This was not her little girl. But that was nonsense. Everyone said this was her daughter, so she would just need to pretend along like she had been doing at work all day. A wave of fatigue washed over her.

"Hello, sweetheart. Tell me about your day."

The little girl's voice became very quiet. "Hello, honey, I can't hear you, you need to speak up." Then Natalia realized the little girl was crying softly over the phone.

"I miss you, Mommy. Please come home."

"I am so sorry, honey, I can't tonight. I have to work."

"But you weren't even with us all yesterday. Don't you like being with us anymore?"

"Of course I do, sweetheart. I adore you and I miss you so much."

"Good night, Mommy."

"Wait! Honey!"

"Hi, Mom." A boy's voice came on the phone.

"I don't care you aren't ever here."

"Oh? Well, you must be having fun then. I am sure your daddy is doing a marvelous job taking care of you."

"Yeah, he is. I like being with him way better than you anyway."

Natalia felt like she was being hit in the heart. The boy sounded like her Allan. "I can understand why you feel like that, my little honey bunny."

"Don't call me honey bunny. I'm not a baby anymore. I am six."

"I miss you very much. I love you."

"What about me?" Another little boy's voice came on the phone. "I bet you love them more than you love me."

Natalia inhaled deeply. "That is not true. I love you so much, sweetheart. I miss you so much. I would love some alone time just with you and no one else."

Natalia heard the little boy call out, "She said she wants alone time just with me and not with any of you!"

Then she heard both other kids in the background start to cry out in protest.

Natalia called, "That is not true! I want time alone with each of you," even though she knew they wouldn't be able to hear her.

Evan took up the phone next. "Great, Natalia, just perfect. Everything was calm and happy before you called. Go back to your party." The phone went dead.

Natalia felt tears streaming down her face. *Evan doesn't sound like himself at all*, thought Natalia. *He sounds like James.* She took a deep breath, went to the bathroom, and fixed her makeup before making her way down to the lobby in the elevator. When the elevator doors opened, there stood James.

"James! Is something wrong?" asked Natalia, panicked.

"Relax, Natalia, I just needed a moment to go back through my speech before dinner." James looked uncharacteristically uncertain.

"Of course. I will leave you to it."

Instinctively she reached out and squeezed his arm as she passed by.

"Natalia?" Natalia turned and paused on the steps.

"You look beautiful tonight." James let his gaze travel the full length of her body.

Natalia felt herself glow. She could not remember the last time James had told her she looked beautiful. She turned and walked back down the steps and stood in front of the man she felt sure she had married.

She looked directly into his eyes and said quietly, "I am certain you will give an amazing speech."

While she spoke, a longing washed over and through her whole body to step closer, close enough to smell his citrus aftershave and feel his lips on hers. But then she remembered Eva standing next to James at the apéro.

Without waiting for a response, Natalia turned and almost ran up the stairs, as if away from danger. With a pounding heart Natalia made her way back into the restaurant.

Whose Life Am I Living?

Chapter 8

"**W**HERE HAVE YOU BEEN, NATALIA? You are late!" hissed Mary, shaking a finger. "You should have been here ten minutes ago! The ballet already started. Now sit down," she concluded, pointing at the only open chair at the table.

Natalia paused for a long moment, looking at Mary. Then she said coolly, "Mary, last I checked, you work for me, not the other way around. Watch your tone." Then she turned back to the table. "How is the wine, everyone?"

Mary looked shocked. Her cheeks flushed and she took a large drink of her wine. Natalia pretended not to notice and, smiling, took a sip of her own wine. Natalia wondered why she had never stood up to Mary before. Was this a new development that Mary talked to her so disrespectfully all the time? Natalia mused that if Mary were her boss, then she would quit working for her after being talked to on a regular basis that way. She had enough of it at home from James—Evan—well, from both of them. The last thing she needed was to be talked to harshly at work too. Natalia sighed. She realized she had just taken out her stress and anxiety on Mary.

"Mary? I said that a bit harshly, I'm sorry."

Mary held Natalia's gaze a moment without replying. Then looking around uncomfortably at the guests seated at their table she said, "No, you were right. I shouldn't talk to you like that. I will try to change my tone. I am sorry."

After the ballet dancers finished their piece to loud applause, Natalia followed the dancers into the bar. She had set up tables with the remaining appetizers and champagne should the dancers want some. She invited them to have a drink before they left. Pleased, the dancers each took a drink and relaxed on the lounge chairs in the bar in the candlelight, snacking. Natalia herself took a glass of champagne and went out onto the terrace. She took a few deep slow breaths of fresh night air.

"Are you staying here tonight?" a voice whispered in her ear.

It was James. She could feel his breath on her neck. He was close enough that she could smell him and feel the warmth radiating from his body in the cold. She knew what it would feel like to take a step backwards, to feel his arms wrap around her, his face buried in her hair.

"I could come meet you for breakfast quite early. Maybe even deliver it personally to your room."

Natalia felt her heart hammering and her fingers tingle in the cold. She turned to look at the man she loved.

"You are with Eva and I am with Evan." Natalia didn't know if it was a question or a statement.

James let out a huge sigh. "Yes. That is true."

"Are you sure?"

"What do you mean am I sure, Natalia? No. Of course I am not sure. Therefore I am standing here trying to talk you into letting me visit you tomorrow morning."

Natalia considered him carefully before answering. "You never fell in love with me all those years ago. You never chose me over her." Tension had crept into Natalia's voice. Her anger masked her hurt, giving her power instead of despair.

Everything suddenly made sense. All those years ago James had chosen Eva instead. And somehow she had ended up marrying Eva's childhood crush.

"Leave me alone, James. Go away."

Natalia turned her back to him and looked out over the lights twinkling on the inky darkness of the river. So he had chosen Eva instead of her.

THE FOOD WAS DELICIOUS but Natalia could not enjoy herself. James had married Eva, the man she didn't remember marrying was furious with her, and worst of all she couldn't even remember her own children. To top it all off, she couldn't decide why on earth she had opened up an event planning agency. She had loved consulting.

While she had to admit she was excellent at the meticulous planning and creativity that made events successful, she knew she was terrible at the small talk parties required. Natalia very much thought she should sell her company and go back into consulting. In her opinion consulting fit her education, skills, and most importantly, personality, much better than working parties did. Why had she ever left consulting?

Suddenly a thought struck her. Maybe she had left consulting to get away from James once he had chosen to ask Eva to marry him. But there were still so many holes in her history that she wanted to fill. She was too impatient to wait for her memory to come crashing back into place, if it ever would. She needed answers now. The best person to get them out of, she realized, was Eva, especially an Eva who had been drinking champagne and wine all evening.

Natalia realized that the crowd around her was laughing. James was indeed giving an entertaining speech. There would be some time for mingling and dancing before coffee and dessert. Then she would need to be at the door to say good night to the guests and help Mike and Mary pack up the equipment and flowers so they could take it all back to the office. Natalia realized her window for cornering Eva tonight was small.

Leaning over to Mike she whispered, "Can you make sure everything in here is going smoothly for the next twenty minutes, Mike?"

Mike nodded at her distractedly. He had been laughing again at something James said up on the stage.

She stood up discreetly and made her way toward Eva's table. Natalia was right beside Eva when James finished his speech and the band began to play.

"Eva, I haven't had you to myself all night," exclaimed Natalia buoyantly. "Come have an after-dinner drink with me at the bar."

Eva stood up, smiling, and said, "Lead the way, darling. We haven't had time to chat in ages."

The bar, as Natalia had hoped, was almost empty. Natalia perched on a chair at the bar and Eva did the same. She ordered two martinis, extra large, hoping it would make Eva a little less suspicious during their conversation.

"Wow, what a night. It is such a shame that Evan couldn't be here. He loves parties," said Natalia.

"Oh yes, that is so true," replied Eva. "He loves a party as much as I do. He would have enjoyed himself tonight. You need a nanny like we have, Natalia. Then Evan can come to all your events. I think that would help your marriage."

"You know things have been a little tense with us lately," ventured Natalia. She tried to frame it as a question and a statement all at once.

"That is putting it mildly," answered Eva. "Such a shame, sweetheart, that you can't be as happily married as James and I are."

Natalia felt like slapping her friend. Worse, she felt like admitting that James had just been kissing her that very morning in the flower shop. Natalia's head began to spin. Nothing was making any sense. Natalia wanted to rest her face on the cool marble of the bar. It was very tempting.

Eva must have sensed her best friend's alarm because she put her arms around her friend, saying gently, "I am sorry, Natalia, that wasn't kind. I am very sorry, you know, that you and Evan have been having a hard time. You are such wonderful people. I love you both so much."

"Remember when we first met?" asked Natalia, leading her in the direction she wanted.

"Of course I do. I introduced you. I remember when you walked into the party James and I put on at our first apartment together. Evan was standing in front of the back door telling a joke and everyone was laughing. That was why I fell in love with him as a kid, you know, because he was so funny. The next thing he knew, you opened the door right into his head. He said, 'There are less painful ways of getting a man's attention, beautiful.' You laughed. And he said, 'Aren't you going to tell me how sorry you are?' and I remember this because it was so uncharacteristic for you: you stepped up, took his face in your hands, and said, 'No' and kissed him softly on the lips. Then you sauntered away to get yourself a drink from the bar. You should have seen his face. I knew you had him hook, line, and sinker."

"That doesn't sound like me...." answered Natalia.

"I know, right! You used to be so studious, serious, reserved. Like Mary, only less charming."

Natalia pushed her friend's arms away. "Hey!"

"Well, it was true, love. But then, I don't know why, all of a sudden you up and quit your job at the consultancy, started your own event planning business, and became the life of the party. You and

Evan together were the perfect power couple. I remember being a bit jealous of you."

"And then we got married."

"Yes. I have to admit, I was even more jealous when you got married before I did."

Natalia was silent for a moment, trying to remember and register everything she was learning.

"I can't believe I walked up and kissed a man I didn't know in front of a bunch of strangers," said Natalia disbelievingly.

"I know, right! I hardly can believe it myself. But I was there. I watched you with my own two eyes. It just goes to show even the people closest to you can take you by complete surprise."

"You have no idea," said Natalia glumly, thinking about her kiss with James that morning. Now Natalia did not know how to feel. Eva was acting like a loving person and a good friend. She almost felt bad about kissing James that morning, but not quite. After all, she reminded herself, you did think you were kissing your husband, not hers. And Eva could utter little mean zingers now and then.

"Sometimes I have thought you would make Evan happier. You two are always laughing together when we go out or are at a party," ventured Natalia.

"Oh for goodness' sake, Natalia, don't be ridiculous. Evan adores you. You just need to take some time for your marriage. Maybe take a break from work for a couple days or something, like James does for me, and have a romantic getaway. You have been working too hard. So hard, I was even worried about you having a nervous breakdown or something. We haven't had a girls' night, an afternoon lunch together, not even a coffee date, in what? Months? Let Mary and Mike take over an event or two. You need a mental health holiday."

"You have no idea."

"Yes, see? I am so perceptive. Now I better go back." Eva hugged Natalia and sashayed her way back into the party.

Natalia felt anger pulsing all the way to her fingertips as she watched her friend walk away. She hated the way Eva's hips were swaying seductively, the way she flipped her shiny hair over her shoulder and smiled at the man greeting her at the door. Why was she so angry with Eva? She couldn't explain why. After all, what had she ever done to her besides make a few underhanded comments? Hadn't they watched each other's children grow up together?

"Eva?" Natalia went to stand up and go after her friend. Natalia wanted to ask her if James really did take a couple days off work to go off with Eva on romantic getaways. He had never done that for her. Why was he cherishing Eva in a way he had never loved her?

Wait. James was never your husband, Natalia reminded herself. You have no right to feel the heat in your chest, nor the pulsing in your temples. Eva is the one who has the right to be angry. In her confusion, Natalia tripped over the bar stool as she went to run after her friend and went crashing to the floor.

"NATALIA, HOW ARE YOU, my love? It's Eva. The doctor will be in to see you in just a moment. I love you. Do you hear me? I love you, darling. You just relax and come back to us when you feel better. I am here for you. Natalia? Natalia?"

Natalia struggled to open her eyes. She felt so tired. She felt so stupid. Who fell over their feet as much as she did? It wasn't normal.

Natalia opened her eyes.

"There you are, honey. I was worried. Should we take you to see a doctor?" asked Eva, her brow creased with worry.

"Oh no, I am fine," muttered Natalia, while struggling to her feet and searching for her heels. One of them was halfway across the bar. She went to go after it but Eva was faster.

"Just take it slow there, Natalia," said Eva.

Natalia smiled up at Eva. "I am fine, really; I am so embarrassed. Let's go back into the party."

Eva looked her over uncertainly, "Well, if you are sure…."

"I am sure."

"Wait," said Eva, reaching out and taking her friend's hand. "You are the sweetest, most loving woman I know. I feel so lucky you are my friend. I love you. Remember that, okay?"

Arm in arm the women reentered the party.

NATALIA MADE SURE she was at the entrance to personally wish each guest good night as they left. She handed each person a small box of Swiss chocolates in her company colors with her company card discreetly tucked under the ribbon. She also encouraged anyone who wanted flowers to take an arrangement home with them.

"What shall we do with the rest of the flowers, Natalia?" asked Mary. "Take them back to the office?"

"Take as many as you would like home with you, Mary. We'll take the rest to the office."

It took over an hour to pack everything up. Natalia offered to go with Mary and Mike back to the office to unpack, but they insisted they could handle it on their own. Natalia went upstairs to her room. After a hot shower she climbed into clean sheets and was asleep before she could summon the energy to set her alarm.

Bury Me in Lies

Chapter 9

"Natalia! Natalia! hello, Natalia, answer me!"

Natalia turned away from the voice. It sounded far away; perhaps someone was at her door. No. It was too much effort to open her eyes. No housekeeping, she wanted to shout. Yesterday was insane. Who worked from seven in the morning until midnight? She fell back asleep.

Natalia heard a phone ringing. She reached for her phone and answered it with closed eyes. "Hello?"

"Wake up, Natalia! We need you. Natalia? It is Tuesday and nine in the morning."

Natalia realized it was Evan talking.

"You are mad at me."

"I love you, honey. Your kids love you. We miss you. Come home."

"I'm sorry I have to work so much."

"Natalia, I want you to be able to come home. I love you so much."

"I am so tired," Natalia mumbled, and without opening her eyes she went back to sleep.

There was sun on her face. Natalia tried to recall if she had left the window open in the night. Yes. She almost always slept with the window open for fresh air. She opened her eyes and looked about her at the hotel room. After a few moments she got up and dressed, pinned up her hair, applied some light makeup, and was out the door in a few minutes.

Hesitating in the lobby, Natalia checked her watch. It was ten minutes past seven. Confused, she paused. Didn't Evan call her and say it was past nine in the morning? It must have been a dream, she realized. Saddened, she continued through the lobby and into the restaurant for some breakfast. Natalia realized how good it felt when she thought Evan had called and, full of love, told her he wanted her home. The waitress came by and asked for her order.

She ordered a black coffee, a croissant, a crusty wholegrain roll, butter, jam, and fresh-squeezed orange juice. A few minutes later Natalia took the croissant out of the basket and realized it was still warm from the oven. Natalia decided to order a cappuccino and a second croissant. She gathered a few newspapers and settled down to read the international and business sections. The modern furniture and indirect lighting were beautiful, in her opinion, especially juxtaposed against the historic stone of the walls. But it was also rather uncomfortable.

Smiling, the waitress brought her a burgundy cushion.

"Thank you," said Natalia, wondering at the excellent service.

"It looks like you are settling in for a while. This will help you get more comfortable," the waitress said, smiling.

"They have excellent service here, don't they?" said a deep voice. "Unfortunately, that is not the norm everywhere in this country."

Natalia looked up to see James standing beside her table. "But then that is why you selected this venue for my event yesterday. May I join you for breakfast?"

Natalia motioned to the seat across from her and James sat down, ordering a coffee and a roll from the smiling waitress.

"So, darling, after sleeping on your decision, do you still want to come back to the consultancy?" James asked.

Natalia took a moment before answering. She registered the *darling*. This must mean that he was trying to endear her to him. Whatever life she had woken up to a few days ago, she needed to start making it her own. Clearly the current situation was not going well. She never saw her family.

Yesterday this had been a blessing. She missed her children dreadfully and she was putting off the moment when she walked through her front door and came face to face with three small strangers. She must have had some sort of mental break. Everyone insisted that this was her life and those three children were her own. Natalia struggled to overcome panic at the thought of how it could be that her husband and mother, in fact everyone she talked to, had no knowledge of Anna, Allan, or Ben. Pushing the panic aside she took a deep breath and looked directly at James.

"Yes. I would like to come back to consulting."

"What will you do with your company?"

Natalia paused and took a sip of her cappuccino.

"I will sell it. I will offer it first to Mary and Mike."

"Do you think they can arrange the capital to buy your business?"

"Yes."

James set down his coffee cup and reached across the table. Instead of taking her hand in his he began gently caressing her open palm with his fingertips.

Without looking up he said quietly, "Perhaps you should retain your business instead. If you come to work for me, then nothing can ever happen between us."

Natalia gave pause. She let James caress her palm and slide his fingers over her inner wrist. James continued, "You are lovely, Natalia, and brilliant. I love your sense of humor and how you are often so close to laughter. I even love your intensity. I see the way you look at me; I know what you are feeling." James leaned in over the table and his voice hushed to a whisper. "I know, right now, you are imagining what it would feel like, to feel my fingers gliding over your skin."

Still caressing her palm, James reached slowly up with the other hand and gently traced his fingers along her collarbone.

Natalia realized that it could quickly become addicting to be so adored. James used to adore her like this, when they first fell in love. The thrill of falling in love with James all over again would be so intoxicating. No one would ever need to know, thought Natalia. It would be so easy. She had not checked out of her room yet. She would only need to stand up and wordlessly make her way out of the restaurant and up the elevator. She was certain that James would follow her to her room. Natalia made the mistake of looking up into James' eyes. Energy passed between them as they sat in silence, an intensity of emotion.

"Sparkling water for you."

The waitress set down a glass of mineral water. Natalia, startled out of her reverie, pulled back her hand as if burned and sat up straight.

"Thank you," answered Natalia, but the waitress was already gone. Natalia reprimanded herself. What was she thinking? She had a husband and three children at home. An affair would bring guilt and most likely a great deal of heartache for multiple people in her life that she loved. Natalia knew deep down that she had loved James from the very first moment she had first met him. Tall and handsome, brilliant and hard working, James had left Natalia a bit breathless. She had enjoyed every moment in his presence; working with him on projects had been wonderful. But apparently James had chosen Eva. So she had ended up marrying Evan instead. And wasn't Evan the better choice? Wasn't Evan more loving, more attractive, more fun? Sure James made more money, but did that matter to her?

Natalia delved down deep into the longing for James and felt anger too. James was being a coward. She didn't want a trashy affair. She wanted a love story. The love story she thought they had had, but that was increasingly proving to be a figment of her imagination. Natalia tried to pull up memories of falling in love with Evan, of their wedding day, of their years together. Nothing came.

"James, I think we can keep our relationship professional. After all, it will not be our first time working together," she answered icily.

James reached into his bag and pulled out a contract. He paused, and then reluctantly, he handed it over to her. "Well, if you are certain, then here is a contract for you to consider. How about you come into my office on Friday at a quarter to twelve, darling? We will meet with my HR manager and then you and I can go out for that business lunch?"

"Perfect. Thank you, James."

NATALIA LEFT THE HOTEL and walked quickly toward her office. She was becoming more and more convinced that she needed to visit a mental health professional. She decided to give herself just one more week.

Then, if I still can't remember my life, I will go in and see someone with a solid reputation.

Natalia wondered if it could really be true that she was married to Evan and James to Eva. Could it be that she had been in love with James all these years, and too much fighting with Evan had caused her to wake up in a delusion? Had she wished history could rewrite itself so badly that her unconscious took over? Maybe it had led her to forget everything about her real life in preference for James and the three beautiful children they should have had together. Was that what had happened? Natalia didn't know. Pausing, she realized that now she was furious with James. How had he failed to declare his love for her all those years ago? She couldn't believe he had chosen to marry Eva instead; they weren't even well suited. Anger and resentment against both James and Eva boiled up inside of her. She would show them. Evan may have been furious with her in the past, but she could fix that. Natalia knew Evan adored her; they had been best friends for so many years. Hadn't she wondered, more than once, what her life would be like if she had married Evan instead of James?

He's way sexier than you, James, Natalia thought vindictively, *and he's funnier too.* There was no longer a line standing between her and Evan. She could go home and step right over it and into his arms. She would build a beautiful marriage with that sexy man, a marriage so happy and tender that both James and Eva would turn green with envy.

On her walk to work Natalia decided that she did not want to arrive for the day in the same clothes as the day before. As she passed by the Gucci store she stopped on a whim and went inside. It was early in the morning, but when the stylist offered her an espresso or a glass of champagne, she accepted the champagne. With excellent service she soon discovered a sleeveless wool blend sheaf dress in sky blue with a belt that crisscrossed around her waist. After making one last stop to purchase a new set of underwear with matching bra, she felt like a new woman walking into her office building.

When the elevator doors opened Natalia expected to see Mary and Mike. Instead, she found herself alone in the office. Sitting down at her desk she opened her calendar and realized that both of her employees had the morning off. She patiently examined every appointment in her calendar for the next week. She was happy to discover there were no events scheduled for that day.

Natalia's mood quickly darkened when she looked at the rest of the week. There was an event Wednesday, Thursday, and Friday night. Each of her days was packed with meetings with clients to pitch venues, menus, entertainment, flowers, guest gifts, and the list went on. She clearly had a lot of work to do the rest of the week.

When am I ever going to see my family? she wondered.

She noticed her heart had started racing and her palms were cold and sweaty. Standing up, Natalia went to the window, looking out over the town. A happy marriage, joyful children, they required overtime hours, too. Abruptly she turned back to her desk and took out her cell phone.

"Call Mary," she directed. After seven rings Mary answered.

"Natalia?"

"Mary, I apologize for calling you on your morning off. But I need to ask for your help. Do you think you could come into the office and prepare for the event for tomorrow? I have some other business I need to attend to."

Mary answered hesitantly, "I was hoping to have the day off after the late event last night and the long nights ahead this week…"

"I understand that, Mary. But here is an incentive. You will be responsible for single-handedly planning the final details for the event for tomorrow night. You have done the majority of the preliminary work for this client anyway. The event will be yours from A to Z. I will not even be attending."

"Seriously?" Natalia heard a swishing noise over the phone as Mary suddenly sat bolt upright in bed. "You have always micromanaged every detail of any event we have ever had."

"I trust you now, Mary. I know you will ensure a perfect evening down to the last detail. I will leave the office in thirty minutes and

I will not be available again until Thursday. We will meet here again on Thursday morning for a post-event report from Wednesday and to check on the status of the next two events."

Mary huffed in surprise, or was it shock? "You will be out of the office for two days before three big events? You will not even need me to check in during the event tomorrow night to reassure you that it is proceeding smoothly?"

"No, Mary. I am handing the responsibility completely over to you and Mike. I trust you. See you Thursday!"

"See you Thursday, Natalia."

Who Owns the Truth?

Chapter 10

Natalia was standing at the stove with an apron tied over a stunning dress when Evan walked in the door. She watched him widen his eyes in surprise when he saw that the table was set, candles were lit, and there were fresh bouquets of roses and tulips on the table and the counter.

"Hi, honey. Lunch will be ready in ten minutes. Why don't you tell the kids to wash their hands and then you sit down and have a glass of wine?" Smiling, Natalia walked over to him, kissed his cheek, and placed a glass of wine in his hand.

Evan carefully placed the glass down on the counter. Wordlessly he turned his wife away from the stove, wrapped his arms around her, and picked her up off the floor in an embrace. A smile spread across his face. Natalia laughed aloud.

"You like my surprise?"

"You chose a very good day for this."

"I had a feeling things were getting desperate," said Natalia, barely touching her lips to his before he pulled away.

"I do a good job with the kids and the house," said Evan, his brow furrowing and his body stiffening.

Natalia surveyed their home. The entire first floor was open and sparkling clean, with everything put away, save a large room in the back of the house that was filled with toys, crafts, and a desk overflowing with books and papers. She knew the bathrooms were immaculate. She turned and admired the rolling green lawn through the floor to ceiling windows, the carefully tended roses and flowers.

"You do an amazing job, Evan. Do we have a housekeeper?"

"Very funny, Natalia."

"No, seriously."

Evan looked at Natalia strangely, trying to appraise if she was making a joke.

"No, I have not hired a housekeeper. I do it all myself. You know that."

"Oh." Natalia paused. "But why?" Natalia reasoned that if she could afford designer clothes and handbags, surely they could afford a housekeeper, but she didn't mention this aloud.

"You know I don't like to waste money like that. I prefer to keep the money and use it to go and do fun things with the kids instead."

Natalia let it go. It didn't make much sense to her that she was freely spending money on luxury items when her husband was doing all the housekeeping. Could that be right? She noticed a guarded look had crept over Evan's face. This was not the mood she was hoping for. She longed to have Evan look at her with love in his eyes. She quickly changed track.

"Thank you for how hard you work, Evan. I am sure it is stressful sometimes with the kids, your job, and all the housework."

Natalia knew only too well how hard it was to juggle work, housework, the children, and finding time to stay physically fit and happy as a parent. She had always been impressed at how well Evan could handle it all and still have energy to laugh and play with his kids. Evan was silent. He drained his glass of wine just as the kids came pouring through the open front door. There was a great commotion as they unloaded shoes, coats, and backpacks and went to wash their hands. Natalia's heart began to race. Her face became hot and she felt herself shaking a little bit. She closed her eyes and prayed that when the children came in the room, they would be her own. Her anger at James and Eva had pushed her longing for her children deep down, shifting it away for a short time.

"Mommy!" a little girl shouted in delight as she threw herself toward Natalia. Natalia opened her eyes and arms to a four-year-old girl with bright blue eyes and blond hair tied up in pigtails. The little girl wrapped her arms around her neck and squeezed. "I missed you, Mommy!"

"I missed you too, darling."

Setting the little girl down Natalia turned to face the two identical boys coming into the room. She had no idea who was Nick and who was Nathan.

"Hey, Mom," said the first one nonchalantly. "What's for lunch?"

The other twin glared at her, his hands clenched in fists. "What are you doing here? I don't want you here."

Natalia didn't let herself get rattled. *He is just like my Allan*, she thought. *He is masking his hurt with anger. Poor little man.*

Natalia crouched down on the level of the blond-haired boy. She looked into his eyes and said, "I missed you very much. I can understand that you are angry with me that I have to work so many evenings and that I go entire days without seeing you. You have a right to be angry. I love you just the same, whether you are angry or not."

Natalia turned toward the other boy, who was already sitting at the table. "I love you too."

"Whatever."

Natalia served lunch. She had made baked salmon, a warm quinoa rice side dish, and green beans with roasted almonds, as well as a fruit salad of fresh strawberries, mango, and pomegranate seeds. She hoped these kids would love the meal as much as her own kids did.

Fortunately they happily sat down at the table to eat. Natalia poured herself a large glass of red wine and tried to act normally. The children chatted about their day and Evan talked about his students at school.

After she cleared the dishes Natalia disappeared into the bathroom. She sat down on the floor and cried. The truth she had to face was that she was either crazy, or everyone around her was lying to her, or she was dreaming. Natalia slammed her elbow down hard onto the floor.

"Ow!"

"Natalia, everything okay?"

"I just hit my elbow," she called back.

Natalia stood up and looked at herself in the mirror. That had really hurt; she decided she was not dreaming. Next she considered that everyone was lying to her in some passive plot. She reasoned that the chance of her husband, her neighbor, and even her own mom conspiring in a massive lie about the disappearance of her children was rather unbelievable.

"How would they find children and convince them to pretend that I am their mother?" Natalia whispered to her reflection in the mirror. "Unlikely. So I must be crazy. What next? Go see a psychiatrist?"

"Mommy! Mommy, I miss you!" The four-year-old was pounding on the bathroom door.

Natalia checked that her makeup had not run due to her tears and opened the door. She resolved she would just have to pretend these were her real children and go do activities with them that she would have done with her Anna, Allan, and Ben.

"Story time!" called Natalia. "I insist, boys!"

Natalia selected a pile of books. Strangely, all of the children's books were exactly the same as before she woke up to this strange life. The little girl settled onto her lap and the two boys grudgingly came in and sat next to her on the bed. After two books one little boy's head was leaning on her shoulder. After five books the other little boy cuddled up close to her and said, "I love you, Mom."

Evan came to the doorway and watched his wife for a moment. Then he said, "Your dad just called from the airport. Their train will arrive here in about an hour and twenty minutes."

"Wonderful," answered Natalia. A wave of relief washed over her. Her father was coming.

"I will go and pick your parents up with the kids. You rest, Natalia. We will be back soon."

Natalia curled up under her duvet and was soon fast asleep.

NATALIA FELT VERY COLD AND ALONE. Her skin felt sticky and her scalp itched. She longed to slip into a hot lavender-scented bath, or to step under a hot, pulsating shower. But her body felt so very heavy with fatigue that she couldn't summon the energy. Then she heard her mom and dad. Natalia's heart leaped. Her parents were here. She needed to get up and say hello. She willed herself to open her eyes and get up, but then her dad was already sitting next to her on the bed, kissing her forehead and smoothing her hair.

"You just sleep, love. You need the rest. I will be here whenever you wake up. In the meantime I have beautiful grandchildren to go and spoil."

Natalia felt her body relax and herself drifting back into deep sleep.

NATALIA HEARD DISTANT VOICES and laughter. She wanted to join her family. They sounded like they were having such a good time. Natalia jumped out of bed and walked down the stairs to the ground floor. Her dad was sitting on the floor and laughing while all three children struggled to fit in his lap at the same time. Sun streamed through the windows running the length of the house and bathed the entire room in bright light.

"Natalia! I have missed you, baby," called John.

"Mom is not a baby," laughed Annabelle.

"She will always be my baby," answered Bren.

"She can't be a baby, babies don't have gray hair!" shouted one of the twins, laughing.

"Gray hair, gray hair," chimed in the other twin.

Natalia frowned. "I don't have gray hair yet. I am only thirty-two years old."

The little girl's face turned serious. "You shouldn't lie, Mom. You go to the hairdresser all the time to blanket the gray with colors."

"Natalia?"

Natalia did not answer. She went to the bathroom and examined her hair in the mirror. She didn't see any gray. But apparently she went to the hairdresser all the time.

"Natalia!" called Bren. Natalia walked back into the room.

"Natalia, you are not thirty-two. You're thirty nine." Bren wasn't smiling anymore. Her normally twinkling eyes darkened and her mouth turned into an uncharacteristic frown.

Just then Evan walked into the room. Evan and Bren shared a look and without speaking seemed to come to an understanding.

"Who wants to go out for pizza?" Evan called happily.

"Well, I do," boomed a voice. Natalia's dad rose from the floor and went over to hug his daughter.

"What about you kids?" asked John.

All three children cheered and tugged on their grandma's arms, urging her to the door.

"No, no, children. Your grandma is tired! You go out for pizza with your daddy and grandpa and bring your mom and me back one to share, okay?"

After a few minutes Natalia was left in the house with her mother. They sat together in silence for a moment. Then Natalia exclaimed, "I am not thirty-nine! That is just ridiculous."

Bren relaxed back on the lounge and said quietly, "But you are thirty-nine."

Natalia stood up and started pacing back and forth across the room. "If I am thirty-nine, then that means I had those twins when I was thirty-three and the little girl at thirty-five."

"Yes!" Bren started to get excited. "It is all coming back to you!"

But then Natalia continued, "No, Mom, I had my first baby, Anna, when I was twenty-five! You were there for the birth! I had Allan at twenty-eight and Ben at thirty-one. Wait a second; if I am thirty-nine, then Anna is fourteen, Allan eleven, and Ben eight. Wow." Natalia paused in her pacing and turned to her mother.

"Natalia, no, of course you did not start having babies at twenty-five. You wanted to establish your career before you started having a family. You only agreed to marry Evan when you were twenty eight."

"Mom, what are you saying! I was married to *James* at twenty three!"

"Natalia, honey, you did *not* marry *James* at twenty-three, but you did start living with Evan at twenty-five. You lived with Evan for years before you two got married."

"That is nonsense. Why on earth would I wait so long to get married?"

Bren laughed. "That is what I have always asked you! I have always thought it was a crazy thing to do. And why you needed to marry a Swiss man at all I will never know. After attending high school and university in Switzerland, you felt you belonged here. I berated you for years to come home to the US."

"Well, I agree with you now, Mom. That is crazy. What in the world was I doing for all those years that I was so disinclined to get married and have children?"

"Natalia, you were working twelve- to fourteen-hour days in consulting in Zürich. You were wasting time traveling around with Evan. You could have been more successful at your job in consulting; in my opinion you were doing something wrong there. Then you opened your own business."

"Mom, I worked in consulting right up until Ben was born. Now I am home with the kids. Wait. No." Natalia sighed, reaching up to massage the stress knots aching in her shoulders and neck. "I was at my event company in Zürich working this week."

Bren said, "Natalia, you need some serious medical attention. We are going to make sure that you get through this, okay? You are not alone."

Bren walked across the room, took both of her daughter's hands in her own, and said, "You just leave it to me. Your mom is here, and I am going to make sure you get the help and attention that you need."

Natalia listened to the seriousness and worry in her mother's voice. "What will you do, Mom?"

"You will need to see a doctor, maybe many of them, in fact."

Natalia considered this and pulled back from her mother. She knew she needed to find out if something was seriously wrong with her, either physically, mentally, or both. Yet she didn't want to see a series of doctors. She was afraid of what they might find out and she detested hospitals. Natalia decided that she wanted to buy herself some time. She looked out the window.

"I have been under a lot of pressure and only sleeping a few hours a night for longer than I can remember. I think the lack of sleep could be the cause of the problem. I am going to sleep nine or ten hours a night for the next week and take a nap every day and then we can see if things improve," Natalia lied.

Bren pressed her lips together and leaned her head to the side, thinking. Then she answered, "Yes. Yes, I think that could help immensely. I am sure that Evan could also do with some more sleep himself. I am happy to be here to help. Your dad is happy to be here too, although I don't know why he insisted on coming. I could have done this myself."

"I am happy Dad came. And you too."

"I love you, sweetheart. Now, you need a hot bath and a good night's sleep. Do you want to eat something first?" asked Bren.

"No, I'll wait for the pizza. Would you like a glass of champagne?" Natalia went to the fridge and took out a bottle of champagne, opening it quickly.

"That would be lovely," sighed Bren.

Natalia handed her mom a flute of champagne and took a glass with her up the stairs and into the bathroom to run a bath.

THE DEEP OVAL BATH was nestled in the corner under windows with a view of the Alp range, dusted in snow, in the distance. Since the bath was big enough to fit two people, Natalia knew it would take a long time to fill up. So she poured in some natural Swiss oil bubble bath and then made her way down the hall to her room to collect a book. Stepping into the silky hot water a few minutes later, Natalia closed her eyes and let out a long sigh. Then she breathed in the fragrant lavender of the bath oil and looked out the window at the sunset. The last rays of sun cast shadows over the Alps, tinting them purple and setting them into even sharper relief. She allowed her entire body to relax. For a few seconds she could let go of all her worry and anxiety. Then it all came rushing back. She needed to talk to Evan.

Wandering downstairs, Natalia called out, "Mom, would you like a bath too?"

"That sounds heavenly. Can you put my pizza in the oven for me? Go ahead and eat without me," replied Bren, already on her way upstairs.

Waiting for Evan to return, Natalia went to the bookshelf. Stacks of photo albums surrounded her on the floor. The books were filled with phantom memories, floating fantasies. Here was a photo of her proudly holding a blond-haired, blue-eyed twin in each arm in the sunshine. Flipping the page revealed a photo of her building sandcastles with what looked like three-year-old twins on a beach. The next photo showed Evan standing in the surf holding an almost one-year-old baby girl.

Natalia picked up another album. The first photo in the book showed a much younger Evan holding her hands across a small table in a little café on a cobblestone street in what looked to her like Paris. The next photo showed her laughing together with Evan as he held her in his arms in front of the Eiffel Tower. Natalia slowly put the album down on the floor.

"We have never been to Paris together before!" Natalia said out loud. More bewildered than anxious and increasingly curious, Natalia opened the album again and flipped quickly through the pages. Apparently she had taken many more holidays with young Evan; her mother was right.

Her unlined face smiled up at her out of photos taken with Evan in desert landscapes, hiking in the Alps, splashing in aquamarine waters, lounging on tropical beaches, as well as enjoying an après ski drink with Evan in their ski gear, smiling with drinks in their hands at a bar in the snow.

She examined some of the photos more closely. She felt certain one of the photos must have been taken in Rome, another in Vienna, and a third in Madrid. Looking at the next page closely, Natalia saw herself in a photo that looked like it was taken in Budapest and the next in London. She tried to discern where the rest of the photos were taken. But cobblestone streets and old buildings left her no clear clues; they could be one of any number of cities in Europe.

"Who lived this life?" Natalia asked herself. She had to admit that she felt very envious of the radiantly happy woman who had been lucky enough to go on so many vacations. Wait. That didn't make sense. She could not be envious of herself. Here was indisputable proof that she had taken these holidays with Evan before they had children together. Natalia willed herself to recollect any moment from any of the holidays in the photos. Nothing. She glanced back down at the photos and smiled. She and Evan looked so happy and in love.

"My wedding! Where are photos of my wedding?" Natalia said just as Evan came in through the door with a pizza box in his hands.

"Pizza for you, Natalia."

"Hi, Evan, where is our wedding album, honey?"

The smile fading from his face, Evan answered, "You know what happened to our wedding album."

"I do? No. I have forgotten. You will have to tell me where it is."

"Natalia"—Evan lowered his voice to a whisper—"you know I burned it."

"You what?" shouted Natalia, rising to her feet.

"Shh. Not so loud. I don't want your parents to hear us. They don't know anything about what happened."

"Why in the world would you burn our wedding album, Evan?"

Evan looked at her seriously, examining her, searching for some kind of evidence. "You really do not remember, do you?"

"Remember what?"

"I burned our wedding album when I found out about the affair," Evan answered through gritted teeth.

Natalia sat down on the floor, stunned, with Evan towering over her. "But what affair, Evan?" Natalia whispered.

Evan crouched down beside her, searching her face. "You know. You refused to tell me at the time. You just insisted that it was over and that it would never happen again."

Natalia was stunned. She would never have an affair; she and Evan looked so happily in love in all of the photo albums. Natalia could hardly believe herself capable of hurting him so deeply. Then with a sharp intake of breath she remembered the kiss with James.

It was James. Wait. No. Natalia thought back. Didn't James say that nothing had ever happened between them before? No. She may have forgotten critical parts of her life, but she knew who she was as well. If she had had an affair, it most certainly would have been with James. But she had not slept with anyone outside her marriage, not ever. Deep down, she felt certain of this fact.

Natalia looked up at Evan; tears were silently rolling down his cheeks. She reached out to take his hand. Just then the kids came running in through the door.

"Grandpa let us go down the slide head first, Mom! Mom! Do you hear us?"

One blond-haired boy came racing into the room and threw himself onto Evan. The other was not far behind. Annabelle walked into the room and cuddled herself into Natalia's lap.

"I'm tired, Mommy," she said.

"Time for a bath, honey," said Evan, and scooping Annabelle out of Natalia's lap, he headed toward the stairs. "Into the shower boys."

"I want Mommy to give me my bath," insisted Annabelle.

Natalia heard Evan explaining to Annabelle that Mommy was not feeling very well, but maybe she would tuck her in and read her a book before bedtime. The boys followed Evan down the hall and up the stairs, begging him to let them stay up and watch a movie with their grandparents.

Natalia picked up the pizza box and walked into the kitchen. She poured herself a large glass of champagne and took the entire pizza with her to the table. If ever there was a time to devour an entire pizza on her own, Natalia decided this was it.

Natalia felt sadness, like a heavy weight, lowering down onto her shoulders, spreading out over her heart. Reaching for the champagne bottle she paused, listening to the rain begin to fall outside, before pouring herself her third glass. Shivering as a gust of rain-scented wind blew in threw the patio window, Natalia resolved not to think about affairs or amnesia for the rest of the evening. This resolution, however, had the strange effect of rolling those exact thoughts over and over again in her consciousness, no matter how hard she tried to push them away. Tears came to Natalia's eyes.

This is all too much for me to handle. She placed her cheek down on the table, the frosted glass cold against her cheek.

"Mommy?" A tiny hand glided back and forth over her back. "Are you sick, Mommy? Mom, are you okay?"

Natalia sat up and gazed at the beautiful little girl in front of her in a pink nightgown. Natalia decided then and there that she was going to be a wonderful mother to this child. She would push down her panic at not knowing where her own Anna, Allan, and Ben were, at least for the time being.

Evan called for Annabelle from the top of the stairs. Natalia scooped up the four-year-old and carried her up the stairs.

"I'll tuck her in tonight, Evan," said Natalia as she reached the top of the stairway.

Natalia carefully snuggled the little girl into her bed, pulling the sky-blue duvet up and handing her the blanket she wanted from the floor. She noticed the worn design and stitching and realized it was her own blanket; she had slept with it when she was a girl.

"This was my special blanket," Natalia said to Annabelle.

"I know, Mommy. You gave it to me. Now it is my special blanket."

Natalia turned to walk out of the room. "Mommy?"

"Yes, dear."

"Will you rub my back? Around and around and squeeze?"

Natalia gave pause. Anna always asked the exact question at night before bed when she was overtired or distraught about something. Natalia had been rubbing Anna's back for the past eight years, ever since she woke up as an infant screaming from colic. Anna loved to have her back rubbed and liked it most of all when her back was rubbed in a circular fashion. Afterwards Natalia had always squeezed the skin together all the way down along Anna's spinal column and then gently moved her fingers up and down her back until she was sound asleep.

Natalia climbed into the bed with the four-year-old and began to rub her back. After just a few minutes the child's breathing grew slow and even. Natalia felt fatigue wash over her. It felt so warm and comfortable snuggled in bed, cocooned away from the twisting reality of her life. *I'll just close my eyes for a few minutes.* Seconds later she was sound asleep.

Natalia semi-awoke and realized that her daughter was no longer in bed with her. She thought she should get up and go and look for her, to make sure she was all right. But before she could summon the energy to open her eyes she heard muffled laughter.

"Well, that is okay then," decided Natalia, letting her body relax back into sleep. "My daughter is laughing."

WHEN NATALIA WOKE UP the air in the room was very cold. Resisting the urge to stay under the warm duvet Natalia counted to three and jumped up out of bed and went out into the hallway. Looking through the bedroom doors she noticed that all the beds were made and the windows were open to air the rooms. She made her way to her own room and selected jeans, a red sweater, and a brightly patterned scarf. Grabbing lacy underwear and a bra she almost ran to the bathroom and closed the door against the cold, enjoying the warmth of the heated tiled floors seeping into her bare feet. Yet the window in the bathroom was also open. Closing it, she noticed the fog swirling outside her window.

Natalia stepped into the shower and turned it on. Water rained down from the ceiling and jetted out of the walls. Frantically Natalia hurried to shut the shower door, but it was too late. There was a large pool of water all over the bathroom floor. Turning off the water, Natalia took a towel and began to mop up the mess. By the time she was done she was freezing. Her entire body was shaking.

Carefully shutting the door to the shower this time, Natalia pulled the handle to turn it on. Hot water rained down onto her. A few minutes later Natalia could feel her body warming up. She found her favorite citrus body wash and a wave of wellness washed over her as she soaped herself up and relaxed back into the hot rain. She leaned her arms forward on the wall and let the rain massage her back.

That was when Natalia noticed a series of buttons on the wall and began pressing them. The first one turned on the jets of water coming out of the wall. The second turned on a waterfall from higher up. The next button seemed to do nothing. But then she noticed the light in the shower had turned to blue. A minute or two later it turned to orange, then pink, green, purple, and back to blue. A voice behind her made Natalia jump.

"Hi, love. What did you do to the floor? It is like a lake out here." Evan opened the door a bit and asked, "May I join you?"

Natalia screamed and slammed the door shut. Her heart thudding, it took her a moment to register that, in theory, it had been her husband standing there watching the water splash down on her naked body. She couldn't help herself. When she saw him standing in the open shower door, her gut reaction was to see him as her best friend.

Opening the shower door she said, "Evan, you startled me. I am just now getting out, sorry."

Turning off the water, Natalia threw a towel around her body and hurried to the bedroom to get dressed.

Natalia found Evan sitting at the kitchen table drinking espresso.

Evan smiled mischievously at Natalia and said, "I love that rain shower. You should have let me in there with you."

Natalia smiled back at him. She wanted a happy marriage; she longed for tenderness and laughter, for appreciation and trust. But Evan's face was darkening.

"Natalia, you haven't asked where the kids or your parents are this morning."

"Oh! You're right. Where are they?"

"Your parents have gone up to St. Gallen shopping for the morning to give us some time alone and the kids are at school. While you slept in I got all three ready and out the door an hour ago. You are taking the day off from work, right?"

"Right," Natalia agreed, reaching out to hold Evan's hand.

"I talked with your parents for a long time early this morning. We are all here for you, Natalia. I will always be here for you, no matter what happens to us. I want you to know that I will always love you."

"How can you be sure?" interrupted Natalia, crossing her arms across her chest. "Just the other day on the phone you were downright mean to me. That didn't sound like an Evan in love; you sounded like you despised me."

Evan came over to her. Wrapping his arms around Natalia and leaning in, he began kissing her neck, his hands in her hair.

He whispered, "I could never despise you, Natalia, I was just… hurt. And lonely. Who have you always relied on to come when you were in need of help? I promised to cherish you until death do us part, remember? I plan on doing a better job at keeping my promise."

Sitting back down, Evan looked pensive. "But your mom says that you still can't remember the children. I simply do not understand that. That would be crazy. I mean you gave birth to them. It isn't like you could forget something like bringing someone into the world! Right?"

Natalia sat back. Evan looked so worried and unhappy again. She didn't want that this morning. And she certainly did not want to be taken in to see a series of doctors at the hospital.

Natalia started babbling nervously. She had to convince Evan not to take her in to the hospital, to give her more time. She told him that everything together had just been too much pressure lately. She missed him and the kids but she had to work hard to ensure that her business continued to be a success. Natalia did not tell him that she did not remember a single facet of her work life in Zürich or anything about having a business. She did not admit that she did not believe the twins and little girl to be her own children. Natalia certainly didn't reveal that she had woken up a few days before convinced she was married to James.

After a long talk and two more coffees Natalia thought she had successfully given Evan the impression of being a sane woman, albeit one near collapse who required sleep, wellness, and recovery.

Natalia could not stop herself from saying, "Evan, what you said before, about an affair…I have never slept with any other man outside of marriage apart from my husband."

"What are you talking about? You told me there had been an affair. You even seemed proud of it, like you were hoping it would lead to a divorce," said Evan as he began pacing the room.

Natalia watched him and noticed the laugh lines around his eyes, appreciating his muscular torso and unruly blond hair. Every time Natalia had seen Evan at a party or in public she had noticed other women looking him over, trying to catch his eye, finding reasons to touch his arm or brush past him. Now she felt herself longing to reach out for him, to push her fingers through his hair, to run her fingers across his skin.

"Well. I must have been very angry with you to admit to a lie. Well, not a complete lie. I did kiss someone one time. But that was all. One kiss. One time."

Natalia watched surprise, anger, and sadness, then once again anger wash over Evan's face.

"Why would you lie?"

"You tell me, Evan," parried Natalia. "Why would I tell you there was an affair if there wasn't one?"

Evan sat back, completely bewildered. He opened up his palms and shrugged his shoulders. But then he frowned.

"I know why. That was when we were fighting about having another baby," Evan answered softly.

This threw Natalia for a loop. She felt out of her depth once again. Deep down, she felt there had been an affair of some kind that related to her, but then again, she didn't think she was the one who had been disloyal. But she had also forgotten her entire life.

"I had an affair because you didn't want to have another baby with me?" asked Natalia, looking up at Evan, puzzled.

Natalia imagined that was the most likely answer. She had wanted four children, or even five. Wait. Natalia shook her head, trying to shake out the confusion from her brain. She had never been married to James, and if she had never had an affair with James, then why could she remember sex with him so vividly? Had she had an affair? Then why did she feel so free from any guilt?

Evan's voice rose louder. "No, I mean you lied about the affair because you didn't want to have another baby with me."

Natalia was baffled. What in the world was Evan saying? She had always wanted lots of children with her husband: four, five, hell, the right man could have talked her into six. Now he was saying she had admitted to an affair that never happened just to avoid having another baby. Did Evan want four children?

Then again, reasoned Natalia, sometimes what we think we want is not what will make us happy. Four children certainly would be a lot. They would have needed a new car, for instance.

Also there was the physical toll pregnancy and breastfeeding took on her body. Natalia knew there were women out there who could have ten children and still remain extremely healthy. Unfortunately for Natalia, she had to admit to herself, she was not one of them. Each of her three pregnancies had exhausted her and impacted her health markedly. It took at least two years after a birth for her to regain her previous vigor and wellness again.

Natalia began to get defensive. Who did Evan think he was, getting so angry with her about not feeling physically capable of having a fourth child that she had felt the need to lie about an affair to find a way out? It was not like he would be the one carrying the baby around in his belly. There was also her career to think about. How would she have continued working through so many pregnancies? But then Natalia remembered that it was Evan at home doing the majority of the childcare.

Confused, Natalia asked gently, "Evan, you wanted four children? Really? Do you think it was fair to insist I have a fourth child if I did not feel up to the intensity of pregnancy and infant?"

"Natalia, what are you talking about? You didn't even want to have *Annabelle*. That is what we fought about at the time. You said the twins were more than enough."

Natalia was now completely lost. None of this sounded like her at all. She had not wanted to have a third baby? Of course she did. She had wanted to have Ben so very much. The third birth had been the best experience of her life. She was an experienced mother with Ben. She could relax and just enjoy the magic of caring for an infant, then a baby, and at last a delightful child. With the two older children she had been so stressed about learning how to be a wonderful mother that she couldn't really relax and enjoy the process of parenting. The third baby was an amazing gift. What could she have been thinking?

Natalia had been silently in thought for a few minutes before Evan cleared his throat. He must have taken the silence for hurt, because he ventured, "Of course you adore Annabelle now, and couldn't imagine her not being part of our lives."

"Annabelle?" Natalia was confused, but she caught herself before she mentioned Ben. "Right. Yes. Annabelle is darling. I was crazy not to have wanted a third baby. Um, it seems so crazy, in fact, that I am having a hard time remembering why I didn't want a third baby?"

Evan looked at her strangely—did he realize she was fishing for information?—but he answered, "You said at the time that another baby would ruin your career."

"I did?"

"Yes. You did. You declared that you couldn't stay in consultancy and be pregnant," he continued, hurt creeping into his voice. "You said the hours were too long and hard to be pregnant and yet you did not want to work any less. You told me I was being selfish, me! You loved consulting and you said having another baby would mean you would need to find a new job, because the physical toll of having an infant and the sleep deprivation would mean your brain wouldn't be able to think creatively, to concentrate deeply, and you would fail as a consultant. Having a baby would mean you would need to find a different job."

"Well, that sounds fair and reasonable," said Natalia, unthinking. Uh-oh. Natalia realized too late that she felt as though she were evaluating the argument as a third party, because she couldn't remember ever having said any of this, let alone having lived through any of it.

Evan exploded. "Don't I have rights in this marriage too? You always told me you wanted many children. I really wanted another baby. The twins were so incredibly wonderful for me. I wanted another baby to be able to benefit from everything I had learned with the twins. I thought that a third baby would be this awesome gift to really enjoy. And she is! I was right. It isn't like I wanted her served up on a platter for me. I did my part. I took a year sabbatical and then I only went back to teaching part time in the mornings when Annabelle was one and a half so I could be here for the children and you could still have your career."

"Wow! I have always told you how amazing I think it is that you are so ready to switch out traditional gender roles and be the caregiver," Natalia exclaimed.

Before Natalia could catch herself she had once again thought Evan was talking about what he had done not for her, but for Eva.

Evan's face and shoulders relaxed. He leaned back in his chair and replied, "I know it isn't easy for any marriage to find a balance and compromise. I think we almost found ours. I mean, during your pregnancy you started your event management business and I stood behind you the whole way. You took just a six-week maternity break. That is unheard of in Switzerland. Almost all the mothers take at least three months. I just didn't realize that you starting your business would mean I would become a single parent the majority of the time. You are always gone. Even on the weekends."

Natalia looked at her watch. They had been fighting for over an hour. She really wanted to feel some cold air on her face and stretch out her legs. The air in the room felt heavy and stale.

"Evan, I think I have a solution so that I am at least here every weekend. Let's go for a walk in the woods and talk about it together."

She took Evan's hand and pulled him out of his chair. She wrapped her arms around his waist and placed her face on his chest, breathing in the clean smell of him. He went to move away but she held on tighter. Eventually he wrapped his arms around her too and pulled her close.

"The good news, Evan," said Natalia, her head still resting on his chest, "is that I have always been loyal to you." Looking up at him and smiling she added, "You owe me a new wedding album."

"True. But we don't have any photos to put in it."

Evan kissed the top of her head and Natalia saw that the realization that there had been no affair was slowly taking hold of him. He pulled slightly away from her, examining her face.

"About that walk, Natalia, I think you are far too worn out. In fact," Evan said, scooping her up into his arms, "I think I should carry you back to bed."

Natalia nestled her head on his shoulder. "Yes. I think you should."

Chapter 11

Natalia felt so cold. *What is wrong with this duvet?* she thought sleepily. Then she felt Evan cuddle in close beside her; she smelled his spicy cologne. The warmth of his body slowly spread to her own until she felt cozily warm again. She listened to his breath become even and slow. And then she drifted back into deep sleep as well.

Natalia sensed that Evan was no longer beside her before she even opened her eyes. Then she heard his voice down the hall, talking to her mother. She decided she was going to get up and tell him that she was going back to consulting so she could be home on the weekends. But then she heard the children coming in from school and she didn't know if she could face them just yet. Natalia felt herself crying. Where were her babies? Where were Anna, Allan, and Ben? And why did no one know of their existence but her? What was going on? She decided to sleep a few minutes more.

Natalia heard her little girl calling, "Mom! We are having lunch together now, Mom. I want you, Mommy!"

Natalia still felt so very tired. It felt like the fatigue had settled way down, deep into her chest, like a weight on her heart, binding her to the bed. Natalia decided she was going to take her sleep deprivation very seriously in the future and ensure that she got her eight to ten hours of sleep every single night. Sleep deprivation, she felt, was the culprit for her current physical and mental health deterioration.

Natalia remembered when she first learned how sleep deprivation affects the brain. She had been sitting at the dining room table with a cup of hot coffee, sun streaming in through the windows, her baby in her arms. Suddenly she rushed out through the open terrace doors and called to her daughter to come back home. She had gotten her all ready for school and sent her off without remembering that it was a national holiday. So she knew firsthand how crucial sleep is to cognitive ability.

Making important decisions, processing information, and thinking creatively during the infant stage of each of her children had been like thinking through mud. Natalia had actually thought that the birth of each baby had made her permanently stupider. She had found it impossible to learn anything new. Luckily, as Natalia recovered from her chronic sleep deprivation, her intelligence and quick wit had returned to her immediately.

Natalia had recently read an article that while sleeping, brain cells shrink dramatically, enabling waste proteins toxic to the brain to be washed away by cerebrospinal fluid. Yet despite the fact that Natalia knew sleep was so necessary, as it was actually detoxifying her brain, she still worked until far too late at night and got up very early.

And now she was in serious trouble.

WHEN NATALIA AT LAST dragged her weary body out of bed, hunger slammed into her stomach and left a painful aching. Natalia stumbled down the stairs and into the kitchen, hoping she was not too late for lunch. However, no one was in the kitchen and the black granite counters and glass table were spotless. Despite her hunger, Natalia's mood lifted to see that the swirling fog outside was gone and she paused to admire the sunshine sparkling on the dewdrops in the grass.

Natalia went to open the fridge door to make an omelet when she noticed a note taped onto the handle. It read, *Lunch for you is in the oven on warm, Love Evan.* Natalia opened the oven door and a waft of spices hit her senses. Natalia took the plate of chicken curry to the table and sat down.

The house was completely still. Natalia wondered where her family had all gone to after lunch. Just as she was eating her last bite a small hand ran down her arm. Natalia jumped. She had thought she was alone in the house. She turned and saw that it was one of the twins standing beside her with his hand still on her arm.

"Hello, honey," she said. "What are you doing home all alone? Where did your daddy and everyone else go?"

The little boy smiled up at her and his eyes sparkled in mirth. "I'm not alone, Mommy, you are here. Can we watch a movie?"

Natalia answered that she did not think that was a very good idea, as she knew Evan liked to limit TV time to the weekends and even then he was quite sparing with how much they could watch. A little too restrictive, if he were to ask her, as it would have given him a much needed break during the week to be able to lie down and read a book while they watched something. The result of Natalia's no to the TV was a tantrum of magnificent proportions. The little boy threw himself to the floor and started screaming like someone was eating him alive.

Natalia heard footsteps on the stairs and soon the other two children were standing beside her, watching with fascination as their sibling convoluted on the floor next to them.

"I want to watch, I want to watch," he screamed over and over again, his arms and legs thrashing around.

Natalia felt the screaming reach her heart and felt her pulse racing faster and faster. But Annabelle appeared completely unruffled by her older brother's behavior. She calmly crawled up into Natalia's lap and let out a contented sigh as she snuggled back and rested her head against Natalia's chest. Natalia was still confused as to which twin was which, but the calm one came and rested his head on her shoulder. Natalia wrapped one arm around him, pulled him in close to her, and kissed the top of his head.

After a few minutes Annabelle slipped off her mother's lap and went over to her older brother.

Placing a hand gently on his tummy she whispered, "Nathan, if you calm down, we can ask Mommy if she will make us pumpkin pancakes."

Nathan's legs stilled. He rested for a moment, panting flat on his back, and then he jumped up. "Yeah! Pumpkin pancakes! Let's make pumpkin pancakes!" cheered Nathan.

Nick joined in his twin's happy dance and began also to chant, "Pumpkin pancakes!" while laughing happily.

Natalia asked, "Do we have pumpkins?"

"We can go to the pumpkin stand first!" shouted the twins in unison.

The chants of "pumpkin pancakes" switched to "pumpkin stand" and the boys each grabbed one of her hands and dragged her to her feet and down the hall. Evan was just coming in through the door as Natalia and the kids were putting on their shoes. Evan bent down and kissed the back of Natalia's neck as she helped Annabelle slide into her rain boots.

"Come with us to the pumpkin stand, Daddy!" said Nathan.

"No, no," said Natalia. "We are going to let Daddy stay here."

Evan gave her an appreciative look and kissed her cheek. Then he went down the hallway and into the kitchen as she bundled the kids out the door and into the car.

NATALIA DROVE THROUGH THE COUNTRYSIDE, looking out at the lake dotted with sailboats. The kids chattered happily in the backseat. In a quarter of an hour Natalia pulled into the roadside stand and let the kids out of the car. Bright orange decorative pumpkins were lined up next to more than ten different types of edible pumpkins and squash in shades of gray, pale yellow, dark green, and various shades of orange. The twins selected a bright orange red curi and a tan butternut squash, while Annabelle chose a carnival pumpkin. Natalia picked up a Cha Cha Kabocha in dark green to add to their assortment.

"Mine is the prettiest, Mommy. Look, it has the most colors on it: green, orange, and yellow!"

Annabelle held up her arms to display the pumpkin for Natalia. Natalia reached down and picked the small blond-haired girl up, her little hands still clutching her newfound treasure.

Annabelle snuggled her head on Natalia's shoulder and said, "I love you, Mommy, you're the best!"

Anna says the exact same thing to me, while placing her head on my shoulder in just that way.

Natalia felt a wave of happiness wash over her as she stood holding Annabelle in the sunshine, feeling the warmth of the sun on her face despite the crisp autumn air. If she closed her eyes, it almost felt like she was holding a four-year-old Anna again. Opening her eyes, she watched the twins chasing each other around the pumpkin stand. Their laughter made her smile. Natalia was still unable to tell the two twins apart. She decided she needed to become more observant so she could learn to differentiate the two boys.

"Mom, can we go cut sunflowers?" asked one of the boys. "Mom! Mom! Are you listening to me?"

"I want a sunflower too, Mommy," chimed in Annabelle.

"Sure, we can cut flowers. We need to put our pumpkins and squash into the car first though."

Natalia paid for their selection, and selecting a pair of shears with which to cut the sunflowers, she followed her children out into the field. Each child selected two sunflowers and she carefully cut them using the shears. Nick and Nathan immediately began using their huge sunflowers as swords. Annabelle started to cry because the boys were breaking the flowers. Natalia managed to stop the boys from swordplay and led them all back toward the car. Just as she was buckling in Annabelle her phone began to ring. Natalia shut the car door and answered her phone, standing at the front of the car.

"Where are you?"

"Who is this?" asked Natalia, even though she knew it was James on the phone.

"Natalia. Natalia, it's me."

"Why are you calling me, James?" asked Natalia angrily.

James paused. There was a long moment of silence. Natalia looked out over the rolling green hills descending to the lake. Natalia noticed how the apple trees were casting longer shadows and the sun was no longer warm on her face. She shivered. It was time to go home and make dinner.

"I miss you Natalia."

Natalia placed a hand over her heart. *How many times have I longed for him to call me from work and say those four little words?* thought Natalia. She felt a glow rising from her heart into her cheeks as she savored the knowledge that James, at last, was thinking of her. He was missing her.

"Natalia? Are you still there?" asked James.

"Yes," breathed out Natalia, beginning to pace.

"Come into town and spend the evening with me. I will take you out to any restaurant in the city, darling. I'll just tell Eva I need to work late," said James.

Natalia stopped in mid stride, her eyes wide, her breath catching in her throat. Everyone, her mother, Evan, Eva, and even James kept affirming that James had married Eva.

Why do I keep thinking he is my husband?

"You'll tell Eva you need to work late," repeated Natalia, and began pacing back and forth in the front of the car.

"Yes," agreed James.

"Because she is your wife. She gave birth to your children."

"Natalia." James softened his voice, almost whispering. "I love you."

"You love me?" Natalia exclaimed so loud that a few people examining pumpkins at the stand turned and looked her way.

Uncertainty crept into James' voice. "I made the wrong choice. All those years ago, I made the wrong choice. It should have been you."

"Why?" Natalia asked, both horrified and curious.

The twins began to pound on the car window, calling for her, their patience wearing thin.

"Listen, James, I have to go. I am married to Evan. He is tender and sexy and fun. But I will see you at our meeting this Friday."

Without waiting for a response, Natalia hung up and climbed into the car. It had felt great to choose Evan over James. She rummaged through her purse until she found three chocolates and handed them back to her children.

"Thanks for waiting for me, guys," said Natalia.

"That's okay!" chirped one of the boys.

The other two children were too busy unwrapping their small chocolates to answer. Natalia wondered on the drive home if it was a good idea to go back into consulting if it meant she would be working for James. Sure, she was mad at him now for having fallen in love with Eva. But she had to admit that her feelings for him were complicated. Deep down there was still a longing, a love. She pictured herself in James' office, late at night, leaning over a desk beside him in concentration, close enough to feel his body heat, to smell his citrus cologne.

She imagined them traveling together to a client for a presentation and overnighting in a classy four-star hotel. They would have a nightcap in the bar; after a few drinks they would walk up to their rooms together. Was she capable of betraying her husband?

Perhaps I shouldn't go back into consulting after all, thought Natalia. *At least, not until I find out why I keep thinking I married James and we have three children together. Perhaps I really should go in for an examination,* she concluded. *But what if they diagnose me as mentally ill? No,* she decided. *I will give myself more time to try to sort this all out on my own.*

NATALIA EXAMINED HER KITCHEN. Pumpkin puree was dripping from the counter onto the floor, flour was spilled all over the counter, and one cracked egg lay on the stove. Cooking with the small children had been exhausting. And now she had a huge mess to clean up.

The children sat at the table with her parents devouring the pumpkin spice pancakes, apples, and scrambled eggs. The children laughed and chattered to each other and with their grandparents, their eyes bright and their cheeks slightly flushed. Natalia sighed and then smiled. It was worth all the effort to make these kids happy, even if she still didn't really believe they were her own children.

"That smells good," said Evan as he wandered into the kitchen. He came up behind her and gave her a hug, burrowing his face into her neck and giving her a kiss. "Good luck cleaning up that mess," he laughed and grabbed a plate full of pancakes. "That is why I do not often cook with the kids. But maybe your parents will clean up the kitchen for you."

You Are Mine to Love

Chapter 12

SITTING IN ANNABELLE'S SOFT PINK BEDROOM, with Annabelle curled up in his arms and Nick and Nathan cuddled up on either side of him, Evan picked up a Dr. Seuss book and began to read. Natalia peeked into the room and leaned against the doorway, watching him reading to his children. Annabelle's eyelids were growing heavy and starting to close. Nick, yawning, rested his head on Evan's shoulder, and Nathan slowly settled back onto Annabelle's pillow. They all looked so peaceful and content.

Natalia watched a moment longer and then descended the stairs. She lit candles all around the living room. Taking the bottle of champagne out of the freezer where it was cooling, she placed it on the counter top. She took out a box of Swiss chocolates and two champagne glasses. Dimming the lights, she filled small glass bowls with nuts and chips. Taking a deep breath, she went back up the stairs in time to see Evan carrying Nick to his bed.

The little blond head was fast asleep. Natalia went into Annabelle's room and found her nestled under her pink duvet, her blond curls spread across her pillow. She picked up Nathan, the only child still awake, and carried him to his room.

"One more story, Mommy," whispered Nathan.

"Tomorrow," promised Natalia and laid him in his bed, pulling the green duvet up and tucking the little boy in under the covers. She noticed how much he resembled Evan. Natalia felt panic wash over her like an icy wall of water crashing over her head. Why didn't she recognize this child? Surely she should have memories of him. At the very least she should feel a mother instinct of love and protection at the sight of him, shouldn't she? Even if she had lost her memory?

"I love you Mom. I love you Dad," said a Nathan, yawning.

Natalia turned and saw Evan standing in the doorway. Wordlessly she took his hand and led him out of the twins' room, into the hall, and down the stairs. It was time to uncover the truth. She turned to watch his reaction as he entered the living room. His eyes widened and then narrowed, as if wary.

"Where are your parents?" asked Evan.

"I thought I would do something romantic. They offered to watch the kids while we went out, but they can do that another night. Tonight I thought they would like to enjoy the wellness hotel in Lindau. Would you like a glass of champagne? I'll be back in just a moment."

Natalia turned and ran back up the stairs to her bathroom. Looking into the mirror, she told herself to relax. If everyone, including her mother, said this man was her husband, then there was nothing to be nervous about. Even if James was never far from her thoughts, she would try to forget him and focus on Evan. Perhaps tonight would resonate with her and she would get her memory, no, her very sanity back.

Natalia put on some lipstick and perfume and as a second thought slid out of her jeans and sweater and into a soft blue dress with beautiful lace straps. Feeling a bit cold in the light dress she pulled on a cashmere sweater before returning to the living room.

"Evan, Nathan is asking for you," Natalia said.

Giving an annoyed grunt, Evan went up the stairs. Natalia felt she needed some liquid courage and she didn't want Evan to know. As soon as Evan was out of sight she took the opportunity to open the cupboard and look through the shelves. A minute later she found a bottle of vodka at the far back, unscrewed the lid, and took a long swig right out of the bottle. She was not a fan of hard liquor and grimaced at the taste.

Normally Natalia was not much of a drinker. She liked a glass of champagne or red wine. But her limit was generally one drink. The hard liquor therefore hit her almost immediately. Tilting her head to consider, she heard Evan coming down the stairs. Taking another huge swig, she hurriedly placed the bottle back on the shelf and took out a bottle of mineral water as Evan came into the kitchen.

"What are you doing?" he asked, frowning.

"Hydrating?" replied Natalia, smiling.

"Forget hydrating, here is your glass of champagne," said Evan, looking her over. "Nice dress."

Natalia took the glass and watched Evan as he walked toward the couch. She followed him but sat on the lounge chair across from him.

"You really are easy on the eyes," commented Natalia, more to herself than to Evan.

"Um. Thank you?" answered Evan. "You are still acting so weird, Natalia. What on earth is going on with you? No, stop, I don't want to know. Let's just pretend that everything between us is normal, I mean, how it used to be. You know, when we were happy."

Natalia felt herself panicking. How in the world could she know what their "normal" and "happy" were? She didn't remember marrying this man and she didn't remember having his children. With surprise Natalia realized it was sadness she felt washing over her. Looking at Evan, she felt a longing wash over her for the life she had seen in the photo albums. She craved the years of memories she had created with Evan as the love of his life. At the very least she wanted the easy companionship they had shared as best friends; there had been none of the tension or reproach then, only smiles and comfort.

All she could picture was Evan with Eva. Images of parties and double dates with Evan and Eva flashed before her eyes. She saw Evan smiling big enough for the dimples to show on each cheek, his eyes shining as he ran his hands through Eva's hair, pulling out the colorful confetti from New Year's Eve. Evan was always ready to tell or laugh at a joke. Natalia couldn't pull up an image in her mind of Evan with Eva looking serious, the way he looked with her now.

Natalia wanted desperately to bring out the laugh lines around his eyes. Unfortunately, she had never been one to tell jokes and rarely to relate funny stories. She envied those who had a natural inclination toward lightness and laughter, like Evan. It must be wonderful, she thought, to be effortlessly able to make people laugh. Natalia sighed. Eva had always been one of those types as well. That was why she was so well suited to Evan, in her opinion. The beautiful couple always seemed to be telling each other inside jokes. Laughter flowed around them wherever they went.

"You deserve someone else, Evan. Someone who makes you laugh," said Natalia. "I have always been a serious type. I just don't think you can have a good time with me, at least not the fun you could have with someone else."

Evan looked up, startled. "Like with who?"

"I don't know. Like Eva?"

Evan laughed out loud. "Eva and I would not make a good couple. We both like to play too much. Who would be the serious one?"

"That isn't true. You did make a good couple. I mean, you would have made a good couple," stammered Natalia, catching herself just in time, "I think. Well, I think you have more fun with Eva."

"Natalia." Evan sighed. "What is this about? I chose you, Natalia. I wanted you. I still do."

"You don't seem happy, Evan," explained Natalia. "I have always loved that about you. How filled with fun and laughter you are. How readily you laugh. The laugh lines around your eyes are testament to how much time you spend having a good time. But lately, well, I haven't seen you smile very much."

Evan considered this for a moment. Sighing again, he answered, "Natalia, it is tough. It has been tough. I work all morning and take care of the kids all on my own. Throw in the housework, the yard work, and I am just too tired to laugh and have a good time. Too tired." Evan closed his eyes and massaged his forehead.

"And I miss you," he whispered. "You are always gone. Even when you are here, I don't know, it feels like you aren't. Do you know what I mean? Like your thoughts, your very being, is in a different life, with someone else. Does that sound crazy?"

"No," Natalia whispered back. She wanted to cry, looking at the exhausted shell of a man sitting across from her. She noticed the dark, almost purple, shadows under Evan's eyes, the sadness in his expression. She knew just how he was feeling.

That is how I felt, thought Natalia, *desperate. Even when James is home, it feels like he isn't.* She had thought quitting her job years before as James suggested would improve things.

"Yes," she had answered James, "perhaps working together is a strain on our marriage. Maybe if I spend more time with the children we will all be happier."

Yet from the moment she quit working James was less attentive, less charming, and less present.

"I know how you feel, Evan," said Natalia, just keeping herself from explaining about her experience with James.

"How the hell would you know how I feel, you don't know what my life is like," Evan snapped. "You have always worked full power at a job. You spend most evenings surrounded by interesting people. You're living the glamorous life in Zürich."

"I'm not sure I like my 'glamorous life in Zürich,'" mused Natalia.

Evan stared at Natalia for a moment, tilting his head to one side in consideration. "You are serious, aren't you? You don't even remember your business? You love your job."

Natalia laughed out loud. "Listen, Evan, I know you insinuate that I am this heartless work bitch, but I think it would be pretty bizarre if I couldn't remember my own children but I could remember my work."

Standing up and going over to Evan, Natalia placed her arms around him and looked him in the eyes.

"Do you remember me? You do remember me, right?" asked Evan.

Natalia buried her head on Evan's shoulder, giving him a big hug, trying to buy herself some time to think. Should she be honest with Evan? How would he react to her belief that she had had three beautiful children with James, that she still looked at Evan and saw her best friend, not her husband? No. She couldn't be honest, not yet anyway. She would need to improvise. What would she like James to say to her?

"I think you are doing an absolutely amazing job with the kids, the house, your job. I appreciate it so very much. I have been distant. I am sorry. I just worry all the time that my business is going to fail; one mistake and the word would get out so quickly. I know my job requires long hours and I am away from you and the kids most of the week. It hurts my heart, really it does. You must know that. I miss you. I miss my kids. Do you think I don't envy you the special moments that you share with the kids? I wasn't here, was I, for any of their important milestones, like learning to walk, to ride a bike. It was you. I know it feels like you have all the heartache sometimes; being a parent is tough. But it hurts my heart to miss my children's childhood while I spend so many hours working to earn this lovely house and provide for you."

Evan nestled his head on her shoulder. The act surprised her. Evan seemed like such a macho man, with his broad muscular shoulders and tough manner. She rubbed his back and the tight muscles in his neck.

"Listen, Evan, we are hiring a housekeeper to come in once a week and scrub the house down. It isn't like there is enough housework to do on a daily basis just to keep it up. And we are hiring a babysitter to come in on Friday afternoons for a few hours so that you can have some time to take care of yourself. Go to the gym, go running, read a book, hell, even go spend the time drinking beer and watching sports down at the harbor. Do whatever you need to do to feel more rested and happy. We are lucky, we can afford it, at least right now. Who knows what the future will bring? Please don't be so proud. And I will mark one evening per week in my calendar where I will always be home. No matter what."

Evan lifted his head, tears in his eyes. Moved beyond words, Natalia looked at her best friend. She thought of all the cups of coffee they had drank together, all the phone calls, and the days spent together playing with and caring for their children as a team. No, she didn't make Evan laugh the way Eva did. It was he who brought her to laughter all the time. They laughed together at the antics of the children, at themselves, at the ridiculousness of life.

Natalia looked at Evan and she remembered all of the laughter and all of the kind things he had ever done for her. When she was ill, Evan was the one on her doorstep with groceries to make lunch for her and the kids. He was the one to bring her medicine and tea. If she had wonderful news to share, she called Evan first; she knew James would either be too busy for her trivial call, or his response would be distracted.

Natalia shared everything with Evan. Evan knew all about the complex relationships she had with her mother, Eva and Mary. He knew she wanted to go back to work in consulting but didn't want to have her children raised by a nanny. Evan even knew about how lonely she was being married to James. In turn Evan opened up to her about his stress at school, his insecurities about being a good father and his longing for a sense of freedom and timelessness that had existed before his children were born, even though he felt they were the best thing in his life. She had spent hours listening to him complain about Eva.

Wait. Natalia shook her head. Had none of that happened? Could it really be true that Evan was her husband, not Eva's? Why was her reality twisted inside out? Shaking her head, Natalia placed her face in her hands. All at once Natalia reached out, taking Evan's face in her hands, and kissed him.

"I'm in love with you, Evan. You are always there for me, in good times and in crisis. You are fun, clever, thoughtful, and well, you are sexy," Natalia ended, her cheeks flushing pink.

Suddenly Evan roughly brushed Natalia's hands away from his face and pulled her to him, kissing the top of her head.

"I adore you, Natalia," he whispered.

Then, without warning, he effortlessly scooped her up in his arms and made his way up the stairs and down the hall into their room.

Natalia began to protest, then stopped, laying her head against his shoulder. All at once Natalia felt completely at peace. Deep down she knew this man loved her. She knew she would change and so would he. They would fight. Life would most likely hit them with the force of a hurricane at some point, and possibly leave them weary and desperate. But she would never need to question if he loved her. She was certain she wouldn't need to run after him, grasp for him, worry he would tire of her. She could let all her insecurities fall away. He loved her. It was even in the way he looked at her when his eyes flashed with anger.

Laying her on the bed, he took her hand, kissing her palm, her wrist, and up along her arm.

"Look at me," whispered Evan, pausing. Smoothing the hair away from her face, Evan smiled. "You are my angel. I'm sorry we have fought so much recently. But I think you and I, we will always be worth fighting for. We are meant to make the journey through life together. And I swear, from this day forward, I will work to make our years together even more beautiful."

No one had ever made love to Natalia in such a slow, trusting, gentle way. Every movement was a question. Every motion was a slow request. Now Natalia felt every nerve still tingling from his touch, as she lay snuggled into his arms, exhausted. Evan's breathing was becoming slow and rhythmic with sleep. She felt herself drifting off as well, with Evan's arms still holding her close.

Is It You That I Love?

Chapter 13

NATALIA OPENED HER EYES, BEWILDERED at the light streaming through her bedroom window. *What time is it?* she wondered. She was accustomed to waking in darkness. An arm reached out. Natalia let herself be pulled back against the warm bare skin of her husband. Closing her eyes against the light, Natalia felt contentment, love and a sense of safety warm her heart. *When was the last time James last held me in his arms in the morning upon waking?* She couldn't remember the last time it had happened.

"Good morning, honey," mumbled Evan sleepily.

When Natalia turned and saw Evan's face she screamed and sat up. *What have I done?* Looking over at Evan, she remembered the previous night and her eyes grew wide. Her heart hammered in her chest, and it took a moment to recall that this, not James, was her husband. Evan looked up at her for a moment in confusion. His eyes grew round too and he leapt out of bed.

"Oh no, Natalia, we are late! How did the kids sleep so long? They will be late for school. School starts at eight fifteen! And you, you are, let's see, what time is it? Eight ten! You are at least an hour late for work! Jump in the shower and hit the road, love."

Natalia continued to sit in bed, stunned. Evan had already thrown on some clothes and hurried out of the room to wake the children.

Slowly she made her way into the shower. Her head cleared a bit once the warm water hit her. Hurrying out of the shower, she threw on a navy blue dress and nylons and selected a pair of red heels to take with her in her purse for the office. Pinning up her hair, she decided she didn't have time for much makeup. Some mascara and red lipstick would have to be enough.

Natalia remembered she needed to take some evening dresses with her for the event that evening. Looking through her closet, she found a garment bag and quickly put in three dresses and packed a bag. Running down the stairs, she threw on a pair of boots, a scarf, and her jacket and hurried out the front door.

A dusting of white lay over the garden. Her boots crunching on the newly fallen snow, Natalia made her way up the front walk and onto the street toward the train station. Taking a left, she hurried along the path beside the lake that wound its way through the park toward the harbor. Natalia noticed the Alps bright white in the distance and the sun sparkling off the waves rolling in the lake. When she reached the Panem she was tempted to stop and hurry inside the café for a cappuccino. Instead, she hurried on toward the train station.

Standing on the platform a few moments later, Natalia realized she had ten minutes before the next train left for Zürich. As she looked out on the lake from the platform, she decided to call Mary and find out if the event from the previous evening had been a success.

"Hello, Mary, it is Natalia. How are you? Did you enjoy your event last night?"

Mary laughed. "Do you mean, was the event a success?"

Natalia smiled and replied, "No, I mean did you enjoy being in charge of executing the event last night all on your own."

"I didn't execute the event by myself. Mike and I did it together."

If Mary had been on the platform she would have seen Natalia raise her eyebrows in surprise. Natalia wasn't used to Mary wanting to share her success with anyone. Or did that mean something with the event went wrong?

Natalia's brow furrowed "So the client was happy?"

"Natalia, you need not worry. The event was such a success that our client requested Mike and I personally execute his wife's birthday party in a month. It will not be a gala for a couple hundred like last night, but intimate events also have their charm, even if they do not have the same payoff for us." Mary laughed.

Natalia was relieved and puzzled at the same time. Mary was in the best mood Natalia had ever experienced. What had happened? Was it so empowering for her to execute an event on her own?

"You sound like you did a marvelous job with the event, Mary. Great work. I have never experienced you so buoyant."

"Buoyant? Oh well...yes. That is true," replied Mary.

"Well, I am taking the train now so I will be in late this morning. I hope you can handle things until I come in?"

"Of course, we just arrived at the office ourselves. We were going to take the entire morning off, remember? Yet there is so much work to do. By the way, I am sure Evan liked having you home this morning for a change."

Natalia tilted her head in thought for a moment.

"Natalia? Did you hear me?"

"Yes, Mary, I think he did. See you soon. Goodbye."

Natalia climbed the steps in the train to the café wagon and settled into her usual spot with a sigh. The cold still clung to her jacket. Thawing a bit, she was happy to see the waiter coming over to take her order. Natalia ordered a latte macchiato, noting that her usual waiter was missing. She was taking a later train, so of course her waiter was on a different train somewhere in Switzerland.

Natalia sat drinking her coffee and thinking about her children. The ache hadn't dulled. It throbbed continually deep down in her heart. She longed to pull her kids into her arms and nestle her chin on their heads and hear their little voices. Tears came to her eyes. She tried to hold them back but couldn't manage.

Pulling out her phone, she started looking through the photos in search of a photo of her Anna, Allan, and Ben. But of course she didn't find them. Instead she came across photo after photo of Nick, Nathan, and Annabelle. Sighing, she put her phone away.

Natalia thought of Anna's last birthday party. She could see her children standing together with Evan's, their arms thrown happily around each other's shoulders. They were all laughing, or shouting, it was hard to tell which. Perhaps it was a bit of both. The memory made Natalia smile, bringing more tears to her eyes.

Blinking through the tears streaming down her cheeks Natalia thought of her children. Somehow she had managed to carry on without them, though how she did not know. The pain was there. Somehow she had pushed the pain down so deep into her heart that she could function normally despite the weight she carried. Wait. Wasn't that what Mary had confided she had to do daily? A wave of empathy washed over Natalia as she thought of her good friend.

Taking a steadying breath, Natalia answered her phone.

"Evan?"

"Hi," said Evan. "What would you think about having Eva and her kids over for dinner on Saturday? Maybe I'll invite a few more people and we'll make it a big party. Actually, I'll go ahead and give Eva a call myself. I'll barbecue."

"But there is snow outside."

"Doesn't matter. I'll put on a jacket to do the grilling. I'll do a mixed grill. That is always a crowd pleaser."

"All right. Wonderful. See you soon."

"Bye. Oh and hey, sexy lady?"

"Yes?"

"I miss you already."

NATALIA PLACED HER PHONE inside her jacket pocket, feeling giddy from her call with Evan. She had to admit that she was totally in love with the man. Smiling, she rested her head on her arms on the table and gazed out the train window. After just a few minutes of watching the rolling green hills, dairy cows, and small towns with church towers pass by, Natalia drifted off to sleep.

Fortunately, the café waiter came and woke Natalia at the Zürich station. That was close, thought Natalia. *If I had slept on I could have ended up in Geneva before I woke up at the end station.*

Natalia walked into the office and stopped to survey her colleagues. They were both grinning from ear to ear.

"Okay. What happened? Let's hear it. The last time I saw Mary smile like that she had beat me for first place in our accounting class."

Mike answered before Mary could say anything. "I proposed last night and Mary said yes."

"You proposed! Wow! Congratulations!" Natalia ran over to Mary and threw her arms around her. "You will be the most beautiful bride."

"You're right. She will," agreed Mike.

"Congratulations to you too, Mike. I am so happy for the both of you." Natalia was beaming. "This means I am taking you both out to lunch in celebration."

"We have our yoga class, Natalia," argued Mary. "I don't want to miss it. We already prepaid for the month."

"I fully support the yoga," agreed Mike. "I don't want to be around a Mary who hasn't done her yoga for the day."

"Hey!" Mary yelled in protest, swiping at Mike. "That isn't nice."

"Just realistic, Mary. If you don't do your yoga you get all stressed out and grumpy by the evening. I want you in a good mood tonight."

Sighing, Mary agreed. "All right, all right, it's true. I admit that yoga calms my nerves and evens me out a bit."

Mike laughed. "Not only you. Natalia is also in a better mood when she gets back. In fact, all women should do yoga over lunch."

"All women! You said that just to get a rise out of me, Mike. Men would benefit just as much from a regular practice. Speaking of which," insisted Mary, "you should come with us."

"And break up girl time, I don't think so. I'll hit the gym instead. You know, throw some heavy weights around like the man I am." Smiling, Mike flexed his arm muscles. "In fact, you two would be better off skipping the yoga and doing some power lifting with me."

Natalia left the two bantering back and forth as she pressed the espresso machine button, enjoying the smell of the coffee pouring into her cup. Walking into her office and shutting her door, she went straight for her computer. She needed to look at her calendar as soon as possible to find out what was on schedule for the day.

As she waited for her computer to turn on she sipped her strong coffee thoughtfully. Images from the previous night kept leaping to mind unexpectedly. Natalia suddenly felt guilty thinking of James. She wanted him out of her head. Turning to her calendar, she saw that there was a charity benefit she was to execute that night. The calendar included a reminder to call Evan and tell him to be at the venue at six in the evening in a tux.

Natalia felt her pulse speed up. Evan was coming to her event? Anticipation coursed through her veins. Picking up the phone, she dialed Evan. Of course he didn't answer; he was teaching and his phone must be switched off, she remembered.

Then Natalia remembered her parents saying something the night before about watching the kids tonight. Natalia caught herself worrying about how she would be a good date while working the charity benefit. Shaking her head, Natalia reminded herself that Evan was not her best friend or a new love affair. He was her husband, even if she couldn't remember any of their life together still. Evan wouldn't expect her to spend a lot of time with him that night, and he loved parties. Unlike her, small talk came effortlessly to him and he thrived on the energy in a room full of people he had yet to meet.

Natalia looked around her desk and in the drawers for a binder of material for the event. Just then Mary walked into the room.

"Looking for this?" she asked, smiling. Mary held out a blue binder to her across the desk. Natalia took the binder and started looking through the contents. Apparently the event was to be held at the Baur au Lac Hotel.

"I have always wanted to attend an event at the Baur au Lac hotel," Natalia enthused.

Mary looked at her strangely. "You have organized many events at that location already."

"Of course," replied Natalia quickly, "but none of the events have been a charity benefit."

Natalia crossed her fingers, hoping she was right about this.

"That's true. A charity benefit is rather classier than a regular event," agreed Mary. "And I like the cause."

"Oh, me too," murmured Natalia.

She had no idea what the cause was. Natalia leafed through the binder, quickly looking over the sections labeled budget, number of participants, guest list, seating arrangements, event schedule, music, entertainment plan, lighting, technical equipment list, parking facilities, and reserved hotel rooms for guests. She switched to the food and drinks section. The welcome drink and appetizers, dinner menu, wine, dessert and coffee, as well as the after dinner drinks, had all been selected. There was also an empty section named "Auction to benefit the nonprofit Child Hunger." She read the note saying that the women organizing the event would be responsible for all details of the auction itself.

"Where is the decoration plan?" inquired Natalia, improvising, noticing an empty section. "And have the seating cards and menus been printed out yet?"

"We are creating the decoration plan today, but everything else has been completed and packed into the car. Yes, including the printed seating place cards as well as the menu. In addition we printed the auction list. You need to head over in half an hour to the flower shop."

"Wait," said Natalia, adding, "You know, you two work so hard. As a bonus for your ingenuity and dedication, and to celebrate your engagement, I want to buy you a night at the Baur au Lac, if you would like that."

"Oh wow," began Mary, and then she looked at Mike. "But you don't appreciate spending so much on a room for a night, do you, Mike? No, I think he would prefer that you use that money to renew a few months of his gym membership. Wouldn't you, Mike?"

Mike beamed at Mary. "Yes, I would prefer that. Is that fine with you, Natalia?"

"Of course. That is very practical of you, Mike. I'll tell you what, Mary. I will buy your wedding shoes so you will have something too. We'll go look for them together."

Mary sighed happily. "Wedding shoes. I'm getting married."

Natalia took her best friend's hands and looked into her eyes, grinning. Ignoring Mary's protests, Natalia pulled her into a huge hug, holding her tight.

"You deserve your happy ending, Mary. I love you, sweetheart."

"I love you too, Natalia. Now let go," said Mary, laughing.

The Secrets We Keep

Chapter 14

UNFORTUNATELY, ANTONIO was unable to accommodate Natalia's request for free flowers. The hosts of the charity benefit wanted the flowers to be provided free of cost. Antonio thought that if the organizers could find the money to rent rooms at the Baur au Lac, they should also be able to find the money to pay for his flowers. She had to admit that she felt that he was right.

So instead of visiting Antonio she was visiting a florist on the Bahnhofstrasse, one she had never worked with before. As she entered the door she was already wary. No one came to greet her and ask her how they could be of assistance. At last she went to the counter and called out in Swiss German.

"Hello? Can someone help me please?"

A woman came unsmiling to the counter and said, "Yes?"

"I am here to pick up the flowers you are donating for the charity benefit to reduce child hunger?"

The woman looked at her for a moment, confused.

"It is being held at the Baur au Lac?" continued Natalia.

"Oh yes, of course, come with me to the back. Do you have a car with you? You will need to make a few trips."

Natalia hesitated a moment before answering. What kind of service were they providing, after all? Antonio always delivered the flowers to the event site personally. And who had made the flower selection? Had Mary?

"Who selected the flowers?" inquired Natalia.

"Oh, we just threw all our leftovers into large vases over here for you. You can take whatever you would like," said the woman and led Natalia to the back of the workspace.

The vases were filled with flowers of assorted types and lengths. None of them went together and there certainly was not enough to decorate all the tables for the 150 guests they would have at the charity benefit that evening.

"This is all?" asked Natalia with raised eyebrows. "That cannot be. None of these match and there are not nearly enough flowers for a huge benefit."

"I am sure you can appreciate that we can't just donate over a thousand Swiss francs in flowers every time someone has a charity benefit?"

Natalia felt the blood rush to her cheeks and her fists tighten. She tried to remind herself that getting angry would not solve her problem. Without a word she turned on her heel and left the shop.

She immediately dialed Antonio's number and started walking toward his shop.

"Antonio, hello! How are you? How is your family?"

"Natalia, no. No and no. I am not donating flowers to those snobby charity benefit ladies for this evening."

"Of course you aren't."

"I want to help hungry children, really I do, but, wait, what?"

"Of course I will pay for the flowers. Tell me, what are the least expensive flowers and greenery that you have on stock? It would need to be enough for quite a few arrangements. We have nineteen tables of eight planned. But of course I will also need flowers for the stage, the entry table, and the bar."

"The easiest would be for you to come here in person, Natalia."

"I agree. I will be there in a few moments."

Natalia put away her phone. She was looking forward to seeing Antonio. He was such a grumpy, affectionate, charming Italian. As Natalia opened the door to his floral shop, she immediately craved a strong Italian espresso from his café among the flowers. She wondered if she had time.

"Natalia, Bella! It is always good to see you! But you know, I am a busy man. Always clients are calling last minute, wanting me to work magic. I ask you, do I look a magician to you?"

"I understand, Antonio. I will go find another florist," said Natalia, turning toward the door.

"Sit down, sit down," continued Antonio. "I'll help you and I'll even bring you an espresso on the house."

"Oh no, Antonio, that isn't necessary," insisted Natalia.

"Nonsense. I know how much you adore my espresso. That just shows that you have discerning taste, as my espresso is the best in town. No. In the country.

"Now," said Antonio, handing her a thick espresso cup, "down to business." He pulled out a binder and turned the pages until he found the flowers he was looking for. "I'm afraid in such short notice, at a lower price point, all I have to offer are tulips, roses, and dusty miller for the greenery."

"But dusty miller isn't green. Gray greenery? I don't know, although it does have a lovely textural pattern. What color are the roses and tulips? Are you sure that is all you have?"

"Red and white," answered Antonio, almost apologetically. "The flowers were to be for a funeral, but the daughter got ahead of herself. Her ninety-two-year-old father was hospitalized for pneumonia and she was sure he wouldn't make it another day. She ordered the flowers for his church service and for the lunch afterwards. But then the old goat recovered. He is already back at home again and complaining because they won't let him walk down in the mornings yet, per usual, to his favorite café for coffee and his newspaper."

"What a terrible daughter to order funeral flowers before her father has actually died. Who does that?"

Antonio thought for a moment before responding.

"This woman seemed really sweet. I have no idea what goes on in some people's minds. But now you can buy her flowers half price."

Natalia was looking through her list. "Mike has the vases. If we bring them straightaway, could you arrange the flowers and deliver them to the Baur au Lac this evening by five? We need nineteen table centerpieces, two high arrangements for the bar, and three runners."

"You will need to arrange and deliver the flowers yourself, Bella. I have a wedding in a few hours' time and the bride just called with some last-minute changes. I'll give you the flowers at less than half; I'll give them to you at cost."

"Deal," replied Natalia, smiling, "if you throw in some candles."

NATALIA WAS HAVING A GOOD TIME. Mike had delivered the vases and then decided to stay and help her arrange the flowers. They had found some twisted branches to include in their arrangements as well as some leftover vines to go with the roses, tulips, and dusty miller. As Natalia started on another arrangement her thoughts wandered to Evan. She had to admit that she had fallen in love with Evan long ago; she just hadn't admitted it to herself. She had always thought Eva lucky to have him as her husband.

True, years ago she had been hopelessly in love with James. Natalia gave a derisive laugh. Hopeless was the right word for her.

Why did I let James take credit for my work at the consultancy? Why have I let him make all the decisions in our relationship? Why have I stayed with him even when he ignores me in the evenings, isn't there for me when I need his help, and never goes out of his way for me, not even on my birthday? Why do I let him make mean comments to me, especially in front of the children?

Why did I ever fall in love with him?

Natalia sighed. She knew the answer. James had two buttons: on and off. Either he was the most charming and adoring husband and father on the planet, or he was cold, distant, and mean. Before they had gotten married Natalia had only ever seen James' on button.

James, smart and handsome, was above all else charming; at least when he wanted to be. Charisma engulfed the man. The few times Natalia had worked up the courage to say she had had enough of James, he had suddenly swept her away to an expensive dinner and took the kids and herself out for a day trip. She wasn't the only one whom James could convince to do anything he wanted. James could sell ice to someone living at the North Pole; no wonder the man was such a success in business.

Yet now everyone was telling her that she had never been lured into James' mirage. She had married Evan instead. So why did she have so many memories of a life lived as James' wife, and why could she remember nothing of her life with her beloved Evan?

"That was a big sigh," laughed Mike. "Are you getting tired of arranging flowers?"

"Honestly, Mike, I have lost my mind. Or at least I have lost my memory," Natalia admitted. "When I woke up on Sunday I couldn't remember that I owned this business, nor that I was married to Evan. I couldn't even remember the children in my house. But don't tell anyone. You must promise not to tell a soul."

Mike was lost in thought for a moment. The he laughed.

"You're kidding. Very funny Natalia. If you lost your memory, you couldn't have arrived at work on Monday morning."

"I got to work on Monday on autopilot. It was really strange. I wasn't sure where I was going until I ended up in a train on my way to Zürich. And then Mary called and told me to meet her straight away at the office. I found Mary's business card in my wallet, so I knew the address."

"So you didn't remember me that morning."

"No. Nor that Evan is my husband, nor my children. Or the fact that I owned a business in Zürich at all," repeated Natalia.

Mike froze, his eyes wide. "And now? It has all came back to you?"

"No."

"What do you mean no? You have been working with us all week. Everything seemed fine. Are you trying to tell me that you still don't remember anything?"

"That is correct."

"But you went to the hospital and they told you just to go back to your life until your memory comes back to you?" asked Mike.

Natalia turned her face away and busied herself with the flowers.

"Natalia? Natalia, you did go to the hospital, didn't you? I mean, if you just wake up with no memory, then you need to go find out why," said Mike.

Sighing again, Natalia turned back to Mike. "No. I haven't been to the hospital. I hate hospitals. It is a phobia of mine you know. I hate the smell, the beeping sounds, the sense of despair."

"Then find a doctor with a practice outside the hospital. There are plenty of those," answered Mike.

"I don't want to. I am afraid a doctor might tell me I am suffering a mental collapse or that I require severe mental healthcare."

"That doesn't make any sense, Natalia. You aren't crazy because you lose your memory," said Mike, patting her arm.

"Oh yeah? Well, when I woke up on Sunday I remembered many things, like my home and my neighbors and my parents. However,

I was certain that I was married to a different man and that I had different children. I woke up thinking I belonged in a different life."

"Wow," exclaimed Mike, "that is bizarre. You told Mary about this, right? You did remember Mary when you woke up?"

Natalia thought back to Monday morning. "Yes, I did remember Mary. Perhaps that is because she is my best friend and our friendship goes all the way back to high school. But when I arrived at work I thought she was my boss, not the other way around," laughed Natalia.

"I didn't realize you had been friends with Mary that long. I asked once and you two answered you had been friends for forever," Mike replied with raised eyebrows, startled into stillness.

"So," thought Mike out loud, "that would mean that you were with Mary when she lost her parents."

"Well, we weren't friends yet when that happened. I think it was the year afterwards that we started studying together once in a while. It wasn't really until university that we became close."

"Still, you know what happened," encouraged Mike, turning back to his flower arrangement, busying himself so as to look nonchalant.

"Well, no, I mean of course she was living in the center after she left them, I knew that, but…"

Mike interrupted her. "After she left them? What is that supposed to mean? They died, right?"

Just then Mike's phone began to ring. Distractedly he answered the phone and then swore loudly. With clenched teeth and furrowed brow he turned back to Natalia.

"The Baur au Lac just called. They said if I want to bring in my electrical equipment I have to do so in the next half an hour, as they have events in the salons and in the restaurants this evening and do not want any 'drafts from open doors or service people interrupting the elegance of our guests' experience with us.' Fortunately I have already loaded all my equipment into the car. I will be back to pick you up as soon as I can. Can you manage to finish all the arrangements on your own?"

Natalia's shoulders relaxed and she let out a whoosh of held in air. *Thank goodness*, she thought, *that I do not need to continue the conversation about Mary.*

"Of course. Go ahead and take your time, Mike. If I manage to get these done before you get back, I plan on taking a break in the café with a café macchiato."

"Hey! I want one of those too."

"Well then, we will enjoy one together."

"And finish our conversation from before," added Mike as he made his way swiftly out the back door toward the company SUV.

Oh, no. Natalia knew she had made a grave mistake revealing that information to Mike. Had Mary really told Mike that her parents were dead? Natalia knew that wasn't true.

IN HIGH SCHOOL SECRETS could travel very quickly. Natalia remembered when someone in school had seen Mary getting on the tram near the Mädchenhaus, a center for abused teenage girls in Zürich. The information had reached her ears quite quickly.

One of the most popular girls in the school had seen Natalia in the library. Natalia was studying alone per usual when Eva came over to her. Tall and curvy, with creamy caramel-colored skin and dark eyes, Eva was as beautiful as she was fun. It was no wonder she was the most popular girl in the school. She was the type of girl all the boys were in love with and all the girls wanted to befriend, or at least emulate.

Meanwhile, Natalia had always been the girl that everyone couldn't help but sincerely like, even if she would never be one of the popular girls. She refused to be mean or gossip and had a difficult time back then making small talk with anyone, let alone telling jokes. Her inability to speak Swiss German didn't help. Serious and studious, she was seen as empathetic, kind, intelligent, and, well, trustworthy. She got told a lot of secrets.

Natalia remembered that despite the fact that she knew gossip could be very hurtful, she had taken a deep pleasure in hearing the inner depths of her classmates' lives. People just loved revealing secrets to her because, while they knew she wouldn't give the information on to anyone else, she was a most appreciative audience, registering emotions such as shock, kindness, anger, or sadness in reaction to their stories at all the right moments.

"Natalia," said Eva in a hushed tone, "I heard the saddest news today."

"Oh?" Natalia answered. She felt a bit of pride that Eva was choosing her, of all people, to spend her morning break talking to.

"Yes. That pretty blond girl, that loner, you know who I am talking about, what is her name?"

"Um, Mary?" guessed Natalia.

"That's right. Mary. Well. I saw her getting on the tram close to the Mädchenhaus this morning. I ran up the Käferberg this morning early, around six a.m., and then I was going to run down and along the river all the way to the lake. But I was slower than usual this morning, so when the number four tram stopped ahead of me, I decided to jump on and take it back down towards the center of town to make up lost time. The strange thing was, I saw Mary getting onto the tram in front of me. I called out hello and she pretended not to hear me and then went and took the seat at the front of the tram.

I went and sat down next to her and said, 'Hi, so you live around here then? You are up and out early this morning!' And she didn't answer me! Just looked at me with these big eyes, like caught stealing or something. Weird, right? Then I realized we both got on near the Mädchenhaus."

Eva looked at Natalia expectantly. But Natalia looked blank.

"I don't know what the Mädchenhaus is," whispered Natalia.

Eva came in even closer to Natalia and whispered back, "It is a house that takes in abused teenage girls. Oh, come on, you know. For example, when a girl has so much violence at home that she needs to run away, well, she goes there," said Eva, widening her eyes at Natalia.

"Oh." Natalia was taken aback. Thinking fast she answered, "Oh, oh, now I remember, I was at Mary's flat one time studying for a team project. I think she lives close to there, wherever that Mädchenhaus is, because she said her mom went and cleaned for the Mädchenhaus voluntarily once a week, you know, a donation of time instead of money. When Mary doesn't have too much homework, she goes and helps too."

"Wow. That is really kind of her," answered Eva, impressed.

"Yeah, I know. I don't ever volunteer. I should though. Just think if everyone gave some time to help out a good cause every week, what kind of world we would have then," enthused Natalia.

"Yeah, yeah, of course. Anyway, good talking to you, Natalia. See you around, darling."

"Bye, Eva."

As soon as Eva had left the library Mary stepped out from behind a stack of books in front of Natalia. Natalia jumped, her face registering guilt and shock at seeing Mary suddenly appear before her when they had just been talking about her moments before.

"You have never been to my flat before, Natalia," she said softly. "Why would you lie to Eva?"

Natalia didn't hesitate. "In case it is true."

"And then?"

"And then you must have a hard enough life without adding in the entire school gossiping about you behind your back," answered Natalia.

Mary paused for a moment. Natalia almost thought Mary was going to cry. Instead, Mary pulled herself up, settled her shoulders back, and lifted her chin.

"Thanks, Natalia. That was very...decent of you. But I am not living at the Mädchenhaus."

"No?"

"No. I really do just live in a flat near there. You and I, we should count ourselves lucky we aren't one of the girls who have to live there. Can you imagine?" asked Mary.

"I can," answered Natalia seriously, looking Mary in the eye. "I think whoever lives there must be really brave to have gotten themselves out of a terrible situation. I admire them. Don't you?"

"Well, when you put it like that, yes? I do? I mean, of course I do," replied Mary, smoothing her dress.

Then the bell rang.

"Bye, Mary. I feel like I almost live in the library, I spend so much time here studying. You can join me whenever you want."

"Sure," Mary replied. "We might happen to be here together at the same time."

NATALIA HADN'T EXAGGERATED TO MARY that morning. She usually could be found both before and after school in the library. Natalia remembered how overwhelmed she had felt, sitting there in that same library, a few hours before the conversation with Mary.

Extremely intelligent, she had still had to study twice or even three times as long as any of the other students to get perfect grades. When she had moved to Switzerland with her parents at the age of twelve she hadn't known any German at all. Her parents had sent her to an intensive German language school where she had learned the language in a group of four all day, every day, for six months. And then they had just thrown her into the normal Swiss school system. Natalia had begged and pleaded and cried for them to send her to one of the private international schools where everything would be taught in English, to no avail. An image of her mother, dressed in a blue sheath dress and pearls, her business jacket over her arm and her heels in her hand, floated into her mind.

"Character building is just as important to long-term success as an excellent education. And you could use some character building, Natalia. Goodness knows you aren't learning grit from one of these international private schools; the work would come too easily for you. I am throwing you into the normal Swiss school and that is that; they have a good public school system here. End of discussion. I will get you a private German tutor."

Natalia had realized there was no changing her mom's mind once it was made up. Watching her mother put on her shoes and head out the door to her job, Natalia had felt fury for the first time in her life at age twelve, real fury, building up inside of her. The minute she heard the front door click closed she had picked up her new schoolbooks and hurled them across the room as hard as she could.

Natalia had felt ashamed of herself after hearing Eva's gossip about Mary. Here she had thought it was a terrible injustice to have to complete her studies in an entirely new language. But she had had a beautiful, privileged life filled with love and security at home. Okay, her mother was a battle-ax, but coming home to her father in the evenings felt like entering a cozy cocoon of warmth, affection, and fun. Natalia admonished herself that her mother had been right. If she had to work harder to do well in school, then so be it. It was not a real hardship, not the kind that so many people had to struggle through.

Do You Know Her Secret?

Chapter 15

NATALIA FINISHED HER LAST FLOWER ARRANGEMENT with tears sliding silently down her cheeks from the memories from long ago. Back at the very beginning of their friendship, Natalia had invited Mary for a glass of champagne in the Grieder bar to celebrate finishing their Matura exams. Sitting on the terrace overlooking the Paradeplatz downtown Zürich, they had drank three glasses of bubbly before Mary admitted to living at the Mädchenhaus and how terrible it felt to carry around pain in her heart over the mother lost to her. The truth was, Natalia had been too afraid to ask any more details. She had just hugged her new friend and told her how brave she thought she was. Still, to this day, she didn't know Mary's entire story for sure.

They had become friends so slowly even after Mary's confession. Mary had always held her a bit at a distance. She held her at a distance even now. Deep down, though, Natalia thought she should have asked more questions all those years ago. She wanted to ask Mary the details now, today. Yet if Mary didn't want to confide in her willingly, then who was she to demand that Mary open up her dark memories?

Mary was alone and had been on her own for many years out of necessity. Natalia just hoped she could let her guard down and admit whatever had happened in her past to Mike, instead of lying to him.

Just then Mike came rushing back into the floral shop.

"Are you done yet or what? Natalia, let's go," he said abruptly.

"Sure, yes, they are done," stammered Natalia, surprised, noting the grim expression on Mike's face and his clenched jaw.

Without a word Mike started placing the arrangements into boxes and then took the first load out to the car. Natalia had a very bad feeling about Mike's uncharacteristic lack of courtesy. She took out her phone and dialed Mary.

"Hi, Mary? It's Natalia. Is everything running smoothly for you?"

Natalia heard a muffled sob and a click.

"Mike?" Natalia went out to the BMW SUV and looked for Mike. He was placing the final box of flowers on the backseat. The back of the vehicle was already full.

"Mike," Natalia asked softly, "did you go and talk to Mary already?"

"I ran into her at the hotel. She was talking to the chef when I dropped off the electrical equipment."

Natalia just waited. She knew that silence could be the best key in the unlocking of secrets.

"I finally got her to admit that her parents are in fact, not dead. But only after she continued to try to lie to me about her status as an orphan for almost ten minutes! It was only after I told her that I knew her parents weren't dead that she grew silent. We just stared at each other in silence for like forever. It was terrible. Then at last she asked me what I knew. I asked her why she had lied to me and asked her to tell me the truth, right then and there, as to why she had lied about her parents."

"And then? What did she say?" asked Natalia, her heart racing.

"She said she wouldn't tell me. I told her I didn't want to marry someone who couldn't trust me and that I couldn't trust in return."

"Oh no!" Natalia's heart was breaking for her friend. Why had she let that piece of information slip? Natalia knew she would need to try to make things right as fast as she could. She knew Mary wouldn't be able to do it and Mike would be too stubborn.

Taking a deep breath, she took hold of Mike's shoulders, looked up into his eyes, and said, "Now you are going to listen to me. Do you know how long I have been friends with Mary?" she asked.

Mike answered, "I don't know. Since high school?"

"Correct. I have been a friend of Mary's since high school. I was at the same high school graduation and we went to the same university. We enjoyed many vacations and countless hours studying together. She came with my parents and me out to dinner to celebrate birthdays, holidays, and at last graduation. We graduated from university in the same ceremony."

"What does that have to do with me?" asked Mike, getting impatient and taking a step back, out of Natalia's grasp.

"I have never seen either of her parents, Mike," replied Natalia.

"Never?"

"No, not at her graduation ceremony from high school, or university, and never at a birthday. Nor did I meet them even once any time in between. And she never talked about them; I just knew she had gone to live on her own at a very young age."

"So? That just means she has lied to you all these years too," countered Mike, an edge to his voice.

"No, she never told me her parents were dead," insisted Natalia. "I just never asked her about them."

"Her parents never came up? You were never curious as to where her parents were?" asked Mike disbelievingly.

"No. I didn't ask her because I knew she didn't want me to," said Natalia, her voice rising and warmth coming to her cheeks. "And as the years passed by and I saw her live her life all alone, with no family to support her in bad times or to come and celebrate her in good ones, well, then I thought...." Natalia couldn't bring herself to finish her sentence.

"What? What! Natalia, what did you think?" yelled Mike.

"I thought it would have been better if her parents really had died!" yelled Natalia back at him. "They were already gone from her life just as if they were dead to her. If they had died, then at least she wouldn't have a secret to carry around with her that she felt she needed to hide from everyone!"

"Like what kind of secret?" asked Mike, his voice soft.

"Oh, Mike," sighed Natalia, the intensity of emotion having drained her of all energy. "No one leaves their parents and never contacts them again for no reason."

With that she took the car keys out of Mike's hand and before he could protest, jumped into the car and began to back out carefully into the narrow street. She watched Mike stand there for a moment with his breath misting in the November air before taking out his phone.

NATALIA DROVE THE FLOWERS TO THE HOTEL. Before unloading the van she decided she would use the restroom and get something to drink afterwards from the restaurant.

"Mary!" exclaimed Natalia.

Mary was collapsed in a heap in the lovely five-star hotel's restroom crying. Her mascara and lipstick were smeared all over her face. Natalia knew she had come down to the hotel to lay out the name cards and the menus on the tables. Now she looked like she was going to be sick.

Abruptly Mary jumped up off the floor and ran into a stall, slamming the door behind her.

"Mary! Come out here!"

"I can't. I'm going to be sick," cried Mary from the stall.

Natalia waited until Mary opened the door and stepped out. Natalia opened her arms and Mary fell into them, still sobbing.

"I know about your fight with Mike. Mary, listen, it will be okay. Really. He loves you. He will think it over and realize that you do trust him. You just need to have a heart-to-heart together and tell him the truth about your parents. Mary?"

"No. He broke off our engagement. It's over. And I didn't lie. My parents are dead. To me anyway," answered Mary between sobs.

"Oh, Mary," sighed Natalia, sitting down next to her beautiful friend and putting her arms around her. "Don't you think it would feel good to let it all out to someone who loves you?"

"No. And what would you know about it, Natalia!" Mary shouted, her eyes blazing as she sat up tall and pushed Natalia away from her. "You with your smart, loving parents and your perfect life! It isn't fair! You work hard, but I have worked just as hard as you! Or harder even! Yet you have the wonderful parents, the sexy husband, the darling children, the picturesque house on the lake, the successful business. And what do I have? Nothing. I have no one," said Mary, her voice weary, her shoulders once again rounding.

"You have me," answered Natalia. "I love you."

Mary didn't respond.

"And you have great shoes," she added, admiring Mary's dark maroon leather pumps with pink stitching and a bow just above the back heel.

"They are great shoes," admitted Mary, smiling just slightly.

"You are right," admitted Natalia, "I was dealt a better hand of cards than you. You have a right to be angry. Life is just not fair. We all take the hand we get and play them the best way we can. For the record, I think you have taken your bad hand of cards and done amazing with them. You have worked hard every day of your life and turned misfortune into fuel for your ambition. You are amazing, Mary. Really. And you can have it all too."

"I am good at bluffing, misleading people, and putting on a perfect facade," replied Mary.

"Well, sometimes we need to bluff to win the game, despite the hand we have been played. But you have certainly worked hard enough. You never bluffed to hurt others or take advantage of them. There is no reason why someone like you can't have a sexy husband and darling children. But you need to be brave, tell the truth, and let down your guard for Mike. Just let Mike love you. Trust him, Mary. Trust that he will love you even if you aren't perfect."

"You know," said Mary, resting her head softly on Natalia's shoulder.

"Oh, Mary," answered Natalia, weary beyond belief. "We both know I have always known, at least in the abstract. You told me a bit at the Grieder bar, all those years ago."

They sat like that together for a long time in silence. Then Natalia kissed Mary on the top of the head and said, "Come, unfortunately, we have a benefit for hungry children to execute this evening."

Mary washed her face and went out into the hotel lobby without any makeup on. She hadn't combed her hair or noticed the rip in her nylons. Natalia didn't know if this was a good sign or a bad one. Just then she realized her phone was ringing. She saw Mike had tried to call her like ten times. She showed the phone to Mary. Mary took it from her.

Mary answered the phone with a faltering, "Hi, Mike," and disappeared into the ladies' room once again.

Natalia headed for the ballroom. She had a lot of work ahead of her, she knew. She still needed to unload all the flowers and set them out on the table, not to mention the rest of the tasks on her list. She worked as fast as she could. Despite the trips out into the cold and back in again she began to get sweaty from her quick pace and carrying the huge heavy flower arrangements. She stopped to wipe her face with the scarf she was wearing and then put her face in her hands. Slightly dizzy, Natalia couldn't remember the last time she had eaten.

"Can I help you with anything, love?" asked a voice behind her. There stood Evan, looking particularly attractive in a pair of jeans and a red long-sleeved T-shirt. He was holding up a brown paper bag.

Natalia's heart gave a leap in her chest and she wished she wasn't all sweaty and stressed.

"Yes, if you could help me lay out the menus at each place setting, that would be great. I will set out the rest of the name cards Mary was working on before, before…" Natalia stopped herself, deciding no one needed to know about Mary and Mike's fight but her.

"Before what?" asked Evan, his green eyes twinkling at her. "Have your workers gone and deserted you?"

"Mary wouldn't ever desert me," countered Natalia.

"Well, you are right," answered Evan. "Mary is like the little sister you never had. She wouldn't leave you in the lurch."

"You don't know how good it is to see you," said Natalia.

"It's good to see you too."

Smiling, he gathered Natalia in a hug and lifted her off the floor.

"Although I must tell you, you have smelled better," he laughed.

"Hey!" answered Natalia, pushing him away, "That's not nice. I've had a stressful day."

"You smell like it, love," replied Evan, winking at her. "Now stop talking to me; this task you gave me requires deep concentration."

"Thanks for helping, Evan," answered Natalia.

"Oh, you think I am doing this for free? I am fully expecting to be compensated for my work."

"Is that so?" replied Natalia. "How about a free dinner tonight?"

"How about a full day of you taking charge of the kids?"

"Expensive drinks?" countered Natalia, smiling.

"WELL THAT IS THE LAST ONE," said Evan fifteen minutes later, stepping in close and licking her neck. "Hmm. Salty. Unless you require more assistance, I am heading up to our room for a nap, then a run around the lake, and a long hot shower. You have the entire rest of the day to think of some more creative forms of compensation than dinner or drinks. And oh, by the way, there is a sandwich and a brownie in that brown bag for you. I know you, you probably haven't eaten any lunch today."

Natalia went for the brown bag immediately and bit into the ham, avocado, and cheese sandwich thankfully, touched that Evan had been so thoughtful. After a few bites the dizziness started to subside. Finishing the sandwich, she saw a bottle of juice also in the bag and took a drink before unwrapping the brownie.

Natalia heard a voice behind her say, "That's not good for you, you know. An apple juice, and a brownie? You do realize you are eating around thirteen teaspoons of sugar, just about double the recommended daily amount for a woman?"

Her head held high, her posture once again perfect, Mary glided over to where Natalia was laying out the last of the name cards. Natalia examined Mary's face for clues as to how the conversation went with Mike, but per usual, Mary's poker face was perfect, despite her disheveled appearance.

"Well?"

Mary broke into a huge grin and threw her arms around Natalia.

"I did it. I told him the truth. I told him everything."

"And it went well."

"He said he loves me even more now than he did before. He

admitted he didn't think it was possible to love someone as much as he loves me," said Mary, tears beginning to slide once again down her cheeks.

"Oh, Mary, I'm so happy for you." Natalia drew Mary into a hug.

As Mary's whole body continued to heave with sobs, Natalia murmured, "Just let it go. Just cry it all out."

Natalia knew Mary had held so much in, for so long, that she just needed a good long cry. Unfortunately, she had only three hours left to set up the greeting table just inside the doors of the ballroom, ensure the welcome baskets were in each of the hotel rooms for the guests that were staying the night, and ensure Mike came and set up all the equipment for the evening and checked that the lighting in each flower vase was functional, among countless other small details. She also needed time to glam herself up.

"Where is my beauty?" asked a deep voice behind her.

"Mike!" Mary was clearly horrified that he was seeing her looking so terrible. Her eyes were red and puffy from crying, she had mascara running down her face once again, and her hair was a matted mess. Mike strode over to Mary and took her in his arms.

"I'm taking you home, putting you in a hot bath, and handing you a glass of champagne. Then I will be back to pick you up just before the event starts at seven. Natalia and I can handle the rest of the work for the event. Right, Natalia?"

"Of course. Go home, Mary, and have a rest," responded Natalia protectively, kissing Mary on the forehead.

As soon as Mike and Mary left hand in hand, Natalia stuffed the rest of the brownie in her mouth and literally ran to get the rest of her work done. A bath sounded good to her too. In fact, sliding into a tub full of lavender-scented bubbles sounded downright heavenly.

Stopping to recheck her list before leaving the ballroom, Natalia saw a note for her. At the bottom of the page, in Mary's handwriting, she read, "Remember you are on the auction block tonight. Good luck."

Does that mean I am helping with the auction tonight after all? I thought these society women were handling the auction all on their own

Sighing at the thought of yet more work ahead of her that evening, Natalia went to the car to collect her bag and gown.

On the way through the lobby she stopped at the reception. "Do you have any lavender bubble bath by any chance?" she asked.

"I am sure we can arrange to have some sent up to your room," the woman responded with a smile. "I do hope things are going well with your event preparations for this evening. If you require any assistance from the staff, please do not hesitate to ask."

"Yes, thank you," replied Natalia.

Open Your Eyes

Chapter 16

NATALIA ENTERED HER HOTEL ROOM with a sigh of relief, placing her gown on the bed and her handbag on a turquoise upholstered chair. Entering the bathroom, she noticed there were fresh flowers not only in her room, but in the bathroom as well. She turned on the bath taps just as someone knocked on her room door.

Natalia opened the door to a young man holding a small bottle of bubble bath out to her on a silver tray. Thanking him, she returned to the bathroom and at last slid into the hot tub. Relaxing in the silky water, Natalia breathed in the lavender-scented steam and felt the tension knots in her neck and shoulders loosening.

Natalia's thoughts drifted to her children. For hours she had not thought of her children. She had been so wrapped up in Mary and Mike's unraveling and the event preparations that she had not had time to worry over any of her own problems.

"I am married to Evan," she said aloud into the steam. "I have two twins, Nick and Nathan, and an adorable little girl named Annabelle."

Natalia waited for a wash of clarity and reality to engulf her, like the warmth of the bath she was enjoying. She tried to remember her life. She closed her eyes. But she didn't see Evan. She saw herself dancing with James on their wedding night. The band was playing "Lady in Red." She could almost feel her white satin dress whispering across the dancing floor as James waltzed her around the room, his hand firm on her lower back. She could even smell his citrus-scented aftershave. Eva, dressed in red, was dancing nearby with Evan, as were her parents.

The memory was so real. Opening her eyes, Natalia could hardly believe it could be nothing more than a fabricated daydream. Natalia closed her eyes again. She would try to remember the birth of the twins, Nick and Nathan.

But instead, she saw herself lying in a hospital bed breathless and triumphant as they placed Anna into her arms. She could almost smell her infant and feel Anna's soft hair against her cheek as Anna nestled for the first time in her arms, skin to skin.

Natalia saw the nurse come over with heated blankets, carefully tucking them around her and the dark-haired baby snuggled in her arms. Exhausted from childbirth, she recalled how the warmth of those blankets had felt so good, like the warmth was seeping directly into her body and relaxing all her muscles.

She heard James whisper, "Look, our angel is asleep, darling. Close your eyes and sleep too." She felt his lips briefly touch her own and watched as he settled down in a chair near them to watch over his new family while they slept.

The memory drifted away and a new one took its place. She heard Allan singing, "Happy birthday for me," in his adorable little two-year-old voice. She saw him gathering balloons in his arms together with Anna and throwing them up into the air, yelling, "Hooray birthday" and then collapsing with his sister on the floor in giggles.

Natalia opened her eyes again. Not one of these memories were of Evan, the twins, or the beautiful little Annabelle. Natalia felt crazy. How could she have all these memories of a life that everyone assured her she had never lived? Relaxing back, Natalia decided to try one last time. Perhaps she would try to remember bad memories instead of good ones and see if that worked.

She felt the sun warm on her skin as she relaxed on a towel at the pool down next to Lake Bodensee with the children. She saw herself turn to talk to her friend, not watching as dark-haired Ben got up from beside her and toddled after his brother, Allan, toward the edge of the pool. She felt her heart almost stop as she turned just in time to see Ben fall and disappear under the water. She could hear Allan calling, "Mommy, Mommy!" as she ran, her heart racing, as she dove into the pool, pulling her one-year-old son up out of the water. She heard Ben sputtering out water and crying as she held his little shaking body in her arms. Guilt and remorse flooding through her, Natalia swore at her inattentiveness to her baby.

She saw Allan at three years old standing on top of the kitchen counter and calling out to her, "Look, Mommy, I am Batman! I am going to fly like Batman!" and jumping. She watched as his little body hit the floor, his head slamming into the stone tiles. Red blood. She felt the stickiness of the red oozing from Allan's head as she picked up his little body and ran to the car, yelling to Anna to jump in as fast as she could. Natalia felt the adrenaline coursing through her veins as she sped to the children's hospital with Anna crying in the backseat and Allan surprisingly quiet. She remembered thinking how little Allan was as she carried him into the hospital, her ragged breathing smoothing only when he lay on the white paper of the hospital table with a doctor sewing his head wound together again.

Natalia felt the bath growing cold. She added some hot water and sat there in the steam, thinking. She decided she no longer cared if she was with Evan or James. She just wanted her own children in her arms. Just then Natalia heard someone calling her name.

"Just a minute," she called. Standing up too quickly, she slipped and fell, smacking her head on the side of the tub. She gazed at the purple flowers on the counter. Then everything went black.

NATALIA FELT SO COLD AND STIFF, but she couldn't seem to open her eyes. She wanted to get up and go find another blanket. She thought she heard Anna come into the room. She felt her daughter crawl onto the bed beside her and snuggle up close. Then she felt her get up again.

She wanted to call, "Come back, sweetheart, come cuddle with your mama under the covers and get nice and warm. It's so cold in here," but couldn't manage it.

She was even having trouble focusing her eyes. The room was so blurry. She gave up and closed them again.

From far away she thought she heard Anna saying, "My mama's really cold. Someone bring me another blanket."

Then Natalia felt Anna snuggle back in next to her with her head on Natalia's chest. She felt warmth settle onto her body as someone tucked a heated blanket over her and her daughter. She wanted to open her eyes and tell Anna it was just like right after she was born, when they had placed heated blankets around the two of them just after Anna's birth, but somehow she couldn't manage to do so.

"NATALIA, LOVE, ARE YOU ALL RIGHT?"

Natalia opened her eyes. Looking around, she saw that she was lying naked on the bed of a richly decorated hotel room. Suddenly she sat up, looking around the room in panic.

"Where is Anna?" she asked.

Evan was standing over her in running clothes. Sweat was running down the sides of his face, his features showing concern.

"Anna? You mean Annabelle? She is at home with your parents.

You know I hate it when you shorten her name. Listen, I just checked in with them," said Evan, holding up his phone. "They just got back from going out for an early dinner with your parents. What are you doing? Shouldn't you be all dolled up and already down completing any last-minute work for the event tonight? Are you sick?"

Evan walked over and leaned in close. He kissed her cheek and smoothed her hair back from her face with both hands, worry darkening his eyes.

Natalia sat in confused silence. Had she just dreamed that she had had her Anna lying next to her? What was she doing before she fell asleep on the bed?

"I think I'm fine," Natalia answered, still bewildered, stretching her body and gently feeling her head with her hands.

Evan reached out and pulled her to her feet.

"Then you best get dressed, love," he said, looking her over carefully. "Hey, Natalia, what is that on your head there?"

Evan gently pulled her damp hair back from her face to get a better view. "You are bleeding a little bit. How did you get hurt?"

Natalia didn't remember hurting her head. What could have happened? Confused, she remained silent.

"Did you fall?" Evan asked, while he went to wet a washcloth, then pressed it to her head to clean away the blood. "Oh look, now it is fine, it is just a small cut. It has already stopped bleeding. Natalia?"

Natalia remembered she was having such a lovely hot bath and when she went to get out…

"I fell getting out of the bathtub," she murmured.

"Well, no wonder you are a bit shook up. But go ahead and get dressed, love. I'll call room service to bring you up a cup of coffee and I have some ibuprofen here somewhere in my bag you can take. I am going to jump in the shower. If you need me just give a shout."

Natalia made her way slowly to the bag lying on a luggage rack near the door. She slowly pulled on underwear and slipped into her nude Christian Louboutin high heels. Unzipping the garment bag at the end of the bed, she took out a shimmering floor-length strapless dress and slipped into it, pulling up the sweetheart bodice and holding it in place. She went to the floor-length mirror by the door and turned. The champagne hue was pretty against her red hair, but the wow factor came from the shimmering open-back design. Narrow glimmering straps crisscrossed her back.

"Evan, will you come and zip me into my dress?" called Natalia.

"That is some dress," Evan commented on his way to the shower, a towel tied around his wait. He walked over to Natalia and ran his hand from her neck all the way down to the straps crisscrossing her spine. "Don't you think that dress is a little too sexy for a charity benefit?" he asked, smiling. "Where is the zipper?"

Natalia answered, "It's here on the side."

She breathed in as Evan pulled the zipper up so it would close. She had to admit that the dress was a bit tight. But better too tight with a strapless dress than risk having it slip down, she reasoned.

"Okay, I am heading back downstairs," said Natalia.

"You aren't doing your hair or makeup?" asked Evan, his eyebrows raised in surprise. "Your hair is still slightly wet. And I ordered you coffee from room service."

Evan walked over, and noticing her jewelry on the side table on the way back to the bathroom, returned to her and fastened her diamond pendant around her neck, handing her two huge diamond stud earrings to put in her ears. A knock came at the door and Evan went to answer it, still in his towel.

A young man followed Evan back into the room carrying a silver tray. Placing the tray gently on the table between the turquoise club chairs, he left the room without a word, shutting the door quietly behind him. Natalia went over immediately and poured coffee from the silver pot into one of the two white china cups on the tray, adding some steamed milk from the jug as well.

Just then the hotel room phone rang. Evan picked it up.

"Yes, thank you, please send her up," he said. He turned to Natalia. "So, you have a professional hair and makeup appointment? She is on her way up to the room. I better go shave and get my tux on in the bathroom then."

Natalia was a bit perplexed. Why had she ordered a stylist to come to her hotel room? She hadn't done that for the last event. Was that something she did?

"Evan?" Natalia asked, following Evan to the door of the bathroom. "Do I usually get my makeup and hair done professionally for events?"

"Well, I can imagine you wanted tonight to be extra special," he replied without turning from looking in the mirror while shaving.

"Why is that?" insisted Natalia.

"You want to spoil your husband by looking drop-dead gorgeous?" Evan smiled. "Or maybe you need some pampering. Listen, you need not worry. I don't care, honey. Go ahead and enjoy yourself."

Natalia heard a knock at the door. She went out to answer it, closing the door to the bathroom as she went.

"Hi, Natalia! Some fancy place, what? Loving the turquoise and warm browns of this room. Where shall I set up?"

A petite redhead with tall high heels, a miniskirt, a loose green cashmere sweater, and large hoop earrings stepped into the hotel room. Without waiting for a response from Natalia she walked over and placed her things on the side table and pulled out a chair. Natalia stood uncertainly still holding the door open, trying to remember the stylist's name.

"Well, what are you waiting for? You told me I would have to do magic in just twenty-five minutes. Sit down and let's get started."

Natalia sat down in the chair and the woman set to work, chatting continually the entire time about the man she had met the night before at the most outrageous party. Natalia didn't need to say one word. A short time later the redhead was finished.

"Go check yourself out in the mirror. You look gorgeous. Loving the dress, by the way. Very sexy. But not in a slutty kind of way, if you know what I'm saying. If they were making that short, why I would wear that out clubbing. Might be a bit too fancy though. Maybe would work for New Year's. Well, that's it." The stylist started packing her makeup and curling iron into a case, just as Evan came out of the bathroom in his tux.

"Never saw the mister before, Natalia. Hello, handsome! You caught yourself quite the fish here, Natalia. I don't remember you mentioning how drop-dead sexy your man was."

Evan grinned. "I like you," he said. "What's your name?"

"Jenny," replied the redhead. "Well, I better scoot. I know Natalia here has work to do downstairs."

Natalia went to her purse and panicked a bit. How much did hair and makeup cost? She didn't know. She turned to find Evan was already paying Jenny for her.

"Thank you, Jenny," called Natalia as Jenny went out the door.

"Pleasure, as always. Call me anytime!"

"You look fantastic," said Evan, turning to admire Natalia's hair half pinned up with curls cascading down her back. Natalia looked in the mirror. She wasn't used to wearing so much makeup. Her eyes were lined and smoldering, her lips painted a deep dark red. She didn't know how Jenny had done it, but even the dark circles were gone from under her eyes and her cheeks glowed.

"You don't think it's too much?" she asked, uncertain.

"Not a chance. Now let's go down. I'm ready for a cocktail while you set to work."

Natalia took the arm Evan reached out for her and they made their way out of their room and toward the elevator.

The Dreams We Dream

Chapter 17

Natalia walked into le petit palais and noticed the chandeliers throughout the room dimming and the lights in the flower vases shifting from orange, red, and yellow, to blue, purple, and red and then over to orange, blue, and pink. She noticed Mike standing up on the stage, intently looking over the room, his head tilted in concentration.

"Hello, Mike. How are you? Are you trying to decide on the best lighting for the evening?"

"Natalia? Wow. You look like dynamite tonight. What is the special occasion? Oh wait, never mind, I remember. So listen, yeah, I can't decide on what lighting is best."

"Can you do orange, purple, and red?"

"Sure. I haven't tried that combination before." Evan used his remote control to shift the colors throughout the room. Each table suddenly glowed with soft orange, red, and purple light. "Exactly! That is perfect. What made you think of that color combination, Natalia?"

"Well, red is stimulating and most people like red. It is the second most popular color on the planet. People also associate red with passion, attraction, excitement, and adventure. Orange, on the other hand, is a definite party color. We associate orange with happiness, fun, and optimism. However, orange can look cheap. So to balance the stimulation of the red and orange and give some elegance to the event, we also needed purple. Purple is associated with dignity, royalty, luxury, and wisdom. Purple is also calming and encourages introspection. The color combination should encourage the right atmosphere for people to really let loose and have fun this evening, albeit, hopefully in a dignified manner." Natalia smiled.

Mike smiled down at her. "Cool stuff that. You need to write me out a guide to color or something so that I can experiment with the different color lighting combinations. Then we can create a brochure with a pre-selected collection of lighting options for our clients to choose from for their future events."

"Brilliant. Actually, you and Mary could work on that together," replied Natalia, smiling.

Natalia glanced through her list, noting that everything was checked off. "Mike, did you finish up all of the remaining tasks on our list all by yourself?"

"Sure. I thought you and Mary could use a break. And I owe you one. You know. For earlier," replied Mike as he checked the technical equipment on the stage.

Natalia looked up and to the right, gazing at a sparkling chandelier as she tried to remember what it was she had done that Mike was talking about.

"Oh, come on now, Natalia, don't make me spell it out for you. You yelled some sense into me at Antonio's. I needed someone to do that. And you know Mary, she is such a proud one, and yet so fragile all at the same time; she was devastated. I don't know if we could have worked it out if it wasn't for you."

Natalia kept a serious face as she answered, "It was completely selfish. I would have had to put on the event tonight all by myself if you two were missing in action. And if you hadn't reconciled, then that would have made for an unpleasant working environment for me."

Mike paused from untangling the wires gliding down the back of the stage and to two huge speakers, grinning. "When you say it all deadpan like that I almost believe those were your motivations. But I know you better than that. Oh hey, a few of our clients have called and assured me they will be bidding on you tonight. So that is great news, right?"

"Bid on me?"

"Yeah, so you can just relax and enjoy the evening, knowing that you can stand up on that stage all confident like, because someone is going to donate a lot of money to the Feed the Children fund for you."

"Oh no," said Natalia, bringing her hands to her mouth and her eyes growing wide.

"Why aren't you happy?" answered Mike.

"Happy! I agreed to stand up on stage in front of one hundred and fifty people and be auctioned! Why would I do that? I can't do it."

Natalia felt shaky. It was one thing if she had to get up on stage and make an announcement. That she could do. It was another thing to stand in front of a meeting and outline the results of a strategic project. If she was well-prepared and imparting knowledge she felt confident in, well then she also could stand up without nervousness and manage to give a good presentation in front of a crowd of people. But to just stand on a stage, as a whole crowd stared up at her, just, what? Posing? That she could not imagine.

Mike walked over and took her hands. "Natalia, listen, we talked about this as a team, remember? We all decided to agree to this because it is such a good cause. Hungry children? How does that not touch the most hardened heart?"

"Oh," sighed Natalia in relief.

"So we will be standing up there together as a team?"

"No, individually. Hey, are you okay? How do you not remember this?" Suddenly Mike smacked his forehead. "Oh wait, you can't remember anything earlier than last Sunday!" he exclaimed. "Of course, I am sorry, Natalia. You just seem to have it all so together, I forgot."

"Mike, someone will hear you. No one can know," said Natalia.

"No one can know what?" asked Evan as he entered the Petit Palais with a drink from the bar still in his hand.

Mike gave Natalia a knowing look and raised his eyebrows. In response Natalia shook her head ever so slightly.

"Know about, well, hmmm, my inventive lighting system!" exclaimed Mike, turning to Evan and reaching out his hand. "Then all the event firms would copy our original lighting experience. Good to see you, Evan. Great tux."

"Good to see you too, Mike. How have you been? Does Natalia have you working the same crazy long hours that she puts in? If so then you see more of my wife than I do!" Evan said, slapping Mike good-naturedly on the back.

"How does that saying go?" asked Mike. "Do something you love and you will never work a day in your life?"

"Don't be angry with me, Evan, not tonight," sighed Natalia, massaging her temples.

Evan walked over and started massaging her neck. After a moment he said softly, "Hey, I was just making a joke. Really. You look gorgeous and I am happy to be with you tonight. There is nothing wrong with a man missing the woman he is in love with."

Natalia straightened and looked into Evan's eyes. Stepping forward, Natalia gently placed her hands on Evan's strong square jaw line, and leaning in, allowed herself to ever so softly touch her lips to his. She had to admit that he looked even sexier in a tux than in his usual wardrobe of jeans and T-shirts. Her mind wandered back to their night together and she felt her cheeks flush.

"Natalia, darling, we are here early. Does the boss have time for a drink before the event starts? How about you, Evan?"

Natalia broke away from Evan, her face flushing upon seeing Eva walking toward them in a bright red floor-length gown with matching red high heels. The gown emphasized her hourglass figure and had a plunging neckline revealing the soft roundness of each breast. Natalia felt her jaw clenching when she saw both Mike and Evan looking Eva over. Striding into the room behind her was James, looking dashing in a tux, albeit unshaven and frowning darkly.

Natalia looked at James, then at Evan, then back at James. She wondered if James had seen her kissing Evan. Her instinct was to feel she had just betrayed James, but after a week of everyone affirming she was indeed married to Evan, and not to James, she quickly reminded herself that it was perfectly normal to kiss her own husband. Despite this, she felt both guilty and defiant while meeting James' gaze.

"That is, if we aren't interrupting you two love birds," added James.

"Eva, you look beautiful, as always," said Evan, ignoring James' comment. Natalia felt her insides twist. She didn't like Evan telling Eva that she looked beautiful.

"Look at these two sour grapes," laughed Eva, motioning wildly at James and Natalia. "Let's ditch these two and go get a drink the two of us, Evan. You can tell me some jokes and make me laugh. I am ready to be in a real party mood and this one is seriously bringing me down," said Eva, her head tilting toward James.

James didn't change his expression as he said, "Life isn't a game, Eva. Sometimes dignity and seriousness are required of us."

"Oh, James, but not at a party, loosen up," said Eva.

Natalia realized she was grimacing and her shoulders had fallen forward. Consciously pulling herself in and up, she stood up straight, plastering a smile on her face.

"It is good to see you, Eva, James," she said, stepping forward to kiss Eva and James on both cheeks.

"Evan, you look amazing in that tux," gushed Eva, as she guided him out the door of the banquet room and toward the bar. "We really need to attend more events like this so I can see you in a tux more often."

James went to follow Eva and Evan and then paused when he realized Natalia wasn't moving. Natalia was angry. She felt her pulse throbbing and her hands clenching. Wasn't it enough that she had a dark and handsome husband of her own? Why did Eva insist on having the adoration of every man she ran across, whether married or otherwise? Natalia decided it was time to stand up to her friend. Without giving a second look to James she strode from the room toward the lobby.

Natalia paused at the entrance to the bar. Eva and Evan were already seated on barstools at the dark wooden bar. Eva was leaning forward, offering an even fuller view of her breasts to Evan as she laughed at something he was saying. Before she could stride across the room to confront Eva, she felt a hand grab her bare arm.

"She isn't doing it to anger you. She is doing it to anger me."

Natalia turned. James stood, his teeth clenched, glaring at Eva.

"In the car on the way here I told her she needed to stop throwing herself at every man in a room at these events, that she is embarrassing me. She told me she couldn't help it if all men are drawn to her sexiness, all men but me, anyway."

They stood together in silence for a moment.

"You were drawn in," said Natalia defiantly. "Otherwise you wouldn't have chosen her."

Natalia almost had added *over me* to the sentence, but caught herself just in time. "You chose to marry her," finished Natalia.

"Natalia, forgive me, it was a huge mistake," said James, running his hands through his hair and looking down at the floor.

He continued, "Can't you believe me? What happened with Eva was a terrible mistake. I just…it was intoxicating for such a sexy woman to shower me with such attention, to seduce me. I only realized later how needy she is. One man's attention isn't enough. She can't let herself relax into quiet love. She wants men desperate for her, thinking about her all the time, she craves passionate love affairs. At the very least, she wants the desire of every man in a room and works until she has them all buzzing around her like little bees."

Natalia didn't say anything. She didn't turn toward James. She stood motionless, watching as Eva's long hair fell toward her martini glass, as Evan leaned over and gently pushed Eva's hair back, his fingers trailing over the beautiful caramel of her bare shoulder. She watched as Eva leaned in, whispering something in Evan's ear, watched as Evan threw his head back in merriment.

Natalia wanted to march over, snatch the cocktails out of their hands, and splash the contents in both their faces.

Turning to face James, she noticed how tall and lean he was, how serious. He looked amazing in his tux, despite the fact that he hadn't shaved in a day and his hair stood on end from all the times he kept running his hands through it in agitation.

Suddenly, Natalia remembered a younger James, a James sitting across from her at a conference table, his hands running through the front of his hair in stress. They were working a strategic proposal. Natalia was finished with her section of the work, but had stayed on to help James. She would do anything to spend more time with him back then. As she sat trying to explain how he should go about tackling the challenge of his section of the work he kept pulling his hands through his hair. He looked uncharacteristically unsure.

"But I don't have time to get this done before the presentation tomorrow," he had said, his shoulders hunched up toward his ears, his brow furrowed. "I hope I don't get fired."

Natalia had been bone tired. Her body hurt from sitting for so many hours. But she felt herself saying, "I will help you. We will stay here all night if we need to."

Then the memory faded and was replaced with a bright-eyed James, standing tall and expansive at the front of a conference room, radiating energy in front of the partners of their consultancy and their client, the executive team of a large company. She saw him presenting her strategy. She saw him taking credit for her hard work. While she sat small and nodding in a corner, all eyes were on James. All the praise and acknowledgment was flowing to him at the end. He'd never admitted that she had been the brains behind the strategy, that she had done the majority of the work. He had just taken the credit. She had just followed everyone out of the conference room afterward, feeling small and hurt.

"Why did I do that?" Natalia declared aloud, lifting her chin and looking heatedly around the room while clenching her fists.

"Why did you do what?" asked James.

"Why did I let you take credit for my hard work at the consultancy? No. Why did I let you take credit for my brilliant and hard work at the consultancy? Was I some kind of pushover fool or what?"

James looked at her, a bit shocked. Recovering, he responded charmingly, "Now, Natalia, you and I know that you have no skill in presenting and even less skill at social intelligence. If it weren't for my fine presentation skills, my ability to win the partners and customer over to thinking the strategy was a good one, well, we would not have been a success at all."

"That is bullshit and you know it. You should have told them I created the strategy, even if you were the one to present the work. You would have had nothing to present if it wasn't for my hard work."

James looked taken aback. "But you didn't say anything at the time. You weren't mad then."

"Like hell I wasn't. But I was a pushover and you knew you could walk right over me. No wonder I left consulting, after having worked with a jerk like you taking credit for all my work and trying to convince me I couldn't sell my own ideas."

"Natalia, come on! Are you really trying to stand there and tell me you think I needed your help because I wasn't smart enough to develop something as good on my own? You are kidding, right? When I was just too tired to get my work done, you helped me. Which was sweet. But we both know who the smarter of the two of us is. Just look at us. I am a senior partner in one of the most esteemed consulting firms in Switzerland. And you. You operate a quaint party-planning service. The truth is, you couldn't cut it in consulting. You weren't smart or tough enough."

Natalia stared unblinking at James, clenching and unclenching her fists. A voice in her head agreed with him. *He's right,* it said. *You aren't very smart. You aren't successful. You must not even be that attractive, as your own husband is over there salivating over another woman.*

"Like hell you are smarter than I am!" yelled Natalia. "I helped you out all the time. You took the credit, all the time. I was in love with you and you took advantage. But you are right about one thing. I wasn't tough enough."

Natalia stepped in close to James, looking him straight in the eye. "I am now though. So I'll tell you what is going to happen. You are going to send me over a generous work contract to sign. Not as a junior partner. But as a senior partner."

"Oh," laughed James. "And exactly what makes you think I am going to do that?"

Natalia stepped in even closer. "I could say because I am brilliant, or I deserve it. I could explain how I will make the firm more money as a senior partner. But that isn't why you will give me the contract to sign."

"Then why will I?"

Natalia was standing so close to James, she could feel the warmth radiating from his body; she could see the way his eyes kept glancing at her lips; she knew she was close enough for him to smell her perfume.

"Because you are in love with me. Karma is a bitch, handsome, and her name is Natalia."

"That doesn't even make any sense," muttered James.

"Natalia!" Mary interrupted happily as she glided toward them in a black Audrey Hepburn–style dress, pearls, and black heels. "It is time to go and man the reception table to greet the arriving guests."

"Perfect timing, Mary," answered Natalia, glaring one last time at Eva and Evan.

You Know the Truth

Chapter 18

As NATALIA FOLLOWED MARY back toward the Petit Palais, she felt her anger melt into sadness, the sadness washing over her like icy water, and she was left feeling hollow and cold. She nodded and smiled as Mary talked about the evening ahead but she wasn't really listening.

Evan or James, it didn't matter to her anymore. She wasn't sure she liked either of them now. Natalia just wanted to hold her children in her arms again. She still hadn't worked out where they were, or if indeed she had amnesia and Evan's blond-haired children were really hers too. It was time, she realized, to take responsibility. It was time to go in and get some professional help.

"Excuse me, Mary, I need just five minutes to make a call and I will be in to help."

Hands shaking, Natalia found a deserted corner of the hall and took out her phone. She searched through her address book for a moment. She had helped Dr. Schmidt complete his business plan while she was still at university during an internship with a small consultancy.

She remembered he had kind eyes and a keen intelligence. She could trust him to help her. She dialed the office, hoping it wasn't too late to make an appointment.

"Good evening, Dr. Schmidt's office. How can I help you?" answered a soothing male voice. "…Hello?"

Natalia cleared her throat. "Yes, I would like to arrange an appointment with Dr. Schmidt, please."

"There is an appointment available in about three months, on Thursday, February 2, at three o'clock. Does this fit your schedule?" replied the man on the line.

"That is the soonest you can get me in? Wow, he is really doing great if he is so booked up."

"Is it an emergency?" inquired the man on the other end. "If you are considering taking your own life, or injuring anyone around you, please stay on the line."

"No, no, nothing like that," replied Natalia, her voice shrill and panicky. "I just, well… I think I am suffering from some sort of amnesia, or something like that. I am having trouble…mmm. Listen, Dr. Schmidt may remember me? Could you ask him if he could squeeze me into his schedule? He might?"

"What is your name?"

Natalia hesitated, then decided to give her maiden name.

"Natalia Scott."

"Hold the line, please," answered the smooth voice. After less than a minute he was back. "Hello? Are you still there? Dr. Schmidt told me to tell you that of course he will make time to see Natalia Scott. But he really is fully booked. So if you wouldn't mind coming in on a Saturday, he will see you at ten a.m."

"Thank you so much. Goodbye."

"Goodbye."

Natalia shook her head and slumped back against the wall. Natalia felt fear, like a hand at her throat, slowly starting to squeeze. She took ragged breaths, slowly slipping down the wall to the floor.

What would Dr. Schmidt say? What if she were severely mentally ill?

Would she loose everything? What would people think of her?

Natalia heard Mary calling for her. Natalia slowly inhaled to the count of six, then exhaled twice as slow to the count of twelve. After a few minutes she felt her shoulders relax down from her ears and her pulse slow. Once again standing up tall, lifting her chin and plastering a bright false smile on her face, Natalia entered the ballroom to stand at the welcome desk for the next hour.

THE NEXT TWO HOURS seemed to go by in a haze for Natalia. Her face hurt from forcing a smile all evening. Her feet hurt from her ridiculously high heels. She was feeling a bit dizzy and kept telling herself it was just due to her too-tight dress. Just before the auction Mary pulled Natalia by the hand into the ladies' room.

"You need to freshen yourself up before the auction, Natalia," said Mary. "You look terrible, like ten years older than your real age."

"Well, you can be a real bitch sometimes," answered Natalia.

Mary turned away from the mirror, her eyes wide. She just stood there, looking at Natalia without speaking. Natalia shrugged her shoulders. She was tired of the people being mean. She wasn't sure if she had even ever noticed it as verbal abuse before. She had usually just believed what James, her mother, and even Mary had told her. She thought she just needed to work harder, be kinder, more helpful, more thoughtful, and they would like her.

Now she didn't care.

Mary said, "Oh, Natalia, don't be so sensitive. I adore you. Put on some lipstick and you will look great. Natalia?"

Without saying a word, Natalia turned on her heel and left the restroom, leaving Mary looking stunned behind her.

"OH THANK GOODNESS I FOUND YOU! You are on stage next," said a plump woman in the hallway. She had a warm smile, gray hair and a floor length blue dress. Natalia followed the woman back to the ballroom and next to the stage. But her heart wasn't hammering. Her palms weren't sweating. When she looked out at the sea of tables in the glimmering room, she lifted her chin; she stood up taller; she smiled. She didn't care anymore what they all thought. Not any of them.

The man on stage announced her name and Natalia gracefully ascended the stairs and stood tall next to him with lifted chin.

"Here we have the lovely and charming Natalia," he began in a smooth voice. "She is the owner and director of Elegant Events, which planned and executed this very event."

A murmur of voices swept the room and someone began clapping. Soon the rest of the crowd joined in. Natalia felt heat spread up her neck and into her cheeks. But instead of a racing heart and sweaty palms she found herself, quite unexpectedly, smiling. In the crowd she saw Evan smiling up at her and she felt her eyes brighten.

"Yes, very talented, our Natalia," continued the auctioneer. "In addition to running Elegant Events she is the mother of three children, loves kick boxing, sailing on Lake Bodensee with her family, skiing, rock climbing, and attending parties."

Natalia looked at the short man standing next to her with silver hair and sparkling blue eyes. She did not understand why he had said she liked to rock climb, not to mention why he had added in the kick boxing and that bit about parties. She had never climbed a rock wall in her life. She couldn't picture herself kick boxing and she found attending parties to be exhausting. She felt her smile faltering and consciously tried to force herself to look upbeat.

"Now, as you can see from your auction card, the bidding for Natalia starts at one thousand Swiss francs, as she is up for auction not as a date tonight like the others, but as an event planner for a party for up to two hundred people. Of course, this includes her expertise only. All event location fees, food and drink expenses, and flowers will need to be paid for additionally to what you donate tonight."

Showing straight brilliantly white teeth in a huge smile, the man paused dramatically, looking all around the room before thundering, "We open the bidding now at one thousand Swiss francs. Do I see one thousand? Remember, your bids will benefit hungry children."

"Yes, number one hundred and fifteen in the back, thank you, sir. Do I see one thousand two hundred Swiss francs? Thank you to number fifty-four in the front. How about fifteen hundred? Yes, thank you, one hundred fifteen. Do I see two thousand Swiss francs? Two thousand? Yes, thank you number three in the middle. Thank you, sir, for your bid of two thousand Swiss francs. Do I see three thousand?"

Natalia's eyebrows rose as she sharply inhaled. Evan had bid two thousand Swiss francs for her to execute an event for him. Surveying the crowd, Natalia spotted Eva at the bar standing with one hand clutching James' sleeve, the other clutching his opposite wrist. Taking a step away from Eva and wrenching himself free from her grasp, James lifted his bid board.

"Thank you, number one for your bid of three thousand! Number three, are you prepared to raise your bid to three thousand five hundred?"

Looking around the room for the last bidder, Evan's eyes at last found James at the bar standing a step away from Eva. Gritting his teeth and clenching his fists, Evan raised his board.

"Thank you to number three. Do I see four thousand? Four thousand Swiss francs?"

James strode across the room and stood directly in front of Evan, his nose so close to Evan's it was almost touching, his eyebrows knitted together, his mouth turned into a tight-lipped smile that didn't reach his eyes. Natalia saw James muttering to Evan but of course couldn't hear what he was saying; she doubted if the people at the table behind them could even hear.

Evan said something back and all of a sudden Natalia heard Evan shout, "She is my wife, damn you," as he pushed James so hard with both hands he crashed backward into the table. The candles, lighting features, and flowers crashed over. A few women let out screams of surprise as glass fell over and shattered on the floor.

Standing up slowly, Evan looked up at Natalia. Then, rolling his shoulders back twice and clenching his fists, Evan pivoted away from the table and landed a roundhouse punch square on James' jaw. Taking a step backward, James held his jaw for a moment then rushed Evan, landing an uppercut punch into Evan's stomach. Evan fell to his knees on the floor, clutching his stomach.

"Thank you, number one hundred and fifteen for your bid of four thousand Swiss francs! Going once, going twice, SOLD to the gentleman in the back! Thank you, sir!"

Natalia turned her attention from James and Evan to the auctioneer and then to the back, looking for bidder one hundred and fifteen. A tall, elegant man gave a small wink and an easy smile as he waved up at her. She had met him at the event she had executed for James. It was the man who had teased her about being a flower thief and had told her to return to a job in consulting.

Natalia looked back to see Evan slowly rising from the floor as James strode toward the exit, his fists still clenched. She noticed Eva standing still at the bar, her eyes wide, looking from Evan to James and back again. Suddenly Eva ran from the room after James, leaving her handbag on the bar counter in her haste, and Evan grabbed the bag from the counter and followed her out of the room.

Natalia felt herself walking down the stairs of the stage as if in a dream. Slowly, she exited the ballroom and started her search for

Evan. Natalia suddenly realized that if anyone could help her make sense of her life, Evan was the one. She didn't understand why Evan would shout "She is my wife!" at James. Did Evan think she was having an affair with James after all? Natalia didn't know if she was prepared for a confrontation, but she knew she was heading for one.

Drifting across the lobby, Natalia saw Evan at the bar. He was waving his hands wildly and shouting at Eva and in the process spilling most of his glass of whiskey all over the bar. In contrast, Eva was standing still as a statue in front of him. All at once she turned on her heel and strode out of the bar, past Natalia.

Natalia took a deep breath and strode into the bar.

"Evan?"

Evan turned toward her, a smile lighting up his face at the sight of her. A moment later his eyes blurred with tears. Swallowing the rest of his drink in one gulp, he blinked a few times and turned to face her. Clearing his throat he said, "I'm sorry about all of that, Natalia. I know how important this evening was to you."

"What? Oh. No, forget about that. What is going on? Why did you shout 'She is my wife, damn you!' and why did you two fight in the middle of a charity benefit? Why were you yelling at Eva? What..." Natalia paused and exhaled, shaking her head. "What is going on?"

"Oh, come on, Natalia. You know I have known for a while now. I just turned a blind eye to the situation."

"What?"

Evan regarded Natalia. Then, motioning to the bartender for two more whiskeys, he said, "Sit down, Natalia."

Natalia took a seat on a bar stool next to Evan. The bartender brought both of them a whiskey and Evan placed one of the glasses in her hand.

"I don't drink whiskey," protested Natalia.

"Well, you do tonight, love. Drink up."

Natalia didn't pause. She lifted the drink and swallowed it down in one go before slamming the empty glass down on the bar again.

"All right. Tell me what is going on."

Evan placed his glass back down on the bar. Turning toward her, he smoothed her hair back from her face, gently caressing her cheek.

"Do you still love him?"

"James?"

Natalia looked down at her hands, examining her wedding ring. She was certain when she had woken up a few days ago that James was her husband and that she was married, albeit unhappily, to the man of her dreams. A memory of an early morning a few weeks ago drifted into her mind.

ALREADY PERFECTLY DRESSED AT SIX A.M., Natalia was waiting for the Nespresso machine to fill her favorite china cup with liquid energy when James had walked into the kitchen dressed for work in a dark blue suit and sky-blue tie. He hadn't even said good morning. He had merely reached for the just filled coffee cup.

"That's my cup," she said.

"Listen, love, I'm in a hurry, can't you just make another cup?" replied James, already turning away and taking a sip.

"No! That is my favorite cup. I drank my coffee out of it the morning we got married. I want it," said Natalia, reaching to take the cup out of James' hand.

James yelled, "Natalia, I don't have time for this. There are like twenty other cups here. You are being so childish."

James yanked the cup up higher away from her reaching fingers just as he failed to see a soccer ball in front of him. Crashing to the floor, James dropped his briefcase, which popped open. And her cup, her favorite china cup, went hurtling to the floor and smashed to pieces, splashing coffee all over James' documents and the floor.

Natalia began to cry.

"Oh really, Natalia. It's just a cup! Now I really will be late and my documents are a mess."

Without one backward glance, James straightened his expensive suit, polished away the few coffee drops from his already gleaming shoes, gathered his papers, and left the house. Natalia was left crying on the floor, surrounded by shards of china. She buried her face in her hands.

Natalia knew she would be asleep by the time James came home that night. And almost every night thereafter would be the same. Thinking back over all the birthdays he had forgotten completely, hers and their children's, she sighed. She thought of the days and nights she had nursed sick children, all alone. She thought of all the hours she had spent in the evening in solitude. Looking around her beautiful living room and kitchen, with its designer furniture and the gleaming windows looking out over the lake, Natalia thought of James, so handsome in his suit this morning.

"How did I get here?" Natalia asked aloud. Then she stood up, picked up her phone, and dialed Evan.

"NATALIA?"

Evan gently caressed her cheek with his fingertips.

"Please answer me. I need to know. Are you in love with James? Do you love him? Or do you love me?"

"But this past week you have been so angry," ventured Natalia.

"Don't think about that," pleaded Evan. "Think about all the beautiful days we have spent together with the children. Or how I am the one who always works hard to make you feel special on your birthday. And that I am the one you turn to when a child is hurt or sick or when you are terribly ill." Evan paused, tracing his fingers down her neck and along her collarbone. "I am always the first person you call when you have great news or suffer a terrible disappointment," he said.

Evan let his hand fall down over her shoulder and began lightly moving his fingers over her bare back.

"Evan, why were you yelling at Eva?" Natalia asked in a voice so soft that Evan had to lean in even closer to hear her.

Evan's eyebrows lifted and his eyes widened.

"Natalia, you know. You know the truth, you just don't want to face it. Open your eyes, Natalia."

But before Natalia could respond, James came striding across the lobby toward them. Carefully examining the bar for any recognizable faces and seeing none, James grabbed hold of Evan's shoulder and jerked him off his stool.

"You son of a bitch!" James thundered at Evan. "I can't believe you punched me in front of some of the most important people in Zürich!"

Evan laughed. "You can't believe I punched you, or you can't believe I had the audacity to punch you in front of a bunch of your so-called 'important people'?"

Natalia stood up abruptly. She knew the look flashing across James' face. He was about to totally lose control.

Standing between Evan and James, Natalia reached out and grabbed James by the shoulder, turning him toward her, their noses almost touching. Natalia stared unblinking at James. James took a step back. Natalia took a step forward, closing the distance, placing them once again face-to-face.

"James? Do you want to tell me what is going on?" she whispered.

"Honestly, Natalia. The innocent martyr act is getting a little old. We both know you are not in love with your husband. This all wouldn't have happened if you hadn't betrayed your husband's trust. So you never slept around outside your marriage. True. But you fell in love with another man and you have spent a lot of time together," said James. "Admit it Natalia. Go on. Admit you are guilty too."

Evan stood up from his chair. Advancing toward James he said, "You leave her alone."

James ignored Evan. Sneering at Natalia, he said, "Kick boxing? Rock climbing? Attending parties? Who do you think you are kidding, Natalia? And that dress, makeup, and ridiculous heels, exactly who do you think you are fooling?" He laughed.

Natalia was taken aback. Crossing her arms across her chest she agreed, "The kick boxing doesn't really seem like me. I was wondering why the auctioneer…"

"She can do and be whatever she wants to be!" interrupted Evan, pushing James hard on the chest. "She can choose her own interests. If she wants to start glacier climbing or deep sea diving she can. Who the hell are you to tell her who she is or what her interests are?"

Natalia looked from one man to the other.

"Oh, come on, Evan, get off it. You know this is all some kind of show. Natalia would rather curl up with a book or OM her way through a yoga class than climb a glacier or attend a party. And since when did she want to trick herself out, like some sex goddess like Eva? She's been doing all of this to impress you. Not because she really wants to be doing these things."

"Well, I think 'trick myself out' is going a bit far, but I must admit I like the sex goddess part," laughed Natalia, trying to break the tension. Natalia glanced at Evan and James. Neither laughed. She rubbed her shoulders. All of a sudden she felt very cold.

"Hello, Einstein. How the hell does your business survive given your level of insight? Have you failed to notice that Natalia executes and attends parties *for a living*?" countered Evan.

Natalia gazed at Evan. His nostrils were flaring, his eyes flashing. She was certain the punches would start flying again at any moment.

"I love you," she said quietly.

Both men froze.

Natalia took Evan's hand in hers. "You asked me, Evan. And I am telling you. I am in love with you. And I know you love me too, but not for what I accomplish or for what I do for you. You love me for me. Just me, as I am. The way I love you."

"Natalia," began James.

Just then Natalia felt a hand grasp her shoulder and pull her around. Natalia had just a second to register Eva standing in front of her before she felt a fist hit her face.

She was falling, the darkness reaching up for her, and as her head crashed against the floor, everything went black.

Bren

Chapter 19

"WHAT ARE YOU DOING? Did you just talk to Natalia? Didn't she want to talk to me too?" asked a tall man with broad shoulders and gray hair. "What's wrong, Bren?"

"Oh, John." Bren sat down on the bed next to her husband and buried her face into his neck. John wrapped his arms around her and held her tight.

"Natalia has been in a serious accident, she is in the hospital," said Bren, jumping up and going to the closet. "I am getting on the next flight to Zürich."

"What happened?" asked John.

"There is no time to explain, I need to get to the airport and on a plane as soon as possible," replied Bren. She took out her suitcase from the closet and began to pack, neatly packing in matching accessories.

"I am coming with you, Bren. I will go pack too," said John, going to the closet and beginning to pack jeans and shirts into his bag.

"But you never fly. You are terrified of flying."

"No, Bren. I am coming. She is my heart," he said.

"You really think you can get on the plane?" asked Bren.

"Well, I better get to the airport early enough to have a few drinks in the bar before we board. That way I will fall asleep before takeoff."

BREN CLUTCHED A GLASS OF WINE in the restaurant wagon of the train. She was going to order a glass of mineral water and at the last minute decided on a glass of wine instead. She felt extremely jet-lagged and yet wired with worry at the same time. She didn't know what to expect when she saw her daughter, but she wanted to be at her side as soon as possible.

Bren found it bizarre that every square inch of Switzerland seemed to be cultivated. The rolling green hills looked more like cultivated golf courses to her than pastures for dairy cows with large bells. When the deep blue of Lake Bodensee came into view, Bren realized she was almost at her destination. It was gorgeous, but she wished her daughter didn't live here, so far away. She missed her so much.

The train pulled into the train station on the harbor. Bren and John stepped out of the train and paused. Standing on the platform, they didn't notice the light sparkling on the water in the harbor, or admire the Austrian and Swiss Alps in the distance.

"Grandma! Grandpa!" Three small children hurtled toward Bren and John and nearly knocked them over as they struggled to all get the first hug. Three little girls stood next to Evan, smiling shyly, watching their friends greet their grandma.

"Hello, Bren, Hello, John." Evan hugged Bren and shook John's hand.

"How is Natalia doing, Evan?" asked John. "Why isn't James here?"

"They're not sure. James said he had to go into the office, so I have the kids this afternoon. It will be great to have some help. I am desperate to go visit Natalia if you are willing to watch six little ones for two hours," asked Evan.

"Well," said Bren, "I must see her myself."

"No, Bren," said John softly, placing a hand on Bren's shoulder and looking her in the eyes.

"You will watch the kids and Evan and I will go visit Natalia," insisted John.

Bren's eyes widened in surprise. "But John," she began to protest.

"No, Bren. Please. You can visit her in the morning. I just have to see her right away."

Bren knew when to listen to her husband. She saw that he was wild with worry, almost unraveling before her eyes. He needed to go more than she did, and someone needed to take care of her beloved grandchildren. They needed her.

"Grandma is going to take you all home and feed you something yummy," she said to the children.

"But you don't know how to cook, Grandma," said Allan.

"But I do know how to order pizza," she replied.

Mary

Chapter 20

MARY WAS SITTING AT HER DESK and poring over a color-coded binder with every single aspect of the evening's event written out in detail. Everything was perfectly organized. Mary placed her hands behind her head and leaned back in her chair while placing her feet up on her desk. She would show everyone that her event service was the best in the city. In the country even. Mary had a detailed order form from the customer on what they wanted for the event and she had ensured that they would get exactly what was on the list. She had even added a few surprises as little extras for them.

Mary felt herself winding up. It wasn't only her worry over her best friend. Mary was agonizing over her recent decision to offer Mike an equal partnership in Elegant Events. She knew having Mike as a partner would enable her to expand the business and hire new employees, but it was a risky step to take. *What if Mike and I fall apart? What will happen to the business I have built from the ground up?*

Mike walked into her office. Mary noticed that today he had on a lime-green tie with his suit. She hated it.

"How are you holding up, Mary? Is everything in line for tonight?"

"Everything is prepared down to the last tiny detail, including the live band. However, I still need to go to the spa and do some quick shopping for a new dress for this evening. I wish Natalia could go with me. I miss her," said Mary, turning to look out the window, lost in thought.

MIKE AND MARY HAD MADE THE SHORT DRIVE up the hill to the five-star Dolder Grand Hotel at four in the afternoon so Mary could enjoy their decadent ladies' spa before the evening work began.

Undressing in the locker room, Mary slipped into a fluffy white robe and slippers, but as soon as she walked into the sauna landscape she hung up her robe, grabbed a towel, and walked around au naturel. Mary noticed immediately the glimmering copper-tiled walls and the slowly changing lights, which cast the copper tiles purple, then green. Walking around, she saw sauna rooms of various temperatures, steam rooms, kotatsu footbaths, aroma pools, steam pots, cold-water basins, and even stand-up sun beds.

Relaxing naked on her towel in the steam room, Mary inhaled deeply, noticing that the steam contained eucalyptus oil. She felt any tension remaining in her shoulders dissolve in the heat. When Mary couldn't take the heat any longer she walked to the rain shower, took a hose, and sprayed ice-cold water over each leg until they ached and proceeded to do the same with her arms. For the finale she jumped into the ice-cold pool of water and, once dry, snuggled into her white robe and melted back onto one of the individual water beds lined up in the relaxing area.

Glancing at a clock, Mary realized she didn't have much time left before her facial, massage, and hairstyling appointment. Walking into the heat of the hottest sauna, she lay down for ten minutes, thinking about the evening ahead, before slipping into one of the aroma pools. On her way to the treatment room for her facial, Mary decided to return to the spa in the morning. She had not had a chance to enjoy the pool or the whirlpool outside on the terrace.

MARY SLIPPED HER GORGEOUS RED FLOOR-LENGTH DRESS over her lace lingerie and surveyed herself in the mirror of her hotel room. The treatments had been expensive, but worth it, she decided. Her hair shone and her face was smooth and radiant. Stepping over to the window, she looked out at the panoramic view of the lake, the city, and the Alps in the distance. Below the castle-like hotel on the hill, the lights of the city of Zürich were starting to twinkle in the dusk.

"I could get used to all this," laughed Mary, turning to Mike, who was lounging on the bed behind her.

"I second that," replied Mike, "but then again, I don't know that it is worth hundreds of Swiss francs for just one night. I mean, it is nice and all, but is it that much better?"

"Oh, Mike, luxury is wasted on you," sighed Mary.

"Why haven't we ever put on an event here before?" asked Mike, sitting up and leaning forward, his left foot starting to shake.

"We didn't think big enough. I pitched the idea to the client and they were excited. And it is so much less work for us! They have everything already available, including flower arrangement proposals, entertainment selections, including amazing bands and orchestras, menu proposals, and amazing service, down to the last detail. They even have all of the electrical equipment and lighting, so we didn't need to lug all of yours from the office and set it all up tonight."

"Well, I am going downstairs for a drink at th bar. Come meet me when you are ready," Mike replied.

MARY WAS HAVING ONE OF THE BEST DAYS OF HER LIFE, even with worries about Natalia circling in her head like background music. Looking at herself again in the mirror of her five-star hotel room, she noted that she not only looked amazing, but she felt powerful, accomplished, in control. *Just look at me now,* she thought, smiling, *I'm standing in one of the most premier hotels in Zürich, about to execute a prestigious event for high society. Look how far I've come.*

The luxury room suddenly felt stifling. Mary went out on the balcony, drinking in big gulps of cold night air, trying hard to suppress the surfacing memories from engulfing her in the past. Mary unwillingly thought of the day when she had found the courage to pack a suitcase and walk out the door of her parents' flat for the last time at sixteen years old.

WITH NO MONEY AND NO CLOSE FRIENDS, Mary felt trapped. Desperation was like a giant hand squeezing the air from her lungs.

She sealed herself away from all her classmates at every opportunity; she had too much to hide to risk getting close to anyone. As a result, the loneliness was almost unbearable. Mary didn't know what she would do if she didn't have her beautifully delicate mother and their shared love of reading to comfort her. Her mother spent hours reading to Mary as they curled up together under a blanket. Books transported them out of the problems of their lives. Books allowed her to temporarily forget the black marks on her arm and the new blue bruise around her mother's eye.

But then her father had lost his job and the violence in her house was intensifying. Books could no longer be a refuge at home when her father was a constant terrifying presence in the flat. Mary lived in a continual state of fear and stress for her mother and for herself. She wished she had a close friend she could run to, but she had isolated herself for too long.

Libraries became her refuge and studying her way out. No one questioned why a student was spending hour upon hour learning; they admired it. They didn't know she was hiding. She knew the teachers at school would help her if she went to them with her reality, but she didn't want to shatter the image she had created of a perfectly dressed, polite, hard-working young woman with the best grades in school. Her loyalty to her mother also kept her silent, even if she couldn't understand why her mother didn't find a way to take them both away, out of her father's reach.

But Mary's mom had tried to compensate for her father. She always found a way to buy her pretty things. She would clean homes in secret, collect cash, and hand it directly over to Mary to buy new clothes, so her father would never find out. Once she even gave Mary her most prized possession: a pearl necklace.

Mary would never forget the short tram ride she took on November 28th, when she saw an advertisement hanging in front of her seat for a center in Zürich that took in teenage girls looking for asylum from their parents. It had taken her four attempts before she had felt enough courage rise up in her to dial the number for the center. They told her she could come right away; she didn't need to return home alone. They could accompany her later to go and collect her things.

But Mary answered she would come in on her own. She knew it was her last chance to stand up to her father, but deep down, she knew she was going home for her mother. She felt certain her mother would come with her, as soon as she saw a way out, as soon as she was forced to choose. She went home to pack her things.

An image of her lovely mother, with her beautiful blond hair and blue eyes, bent over weeping in the doorway of her childhood flat, now floated into her mind. She gritted her teeth to keep the tears from coming to her eyes at the memory. Then she remembered her dad standing in the doorway, screaming at her and waving his fist.

"Mary, don't go, please don't go," her mother had sobbed.

Mary had knelt down and whispered, "Mom, you can come with me. Get away from him. Come with me."

But her mother had just looked up at her helplessly as her father had lunged to grab her. Mary had leapt back, stood up straight, looked her father right in the eye, and said quietly, "You will never hurt me again."

Then with her head held high she ran down the stairs to the street, her heart thudding louder than her feet on the stairs, and ran to jump through the closing doors of a tram.

As soon as she sat down she collapsed forward, her whole body shaking. She sobbed all the way to the center. She loved her mom so much. She couldn't understand why her mom let her father beat them. Even up until the last moment, Mary had felt sure her mom would come with her and flee the violence, the constant fear. She had pictured it so often in her daydreams. She would rescue her mother and herself and they would build a new life for themselves. Shock and hurt swirled within her when she arrived at the center.

They had taken her in, given her a room and support. At first she had spent hours gazing out the window of the Mädchenhaus at the pale blue house across the street, imagining her lovely mother and herself living there on their own. She pictured them cozily drinking afternoon tea together and taking turns reading aloud to one another. She imagined what it would be like to cook dinner together and curl up afterwards happily, without the weight of fear bearing, always bearing down upon them.

There were many times when she wanted to run back to her mom. She had still held out hope back then that her mother would arrive one day announcing that she, too, had fled; they could now, at last, start again just the two of them.

But it hadn't happened. And as the days passed by, one by one, the hurt had been too much to bear. The hurt shifted to anger, the anger to determination. If her mother could forget her, then she could forget her mother. Or at least she could push the pain so deep down, closing her heart up and over it, burying it there, so that she could continue forward.

SHE HAD HAD TO MEET WITH A PSYCHIATRIST at the center. They had discussed the darkness of her home life, of course. He had also explained to her that she used perfectionism as a way to hold herself in, away from people, away from herself, which made her feel safe.

She remembered him telling her, again and again, in his soft, understanding voice, that she didn't need to always look perfect. Her room didn't always need to be in order and clean of every bit of dust, she didn't need to have perfect grades in every class, and she didn't need to hide away her negative feelings from the other girls and the personnel in the center.

She had watched his face as he said this. She remembered he had all these lines around his eyes, which she knew meant that he had spent his lifetime smiling and laughing.

Mary liked Doctor Brown. He was American, tall, friendly.

She said, "You are a good man, Dr. Brown, and I know you want to help. But whatever you want to call it, it has gotten me this far. I'm the best in my class. This is who I am."

Sighing, the doctor leaned forward and patted her arm. "You're doing great in school, Mary. Just try to let people in. Make some friends. Let your emotional and social intelligence develop. Let people love you. No one succeeds in life alone."

Mary had left the room reeling. She was intelligent and clever. She knew he was right. Few succeeded in life without friends, colleagues, and well, admirers. She went straight to the library and checked out an armful of books on social intelligence, emotional intelligence, body language, and the classic *How to Make Friends and Influence People* by Dale Carnegie.

She would learn to be successful socially the way she had learned math and economics, she thought. It was, she decided, just about reading, studying, and practicing. Somewhere in the back of her mind, though, she was astute enough to know this was not what Dr. Brown had intended.

Standing in the library in the pale light, bent over her books, Mary had more than once allowed herself to daydream for a moment that she had two or three close friends. She saw herself unburdening the truth of her life history to these dear friends and imagined how it would feel to have them come forward, hugging her as she cried, telling her she was so brave and everything would be okay. But what if they left her; what if they were even cruel to her? Could she survive that too?

No. She had spent her life on the outside watching in. She knew how selfish and mean people could be even to their best friends. Mary slammed her self-help book closed. She could learn to dazzle them without falling in, without opening up.

THE UNWELCOME MEMORIES FELT HEAVY, pulling her shoulders forward, into herself. She still felt the ache of her love for her mom every single day; she hated it. There were too many different emotions associated with her mom to reason through. Mary drained her champagne glass and set it down next to the sink. She shook herself, stood up straight, and put on some extra perfume. Then, as she slammed the door shut to the room, she shut the painful memories away again as well. She wouldn't let them ensnare her, not tonight.

"You did it, Mary Louise. Look where you got yourself, all on your own. You have a gala in a five-star hotel to execute."

And lifting her chin, Mary made her way down to the bar.

Mike

Chapter 21

MIKE TOOK THE ELEVATOR down to the lobby and went through to the bar. Looking around, he had to admit that the indirect lighting and the leather chairs gave a luxurious ambiance. He ordered a gin and tonic and settled down comfortably into a chair in the corner where he could survey the room.

Mike thought about their room upstairs. He certainly would not spend all the extra money to overnight here when he could stay at a perfectly respectable three-star hotel in town. Or even a two-star hotel. And while he appreciated the fantastic views from the windows of the room, the rest of the details were not important to him. But he knew Mary was enjoying every minute of the luxurious experience.

Mike sat up straighter and rubbed his hands. Generally he created a new private website for each event they created so guests could access all the relevant information about the evening. However, Mary had said this was unnecessary because she didn't think the guests would use this service. They could just as easily call the Dolder and gather any information they needed from the front desk. Mary didn't realize he had already built a website for tonight's party the week before. Mike had felt at loose ends for a while that morning. He would have liked to start working on the websites for upcoming events or organizing his lighting proposals for the venues for other evenings. Mary had said it could wait until the next day; she had insisted he needed a day free from stress.

He had not listened to Mary and instead had organized the flower arrangements and lighting on his own accord while she had spent the afternoon in the spa and getting ready for the evening in their room; she wouldn't like him making changes to the event without consulting her first. After all, it was the business she had built up all on her own and she was still nervous about changing her firm into a partnership. She was used to being the boss.

He knew Mary had shown her trust and respect in him by recently inviting him to become an equal partner in Elegant Events. He wanted to reassure her that she had made the right choice by making him an equal partner. Yet he didn't want to act like her employee anymore. *I need to insist Mary treat me with more respect*, he admonished himself. *If we are going to be a team, we need to start acting like it.*

The bartender glanced over and Mike gestured for another drink. A woman clad in a strapless gold dress sitting at the next table glared at him and then looked down at his foot. He had been unknowingly tapping his foot against her chair leg. The truth was, he wasn't nervous about Mary's reaction to his changes to the event. He was redirecting his anxiety in another direction as a coping mechanism and he knew it. His heart was beating faster than a humming bird in anticipation of her reaction to one simple question.

An image of Mary pulling her dress up over her lacy lingerie flashed in his mind and he thought of his plans before the event and the luxurious room upstairs, waiting for their return.

Mike placed his hand in his coat pocket and ran his fingers over the small box. *Okay, she is bossy, perfectionistic to the point of crazy, and sometimes a bit grumpy, but I can handle that,* he reasoned to himself. *Can't I? But can I deal with how secretive she is? She needs to trust me a bit more. Am I making the right decision?* Mike began drumming his fingers on the armrest.

Mike inhaled sharply. Mary had just entered the bar and she looked stunning. He wasn't the only one staring, he noticed. Mary's blond hair was pinned up intricately and her makeup flawlessly applied. She looked sexy in her dress. Most of the men in the bar had looked over at the blond sashaying her way over to him.

Damn, she looks good, he thought. Mike placed his hand in his coat pocket and ran his fingers over the small box. *It's decided then; She is classy, intelligent, cunning, and hard working. I am in love with this woman. Tonight is the night.*

Mary

Chapter 22

MARY STOOD AT THE ENTRY TO THE BAR for a moment. She couldn't see Mike. Where was he? Then she noticed he was sitting in the back corner. She didn't notice the appreciative glances of the other men in the bar. It wasn't that she was unaware of how beautiful she looked tonight. When Mike was in a room, she only had eyes for him.

She had many colleagues and friends, but all of those relationships were built on a brilliant facade. Mary knew Mike was the only one who really knew her and loved her despite her intensity. Well, Natalia also loved her, she knew.

And, well, she knew she could be snappy and bossy to them when her guard was down. Mary still had a hard time believing Mike loved her despite these traits.

She had thought of ending the relationship numerous times. She couldn't manage her emotions around him. She couldn't maintain her usual facade as they spent too much time together and she didn't want him to find out about her past.

The truth was, Mike scared her, made her feel exposed. She hated how much power he had over her heart. If he left her, well, she refused to stop and even analyze what that would do to her. No matter how vulnerable the relationship made her feel, no matter how much she cautioned herself away from weakness, she couldn't help herself. She was completely in love with Mike.

She saw Mike stand up and come toward her. She noted that one of the trouser legs of his tuxedo was stuck into his sock; his tie wasn't straight; he had missed the tiniest patch of scruff while shaving just below his chin. Mary had no idea why she found this so charming. Wordlessly she slid a hand down his leg, pulling his trouser out of his sock, and gracefully standing back up, stood in close to straighten Mike's tie.

Mary noticed the warmth spreading over Mike's cheeks. Everyone in the bar was looking at them and she knew he was not one to enjoy being the center of attention. A few of the men glanced over enviously, the women with them feigning disinterest while silently noticing every detail of Mary's dress. A couple with gray hair paused while walking by.

"You make a lovely couple," remarked the elegantly dressed woman.

"She always helps me with my tie too," laughed her husband.

Mary's smile grew bigger as she recognized the couple.

"Mr. and Mrs. Chinchinian, hello. I hope you will enjoy your evening. I am the event manager from Elegant Events who planned and will execute your event. If you need anything at all please let me know."

Mary noticed that the blue of Mrs. Chinchinian's floor-length dress brought out the bright blue of her eyes and contrasted beautifully with her short silver hair. Diamonds glittered around her throat and her sapphire earrings sparkled in the light from the chandelier hanging over them in the lobby.

Mr. Chinchinian was wearing an obviously expensively tailored tuxedo. Most men seemed to look like their tuxedo was wearing them, instead of the other way around, in Mary's opinion. But Mr. Chinchinian looked like he was relaxing in a sweat suit instead of a tuxedo. He was obviously quite comfortable in his formal evening attire.

Mr. Chinchinian cleared his throat uncertainly. "Where is Mike this evening? Does the boss not deem it important enough to handle my event personally? I am severely disappointed. Can you believe that, dear?" he said, turning toward his wife.

"Now Harry, dear, I am sure this young lady is very good at her job. Aren't you, hmm, what did you say your name is?" Mrs. Chinchinian asked, turning toward Mary while laying a hand gently on her arm.

"My name is Mary Davina. And I am the owner of Elegant Events. I assure you, I am even better than Mike is," answered Mary.

Harry Chinchinian laughed in surprise. "Well, you do have confidence, I'll give you that. Now show me the way to the bar. I am ready for my cocktail."

Mary led the way through the hotel to the gallery where Mr. Chinchinian's company event was taking place. As they entered the space Mrs. Chinchinian turned to her and said, "Mary, it is elegant. It isn't unique, but beautifully done."

Mary smiled at her in response and examined her work for herself. Each white-table clothed round table was decked with many long stemmed glasses filled with floating candles. In the center of each table stood tall vases holding arrangements of tall bright white orchids, white roses, and lilies of the valley. On the far wall stood the bar they had set up with indirect lighting under the bar and behind the shelves. The same tall vases filled with white flowers were also placed on the bar. Meanwhile the entire south wall of the room featured floor to ceiling windows looking out over the rolling green lawns and the lights of Zürich twinkling below. Crystals hung down above the tables, sparkling in the candlelight.

Mr. Chinchinian surveyed the room along with Mary, Mike, and his wife. He did not look pleased.

"My wife is being polite. This looks exactly like the innumerable weddings, social celebrations, and corporate events we have attended over the years. We hired your company to ensure our event would stand out from the rest, to really blow the socks off even the younger generation attending tonight."

Mary felt her smile freeze on her face. She had no idea what to answer. He was right. Why on earth would they pay all that money for the same tired idea? What had she been thinking with the all-white flower arrangements? True, it was elegant. But it had been done countless times before. She had no idea what to answer Mr. Chinchinian. Should she apologize? Offer a refund? Think of an improvement she could make in the next twenty minutes to add to the uniqueness of the presentation?

A moment before, she had felt confident, powerful, and glamorous. Now she felt cold sweat on her palms and under her arms, despite her sleeveless dress. And what must Mike think of her? He had already voiced his concerns this morning about her laid-back approach; he had disagreed with her on how to handle this event.

Mary glanced over at Mike, her eyes communicating her fear and stress while the smile remained plastered on her face.

Mike looked back at her and winked. Smiling, Mike said, "Of course you didn't hire us just to give you elegant. You hired us to give you this."

Mike took out a remote control from his bag and pressed a button. Instantly the tables were bathed in rich purple, deep blue, and bright red lights and the white flowers took on lavender, red, and blue hues. The lights hit the crystals, scattering prisms over the tablecloths. Deep purple, red, and blue light bathed the walls and set a glow to the ceiling.

"How did you do that?" asked Mr. Chinchinian.

"Well, that is something I've never seen." Mrs. Chinchinian said.

"There are lights set up around the room and on the bar, as well as tiny lights located in the base of the flower vases," answered Mike.

Mr. Chinchinian considered the room. "But I hate purple," he said.

"No problem," Mike replied. He pressed another button and the room was bathed in a soft blue, warm red, and pale yellow light instead.

"Wow. No, I like the other one, dear," said Mrs. Chinchinian to her husband. "The colors feel more luxurious."

Mr. Chinchinian frowned, but before he could reply, Mike spoke up. "Another option would be to start the evening with the soft palate of colors and then switch over to the deep purple, red, and blue for the dessert course as a transition to the evening music and dancing."

"Good man. I am very impressed," declared Mr. Chinchinian as he clapped Mike on the back. "And I loved the website you set up for us for the event, by the way. I'm glad you talked me into hiring the professional photographer to come and take our picture for the homepage; I love it. Now it is time for my cocktail. Ready, love?" The tall, handsome man held his hand out to his wife.

As the older couple made their way to the bar Mary stepped directly in front of Mike, her hand on her hips.

"You didn't listen to me," she said.

"I'm not always going to listen to you, Mary," parried Mike.

"You could have at least told me you were going to do all this," said Mary, the corners of her mouth twitching upward.

"You're just mad because you didn't come up with all this yourself," laughed Mike. "Come on, admit it: I totally saved you tonight."

Mary broke out in a grin. "Maybe. When did you have time to install all the lighting elements, not to mention building the website I told you we didn't need?"

"The website was already up last week. I set up the lighting while you were shopping and in the spa today. I've been working on this idea for quite some time." Mike slipped his arms around Mary's waist and pulled her close.

"How did you get the lights into the flower and candle vases?" asked Mary, looking up at Mike.

"I specially commissioned them from a glass blower I contacted at Hergiswiler Glass. He made a hollow on the bottom of each vase big enough to fit the lighting element underneath, which is battery operated. And you are already familiar with the spotlights I placed around the room and set up at the bar."

"It's amazing, Mike, really," Mary said, gazing up at him. "Why don't I know about this creative lighting of yours?"

"I was going to tell you about it this morning, but then you refused to listen. Then I attempted to tell you in our hotel room, but you were still in one of your bossy, know-it-all moods, so I thought…"

"Oh, Mike, I am so sorry!" Mary interrupted, throwing her arms around his neck and looking up into his eyes.

"Do you forgive me? I shouldn't be like that; I know I shouldn't. We should be a team. I would be devastated if the first event we have responsibility for as partners was less than an absolute success."

Mike took her hands and silently led her out of the gallery. As he led her into the glass elevator Mary began to protest.

"Mike, where are you taking me? We really need to be at the reception now to greet the guests. They should arrive in less than an hour. I am sure it would be a good idea to look back over the details for tonight."

"Mary, hush. Everything is ready for the event. Can you trust me?"

Mary went to say something more and caught herself. *He is right. I can't always be trying to control everything. I need to relax a bit and give Mike more trust.* Mike led Mary out of the elevator and then took out a blue silk scarf and went to bind it over her eyes.

"Mike, no. You will mess up my hair. And second of all, someone could come up here and then how would that look?"

"It would look like a beautiful woman with a blindfold over her eyes?" Mike stepped forward and proceeded to tie the scarf tightly over her eyes. "It will be worth mussing up your hair a bit, I promise you."

"Mike, I said no! This is too scandalous, we shouldn't even be up here. Someone will see us."

"Trust me, Mary."

Finally Mary nodded and let Mike guide her into the lounge. He encircled his arms around her waist and then slowly turned her around. His fingers trailed along her shoulders and up into her hair. She could feel his breath on her neck and then his lips caressing her bare shoulders. He turned her to face him, his lips and tongue gently caressing the skin along her collarbone. She felt her face flushing, her whole body starting to pulse.

Suddenly Mike stopped, whispering in her ear, "You are a naughty minx. I take out a scarf and you immediately think it is insinuating something scandalous. But that is not why I brought you here, for a moment I just couldn't resist." Laughing, he took off her scarf.

Mary stood for a moment blinking her eyes. They were standing in a gallery lounge in the middle of a circle of high vases filled with long-stemmed white, pink, and deep red roses. Mike was down on one knee. He took out a remote and clicked a button. The vases and the room were wrapped in a pink glow. Candles flickered from large candelabras around the room.

"Mary, you are the bossiest person I know. You can be manipulative, arrogant, secretive, bossy, and downright grumpy."

Mary didn't know what to say. She stood still as a statue, anger starting to well up inside her. A smile spread across Mike's face, his eyes twinkling up at her.

"I know your weaknesses and your failings. And I love you. Do you understand me, Mary? I know all of your darkest places. And I adore you. I want to spend the rest of my life with you. You are clever, hard working, classy, and incredibly smart. You also are thoughtful, tender, and loving. More importantly, I have fun with you. You make me laugh. Last of all, I know that I am my best self around you. You encourage me. No, you insist that I work hard to achieve my goals, whatever they are. Please, Mary, would you be my wife?"

"What about beautiful?"

"Excuse me?" Mike looked up, a bit bewildered.

"You forgot beautiful. You know. In your list."

Tilting her head to one side and tapping her foot, Mary considered Mike kneeling before her.

"And what kind of ridiculous proposal was that? You start out by naming all my worst qualities? That certainly is no way to sweep a woman off her feet."

"Oh hell, Mary, I was trying to be romantic; look at the room. Now how long are you going to leave me down here on my knees? Just say yes so I can stand up."

Mary began to laugh and then she couldn't stop herself. Mike began to laugh with her. Mary laughed so hard she lost her balance a bit and sat down on Mike's knee. Putting her arms around Mike's neck, she leaned in and touched her lips softly to his.

"You are something else, Mary Davina."

"Are you certain I am that something you want? Are you sure? I mean, I know you said all that about knowing my darkest places and such but there is more you don't know…"

"Mary. Mary." Mike took her chin in his hand and forced her to look in his eyes.

"Shut up and say yes. I adore you and I always will."

Mary paused. There was so much she hadn't told him. He didn't know about her abusive father, her complex feelings toward her mother, nor her running away and never seeing them again.

He knew none of it.

She had led him to believe her parents were dead. What would he think if she were to tell him the truth?

"Yes," whispered Mary, large tears rolling down her cheeks. It was so unfair that even now, in what should be the most perfect moment of her life, her past was squeezing out some of the happiness that should be filling her whole heart with joy. Why did part of her need to, already, mourn the fact that her mother wouldn't be at her wedding?

Mary stood up and reached out her hands to pull Mike to his feet. She turned around, taking in more fully the ambiance of the room.

"I thought you were having an affair the past few weeks, you have been so secretive. So you were planning all this?"

Mike looked at her protectively while standing up and drawing her tight into his arms in an embrace. For a moment they stood in the flickering candlelight in the pink room, surrounded by roses. Mike pulled her even tighter to his chest.

"Oh, Mary, my beautiful orphan. I would never have an affair. You sure seem such a tough act, but deep inside, you have a tender heart, don't you?"

"You have no idea."

"You know, someday," replied Mike, pausing to kiss her forehead, "you will need to tell me about how your parents died."

"Hey," said Mary, brightening, changing the subject, "do you have a ring for me?"

"Oh man, how did I forget that part?"

Getting down on one knee again, Mike reached into his tux pocket and took out the ring box. Sliding it open, he revealed a huge sapphire surrounded by glittering diamonds. Mary gasped. It was exactly like the one Princess Diana wore, the one that William gave his Kate. Mary was speechless. It was the ring she had always wanted. How could he have known? How could he afford it for that matter? Mike took her hand and slipped the ring onto her finger.

"Natalia told me weeks ago," was all he said. Then, stepping out from the ring of roses, he went over and handed Mary a glass of champagne. He pretended not to notice the tears running down her face.

"Drink up, love. We need to be downstairs in five minutes to greet the guests."

MARY STOOD UP AND STRETCHED. Sashaying her way to the coffee machine, Mary couldn't help but admire her ring the entire way. It was so beautiful. She could still hardly believe her luck. Mike's proposal had been a complete surprise. In truth, Mary hadn't really thought he would ever propose and she hadn't cared. Or she hadn't thought so. She was so caught up in worrying about him leaving her at any moment that she hadn't had much time left over to dream about what it would be like if he were to propose.

Taking a sip of her coffee, Mary smiled. How had she not realized how amazing the coffee in their office was? Taking another sip, she realized everything this morning seemed richer, more deeply hued and satisfying. She even noticed how smooth the satin of her dress lining felt against her skin, how soft her cashmere scarf around her neck.

"Hi, beautiful," said Mike, walking toward the coffee machine. "How are you feeling this morning? Tired from the late night and the early morning? Why we had to get up so early to go for a swim and visit the wellness landscape, I have no idea."

"Tell me you don't feel fantastic now after that swim, steam, and sauna!" Mary protested.

"I think we could have spent the morning in bed," countered Mike, smiling. "But I do feel great this morning."

Mary just stood there smiling up at him. She didn't want to go back into her office. If she had the choice they would go home right now and spend the entire day snuggled up together in bed. Her uncharacteristic vulnerability to someone made her feel shy. She felt her cheeks warm.

"Mary, are you blushing?" Mike teased. "I haven't known you to ever blush. What has happened to you?"

"You," whispered Mary. "Everything is almost perfect."

"Almost?" asked Mike, pulling her close.

"I am so happy and I keep wanting to tell Natalia and realizing I can't," whispered Mary, wiping the tears from her eyes.

"Of course you can," answered Mike. "We will go to the hospital together."

James

Chapter 23

JAMES SAT IN AN ALL-WHITE CONFERENCE ROOM with silver office furniture listening to a junior associate present. He was having trouble concentrating though. First there was his wife to worry about. He knew he should only be thinking about his wife, especially given the circumstances. Yet every few minutes he caught his mind wandering to a night from the week before, reliving the feel of the warm silky skin of the woman he loved, the smell of her.

James' thoughts drifted back to his wife. This had never happened to him before. Of course he had had his temptations in the past. But his steely mind had been equally capable of shutting them down. Putting them aside. During phases of temptation he threw himself into focusing on his work. He had never betrayed his wife's trust, never once, until he fell in love with her friend.

James thought of the years leading up to his affair. How long had the unhappiness pressed down on his chest, like a fist grasping his heart, his lungs, squeezing slowly? At times he literally felt breathless, struggling to the window or rushing outside to take ragged breaths of fresh air. He knew he was a showman, a blender. He had just enough intelligence, talent and knowledge to be very convincing when put in front of an audience. The problem was, that behind the scenes, in the dark, he knew he didn't possess the capability and capacity to get the real work done. He didn't know exactly how he had managed to use his charisma to benefit from the brains and talent of his co-workers, his team mates, and afterwards, his employees.

He would have liked to be able to open up to Natalia, to drop his game and have her reassure him that he, that they, would be okay. That he was smarter than he knew. Or that his charisma and leadership served important, vital roles in the success of his firm. But he couldn't be honest, not with his wife. Natalia, more than anyone, believed completely in the showman version of himself. It was exhausting to uphold the mirage all day, impossible to maintain it at home anymore. Instead of opening up to Natalia, he closed down. He stopped talking to her at all. He found reasons to come home after she would be asleep.

James thought of the night he had gone to Eva's restaurant and he had stayed late, past closing, drinking wine with her at the bar. He remembered the unbelievable relief of letting go of the game and confessing all his fears and transgressions. Talking to Eva felt like the icy chill of diving into an alpine lake on a hot day. He felt clean, refreshed. When he was all done talking, James remembered how Eva had taken his hand, looked him in the eyes and said, "You would be a jerk if you didn't feel unsure of yourself sometimes. So you take credit for others' hard work. Lots of managers do just that. You need to continue to put on the show of being the perfectly successful man. But with me you don't. I have never liked you more than I do tonight."

Suddenly, he could breathe again.

The high of their affair began in that moment. He hadn't thought of the consequences. He was intoxicated by Eva's presence, the mere anticipation of being with her. He couldn't get her out of his mind from that night onwards.

Guilt started pulsing through his veins, an unrelenting throbbing pulsing from his heart so loud that he looked around, worried the others in the room could hear it. He was having trouble breathing. The giant fist was back, clutching at his chest. Suddenly drenched with sweat, James realized he would need to change into a new shirt at the first opportunity. Luckily he had an extra in his office.

No, he couldn't go see the woman he loved, even for a few minutes. It wasn't only that he shouldn't. It was that he felt he didn't deserve the comfort of her embrace.

Thankfully, the meeting was ending. Forcing a smile James shook hands with the attendees and forced himself to appear casual as he walked back to his office. As soon as he closed the door to his office and locked it he ran to the window, opening it, standing in the cold rush, gulping air as if he had finally broken the surface after being held beneath water.

He missed Eva so much his heart hurt. If he had his way he would be this very minute at her side. But he couldn't see her. Not now. No matter how much he wanted to hold her in his arms and never let go.

Feeling guilty, James let his thoughts wander back to when he had admitted his love for the first time in that restaurant in Rome. They had both lied about work events and caught an early flight out of Zürich on Friday afternoon, returning on Saturday. He could almost smell the scent of her hair mixing with that of the coffee and amaretto they were served at the end of their meal.

He relived the feel of pulling her gently toward him in the piazza on the way back to their hotel, how his hunger for her grew, then how it felt when she slowly pulled away. After their kiss he couldn't stop the words I love you from rushing out from somewhere deep in his chest. It had been spontaneous and unrehearsed. He would never forget that evening, or the night that followed. The worst of it was that he could think of nothing but her after he returned home from Italy.

His wife needed him more than ever. He knew that. His children needed him. The shame of what he had done to Natalia, of how little he felt for her, haunted him. James took a long, deep, calming breath and blew it out as slowly as he could. The children would be with his wife right now, with her parents.

He knew he should be with his family, with his wife, but he couldn't bring himself to spend more than a few minutes with Natalia each morning. He reasoned to himself that he still needed to spend long hours each day in the office and couldn't afford more time with Natalia. He chose to ignore the fact that he had always, no matter how much work was piled on his shoulders, found time for Eva.

Evan

Chapter 24

EVAN TRIED TO FOCUS ON THE ROAD. It was difficult. All he could think of was why? *Why?* Like a continual loop the question came up over and over again. *How could Eva betray me this way,* he thought. *How could James do this to Natalia? Why did Natalia, my lovely Natalia, have to get hurt? How will I face Eva and James when I see them tonight?*

Layered on top of this soundtrack were other worries. He was wondering how he could get those papers graded by Friday, he was trying to decide what to make for lunch for himself and the kids, he was trying to recall if the kids had any activities for the afternoon, and he was worrying about whether his daughter should be taken to the doctor because she kept complaining about recurring stomachaches. Evan sighed.

His youngest daughter had woken up in the night at around four with a nightmare and had spent the rest of the night in bed with him. He had not been able to fall back asleep until shortly before his alarm clock went off. He felt the fatigue settle down somewhere deep in his chest. He was so tired he didn't even feel tired anymore. Evan pulled into the driveway just as the kids were walking up the block home from school. He knew he was running late and would need to cook fast while listening to loud protests of hunger.

This is not how I imagined life would be ten years ago. If only I had made a different decision, all those years ago, things wouldn't have come to this, he thought.

Opening the door, he took off his shoes and rushed into the kitchen to start cooking. His life might feel like it was falling apart, but he still had children to feed and another three to go take care of this afternoon, before the babysitter came and he went to the hospital.

JAMES, IN HIS EXPENSIVE ARMANI SUIT, paced back and forth in the conference room while Evan and Eva sat around the table along with a few men in white coats.

"I want answers and I want them now. Why does Natalia think Evan is her husband? How the hell can she not remember I am her husband? We have been married for over eleven years, dammit. When is she going to be able to get out of here and back to her normal life? I want answers," yelled James, stopping his pacing and pounding his fists on the table.

He began rubbing his neck while tilting his head from side to side. He stared down at the table, refusing to look at Eva.

One of the men at the table stood up and said, "As you know, Natalia suffered a few broken ribs, a broken arm, and a few lacerations that needed to be stitched up in the accident. I am afraid that although she has woken up from the coma, she has not regained full functioning and she will most likely have a long road to recovery ahead of her due to her brain injury. This is normal. Perhaps you have seen TV programs in which a patient wakes up from a coma and almost immediately regains full functioning? Unfortunately, that scenario is rare. Memory loss, especially memory loss of recent events, and confusion is a normal process after awakening from a coma."

Closing his eyes, Evan said, "Shut up, James. Natalia wouldn't even be in this place if it wasn't for you and Eva."

"Are you trying to say this is all my fault?" James thundered. "You're the one who put crazy ideas in her head. Why would she attend that charity event without asking me? This wouldn't have happened if she hadn't been at the hotel."

"Do you hear yourself? You sound like the idiot and jerk you truly are. Ask you? What is she, a child? You didn't tell Natalia where you were going to be that night. Mary gave Natalia an invitation to help her work the event, so she could better decide if she wanted to start working for Mary full time. I thought it would do her good to start working again, so I encouraged her to go and offered to watch all the kids. I thought Eva had to work late," added Evan, glaring at Eva sitting next to him. "Little did I know that was a lie and she was at the hotel with you."

Eva spoke up. "I think we should stop fighting and start listening to the doctors."

"Shut up, Eva," said both men at the same time.

"Don't tell her to shut up," yelled James.

"She's my wife," said Evan.

"Well, she's my..." started James.

"That's right. She's your what exactly?" asked Evan, his voice quaking. "Your mistress? Girlfriend? Love of your life? Passing fling?"

"Evan, stop," pleaded Eva, near tears, her body shaking. "We are here to learn how we can help Natalia."

"Oh, don't you go acting like you are the concerned, loving

party here," said Evan, bringing his hand to rest over his heart. "I love Natalia the most. Me. You two are the culprits who caused all this. And now I have lost her forever," said Evan, burrowing his face in his hands and beginning to rock back and forth in his chair.

"She isn't dead, Evan," answered James, his voice choked with tears.

"It won't ever be the same, she won't ever be the same," Evan cried. "Don't you understand? She was my best friend. She knew what I was feeling. She was always the one I went to for support when I wanted to share something beautiful. She understood me. It's not the same anymore. She's different now, she's so confused."

In the long pause that followed, a tall doctor shuffled some papers. Frowning at James and looking around at the others sternly, he asked, "If you are all through? I can continue?"

When no one replied the doctor said, "We will place her in a program of high intensity where she will undergo a range of rehabilitation services. This will include physical therapy, but she will also have language therapy, recreational therapy, neuropsychological treatment, and even occupational therapy. I cannot tell you how fast she will progress in her treatment, as there have been significant differences in rates of improvement among patients.

"However, all the nurses can confirm that Natalia has yet to exhibit anxiety, depression, sleeplessness, or even the irritability that often occurs with a traumatic brain injury. She is downright cheerful and positive about working toward regaining her functioning. Now, you must be aware that these symptoms could surface in the future. But considering that her brain injury was mild and she is young and otherwise very healthy, we can certainly allow ourselves to hope for the best outcome."

"Which means?" asked James, beginning to pace the room anew.

"That she will regain functioning, but it will take time, and the insurance will only pay for rehabilitation services for the duration of her stay in the hospital. Her level of cognitive functioning on the Rancho Los Amigos index is at a six out of ten and we hope she will show marked improvement by the time we send her home. However, once she is sent home, she will still not have regained full functioning. You need to think about how you will arrange for her care at home. You don't need to know the answers now. You just need to think about making some decisions in the next two to five days. I have an information packet here, and you can read through the levels on the index we hope her to work through. We are available to answer your questions when you are ready."

Another doctor at the front of the table stood up stood up and smiled compassionately. "It is quite normal for loved ones to grieve for the injured party. We are used to shock, denial, depression, mobilization, and fatigue before arriving at acceptance. But it sounds like more than that is going on here.

"If you are going to really help Natalia recover, you need to work through your emotions and any other issues you all are having. I will refer you to a psychiatrist for a group session. I would also recommend individual sessions. Helping a loved one through a recovery takes its toll. Fortifying yourself is a good idea. Be sure to exercise, eat healthy foods, and get enough rest. Allow yourself to laugh and have fun and not feel guilty about it. You will get through this."

The doctors wished each of them the best and left the room.

"WE SHOULD DO IT," said Evan. "If anyone needs therapy, we do."

"Yeah," sighed James, staring down at the table, unable to meet Evan's gaze. "Sure. I'm in. Eva?"

"Definitely."

"What are we going to do about Natalia?" asked Evan. "She could go home soon, you heard the doctors. But she needs care and someone needs to be there for the kids. Can her parents take care of her and the kids for a while?"

James sighed and slumped into a chair, wrapping his arms around his stomach. "Natalia's parents have to go home soon. They both have jobs and her mom has a top executive position. They are on leave due to the emergency, but they don't think they can stay much longer without losing their jobs. And, well, I don't want them to stay. I love my in-laws, but it is tough having them in the house."

"So what are we going to do when Natalia goes home?" asked Evan, forming his fingers into a steeple. "You work crazy hours. You can't be there for her."

"I could pay for at home care," suggested James.

"Can you afford that?" asked Eva in a shaky voice. "That can be really expensive, James. The doctor said insurance will not cover out-of-patient rehabilitation services. You would also need to hire a nanny. Natalia will get better, you heard the doctors, but it will take time for her to regain full functioning. She can't take care of the kids and the house. She needs to attend therapy sessions and rest."

All three fell silent for several minutes, each lost in their thoughts.

"You never answered my question," said Evan, once again staring at the table.

"What question?" countered James while rubbing his eyes.

"What is Eva to you? Do you love her? How did this"—Evan waved his hand in their direction—"even start?"

James froze. He slowly lowered his hands. "Damn you, Evan…" he began, his voice cracking. "I feel so terrible, if you only knew how sorry I am, about all of it. Not just Natalia's accident, although that is the worst. But I am sorry for what I did to you too."

Evan lifted his palms upward and looked at James. "James, look at me. I need to know, James."

"Why aren't you asking Eva?" parried James.

Evan sighed. "Because I already asked her and she just started crying so hard I couldn't understand anything she had to say."

James shifted his gaze to Eva. Eva looked down at her perfectly manicured nails, biting her lip, her body still shaking.

"Yes. I love her. I admit it. There, you succeeded at making me feel like the villain I am. My wife just woke up from a coma from a head injury she suffered due to me falling in love with your wife," James shouted. Rubbing his forehead, James lowered his voice and explained, "It started in her restaurant. I started going to eat late at night and stayed talking to her after she had closed up, just the two of us enjoying cocktails at the bar.

But it was during a one-night trip to Rome that I knew I was in love with Eva. I looked over the table, her skin golden in the candlelight, her eyes sparkling with laughter, and I was so overcome with emotion, I just had to tell Eva I had fallen in love with her in the piazza on our walk back to the hotel. That is when it really began."

"Tell me what happened the night of Natalia's accident," demanded Evan through clenched teeth.

James became very still. In a voice almost a whisper he began, "Eva and I had arranged to meet at the hotel at seven. Eva had already gotten the key to the room and was waiting for me near the elevators. I came in through the back service doors so no one would recognize me from the restaurant or in the lobby, saw Eva waiting for me, and we went up to our hotel room. At around eleven we came down in the elevator. Stupidly we rode down together. Eva gave me one last kiss goodbye just as the elevator doors opened and then asked me when we would be able to meet again. Before I could answer I heard a cry. And there stood Natalia in front of the elevator, staring at us.

"I don't know whose surprise was greater. Natalia turned on her very high heels and ran blindly through the lobby and out the front doors. It was a moment before we could shake ourselves free from our shock and run after her. We were too late. In those few moments Natalia had already run down the steps and failed to see the Ferrari pulling up in front of the hotel. The car had hit her, slamming her up and onto the hood of the car, her head smacking against the glass of the windshield. She lay there knocked unconscious. Blood was everywhere. The driver had already called for help, we could hear the sirens. I was in shock, just standing there. It had all happened so quickly. The staff came outside, people swarmed around the car, calling out to Natalia, trying to help her. The paramedics arrived and I got into the ambulance with Natalia to drive to the hospital. All I remember thinking is she looked so pretty lying there, even with all the blood. Angelic."

James rested his forehead on the table and began to sob. "It is all my fault. It's not true what I said before, of course it isn't. Natalia is an angel and she was hurt so terribly because of me."

"I would be lying if I said I am not furious with both of you. Because I am," said Evan, pausing to find the right words. "But this isn't about you. It isn't about me. It isn't even just about Natalia. It is about our children. All of them."

Nodding and grimacing at the same time, Evan continued, "We need to know what we want to do. I don't want to stay with Eva anymore when she is in love with someone else. But I don't want my kids, or your kids, to suffer through a divorce."

"I am not leaving Natalia. Think what you will, Evan, but I am no monster. I would never leave Natalia when she needs me the most. Or my kids," said James, raising his head just enough to look up at Evan.

"I know," responded Evan, swallowing. "I have given this a lot of thought and I don't want either of you to respond to my proposal for at least ten minutes. We are just going to sit here and think it over, okay?" Evan waited for both James and Eva to nod their agreement. "I think we should all move into the same house so I can take care of Natalia and all of our kids."

James' mouth fell open. Eva gasped. But they kept their promise and remained silent, thinking, for ten long minutes.

"Evan," began James, his voice choked with tears, "you must really love Natalia. But I say no, you aren't thinking straight. The idea is just crazy and well, wrong. Eva? What do you think?" James turned to Eva.

Eva drew in a deep breath, then releasing it all at once said, "Yeah, it is a crazy plan but I will agree to whatever Evan wants. I want you to really think about this for another night, Evan. It is taking on so much: six kids and the care of someone with a head injury. Fortunately, we can afford to hire someone to come in and clean twice a week as well as a nanny to come in a few hours a week. Someone needs to take the kids to their activities and out on day trips, to go grocery shopping. How will you do that all and teach?"

"I have already called the school. I can take a year sabbatical."

"No," cried Eva, slamming her fist down on the table. "That doesn't work. You need to be able to get away from the house and have your own life for a few hours a day. You love teaching."

"They will hold my job for me, they promised," Evan insisted. "And don't act like you care, Eva. I am certain you would just as soon get a divorce and run away from all of us with Mr. Money here."

Eva sat up straight. "I love my children and I sure as hell do not want to run away from them! I have betrayed you, Evan, sure, but we both know you have been in love with Natalia for years."

"What?" asked James clearing his throat and turning to look at Evan. Evan held his gaze steadily until James shook his head and looked at the floor again.

"Yes, I am in love with Natalia. I don't even know how long I have been in love with her, honestly, but I think for a long time now. There, I've said it out loud..." Evan paused, looking from James to Eva, gaging their reactions before he continued. "There was no affair, and there was never even a kiss, okay? We have just spent so much time together over the years with the children. She has been such a good friend to me, and I to her. I was always there for her in times of trouble and heartache. And well, she is lovely. And even though everything has changed now, I still am in love with her. I want to take care of her, to be there for her."

Cocking her head while raising her eyebrows, Eva asked, "Doesn't that sound rather crazy? Would that be good for our children, all of us living together in one house? How would we explain it to them? Furthermore, Natalia just woke up from a coma. She used to be crazy in love with you, James. She may be in love with you once again, once she recovers from her head injury, and despite knowing about our affair. Sure, she thinks she is in love with Evan now, but who knows? She just woke up from a coma; she is confused. She might end up wanting her husband back and despising me for the damage I have done to her marriage. This may just be a recipe for disaster, placing us all together under one roof."

"Not to mention what people will say when they hear about this crazy setup of us all living together. How will we explain to the children the fact that Natalia is no longer sleeping with me, that Eva is no longer sleeping with you?" asked James.

Clearing his throat, Evan replied, "Well, we would explain it to begin with by saying that Natalia needs our help so we are all moving in together. That they will all understand. And for the rest, well, it won't be for a long time…"

Evan swallowed, his shoulders slumping forward. "You're right, Eva, Natalia may decide she is in love with James. Don't think for a moment I will rush things. I plan on giving her time and space to know her own mind and heart. But until Natalia recovers she will need help. My help, as you two are never at home. You work until after the children have been put to bed. You are often up and out the door before they awake. The kids won't know where you sleep.

"If we move into your house, James, well, then there are two guest rooms. I will take one and Eva can take the other. The kids will take a very long time to even notice if you both get up before they do in the mornings. In the meantime, we can share the care for the children and Natalia. It will be hard. I am not going to be a martyr of some kind. I want every Saturday, with no exceptions, completely free to get away from all the kids, Natalia, everyone."

James declared, "I think the plan is crazy. But temporarily we can go ahead with it. You can move in with us. When would you like to move in? I think we will need to do that within the next week, so that Natalia can come home, right?"

Eva spoke up, "I will organize the move, everything. Don't give it another thought. I'll pack up the kids' rooms. Do you think Allan and Ben could share a room? Then I would put Lindsay and Lauren in one of the rooms together and put Holly in with Anna. Anna and Holly are best friends. I think they will love sharing a room. But I am keeping our place until we have made a permanent decision."

"Sure," agreed Evan.

"Someone needs to explain everything to Natalia," said James. "Who should do it?"

"Who do you think is best?" asked Eva, looking at the floor.

Evan sighed. "Okay. I'll do it. I will explain what happened, though I think it should be coming from you, James, and I will ask her if she agrees with our plan." Evan got up and made his way toward the door. "And by the way, James, you go arrange the first therapy session for us. Seeing as I still hate both of you, I think we could do with some professional help if we are all going to live together."

The door slammed behind Evan on his way out of the room.

Natalia

Chapter 25

NATALIA OPENED HER EYES with a sharp intake of breath. She looked blearily around the room, registering the white walls, the flowers next to her bed, the beeping of the monitors, and the feel of sheets, scratchy against her skin. Her head was pounding. Then she heard Anna talking to her; she was lying on the bed next to her.

"I want you to come home, Mommy. I miss you so much. The doctor told me I should talk to you. Daddy is with the boys in the cafeteria eating French fries. Today at school I had my multiplication test and got every single answer correct. But when I told Dad he just nodded and said, 'That's nice, dear.' I worked really hard at school so I could do well on the test. It made me sad when I felt like he didn't care that I did so well.

"I don't like the tubes you have everywhere, Mommy.

"Dad isn't used to taking care of us all the time on his own. I think it's harder for him than for you. We've eaten a lot of pizza and he asks me all the time, 'How would your mom do it?' and 'What would your mom say?' But don't worry because I told him we need lots of vegetables and I peel and cut them up for us every night.

I know that we are supposed to let you rest as long as you need to, but I was wondering if you could think about getting up soon? You've been asleep for five days and that is a really long time."

"You don't have to worry about when you come home. Grandma and Grandpa are here and they will help. Evan will help you too, he has been here to see you almost every single day. Mary has been here too, all the time, with Mike. Mike's funny, I like him. And when Grandma and Grandpa have to go home I will help you with everything. When Dad wasn't looking I looked up coma. There were a lot of big words I had to look up, but it said you would be confused when you wake up. Don't worry, Mommy. I know how you do everything. I'll help you just like I'm helping Daddy with Allan and Ben."

Natalia looked at the white walls of the sun-filled room. Looking down, she could just make out the dark hair of the top of her daughter's head and the white of the blankets laid over the two of them. She smelled antiseptic and heard faint beeping and shoes squeaking as they walked down the hall. Her head was pounding; her body was aching; every breath hurt. She noticed how stiff her joints felt, how tight her muscles. Her skin felt sticky and her mouth had a terrible taste in it. Metallic. Her thinking felt hazy, murky.

Yet her daughter was snuggled beside her on the bed. Here was her little girl she had been longing to hold by her side once again. Heart filling with joy, Natalia struggled to say something, to sit up. Yet suddenly even the effort of keeping her eyes open felt too great. She felt herself once again drifting off toward blackness.

WHEN NATALIA AWOKE AGAIN Evan was in the room. She smiled at him. Upon seeing her smile Evan broke into a wide grin. With wide eyes he turned and ran out of the room. A few minutes later a short balding man in a white coat entered the room.

"Natalia, can you hear me?"

Natalia tried to say something and couldn't. She nodded.

"Good, good."

The doctor approached the bed, took her hand, and squeezed. "Do you feel that?"

Natalia nodded again.

"You are safe. Your family is safe. You are in the hospital Hirslanden in Zürich. You were in an accident and suffered a brain injury, fortunately not a severe one, and you have been in a coma for eight days. We will contact your family right away to let them know you are responding to stimuli. In the meantime you just try and relax."

The doctor patted her arm and left the room.

Natalia lay alone listening to the sounds of shoes squeaking down the hallway outside her door and the murmur of voices. Where was Evan? Why wasn't he coming back to her? Natalia tried to keep her eyes open, yet she found it increasingly difficult.

WHEN NATALIA BECAME AWARE of the hospital room again it was dark. She couldn't remember falling asleep. Where did the doctor go? Didn't he say her family was coming to be with her? She could hear the beeping of machines, but otherwise everything was quiet. She decided she wanted to get up and take a long hot shower. She tried to sit up, thrashing to get rid of the tubes, but the effort exhausted her. A beeping started and a nurse rushed in.

Then Evan was at her side, smoothing back her hair, and Natalia felt herself calming down. But the nurse pushed him back from the bed, restraining Natalia so she could replace the tubes going into her arm.

"Evan," Natalia said.

The nurse turned to Evan and said, "Go ahead, go to her on the other side."

Evan walked around the bed and resumed smoothing her hair. It felt so soothing.

"You are such a good husband," she said. "Have you been here all night with me?"

Relaxing once again on the bed, she closed her eyes.

"NATALIA?" Natalia looked up. Evan was standing at the side of her bed. He looked terrible. The circles under his eyes were so deep they were purple. His shirt was rumpled and his hair stood on end.

"Evan! Why am I in the hospital? How did I hurt my head? How long was I in a coma? Where are my children? I am going to go find them right now."

Natalia moved to get out of the bed. Evan gently pushed her back. Running his fingers threw his hair, he came to stand closer to the bed.

"Natalia, I am so happy you are awake, that you are okay," said Evan, shifting from one foot to the other. "Let's just slow down and wait for the doctor to come, okay? Then you can hear the entire story."

Natalia smiled at him, opening her fingers, reaching for his hand. Noticing, Evan took her hand and held it.

Just then she heard Anna's voice in the hall. She struggled to sit up again. Then Anna was in the room, running toward her, jumping up onto the bed, and burrowing her head into her shoulder. Evan squeezed her hand and quietly left the room.

Natalia's whole heart filled to see her daughter, to have her so close. Her eyes filled with tears. The relief of seeing her child again was so great that all other worries washed away from her mind, like a sandcastle pulled away by an ocean wave.

"Mommy, why are you crying?" asked Anna. "Does it hurt a lot?"

"Anna, I said stop!" said James as he breathlessly entered the room. "You have to be careful with your mom. Hop down here, please. We need to go and talk to the doctor."

Reluctantly Anna followed her father from the room. Natalia didn't want Anna to go. She wanted to shout for her to stay, but couldn't find her voice.

Why didn't James come talk to her? Why did he take Anna away? Exhausted, Natalia closed her eyes and fell asleep.

WHEN NATALIA OPENED HER EYES it took her a moment to recognize the hospital room. She saw Evan by her side, now sitting in a chair by her bed.

"Hi," she said.

Evan leapt up out of his chair, looking at her and then at the door.

"No. Stay," pleaded Natalia.

Evan sat back down while reaching out to take her hand.

"How are you feeling?" he asked.

"Yucky," she answered. "I want a shower."

Natalia tried to lift her arms and sit up.

"Wait," said Evan. "I will go get a nurse to help you take a shower."

Evan disappeared down the hall. It felt like he had been gone for hours when the nurse finally came in.

"So I hear you would like a shower. I can help you with that. Let's see if you can stand up out of bed for me and sit down in this wheelchair."

"I don't want to sit in a wheelchair. I don't need one," replied Natalia.

"I can understand that it is frustrating to sit in a wheelchair," the nurse said. "You have been lying in bed for a long time. How about today we take the first step by having a ride to the shower in the chair, and tomorrow you can try walking there on your own?"

Natalia stood up, holding the nurse's outstretched hand. She felt immediately dizzy and was happy to take a seat in the wheelchair. The nurse wheeled her into the bathroom and helped her out of her nightgown and onto a bench in the shower.

"Can I have a really long, hot shower please?" asked Natalia.

She felt overwhelmed. She wanted to shower alone.

"I am so sorry, miss, but I have other patients to take care of too and I can't leave you in here alone yet," answered the nurse.

Natalia began to cry.

Just then she heard James' voice at the door. "What if I stayed with her, and pressed the emergency button here if anything goes wrong?" he asked. "Natalia, it is so good to see you awake and out of bed, love."

"Yes, that would be okay. Stay in here as long as you like then, Natalia. And look, your friends and family brought some lovely soaps and lotions for you to use."

Natalia watched as the nurse carefully put the bottles next to her on the bench.

"I'll just wash your hair and your body for you, and then leave you to enjoy the hot water with your husband here," continued the nurse.

"He's not my husband," insisted Natalia. "James, please go find Evan."

The nurse looked at James and James shook his head.

"I am her husband," he said.

The nurse nodded, and after Natalia was all clean she left the room. It felt so blissful to feel clean again, to have the hot water running over her skin, that Natalia didn't notice the nurse leave the room or James still standing in the doorway for a few minutes.

"Oh! What will Eva think, you standing here watching me in the shower?" asked Natalia.

Tears came to James' eyes. "Natalia..." But he couldn't finish his sentence. He closed his eyes for a moment, struggling to compose himself. "I love you, Natalia. You know that, right?"

"Oh," answered Natalia. "Where is Evan?" she asked again.

"He will come visit you later today," answered James.

"You're such a good friend to be here with me, James."

"I am your husband, Natalia, of course I am here," answered James quietly, looking at the floor.

"You're my husband?" answered Natalia, her body growing rigid. "Where is Evan…"

"Just enjoy your shower, darling," said James. "Afterwards you can slip into your favorite lounge outfit I brought for you from home and when you are comfortably in bed again, we will call for Evan."

But by the time Natalia was dressed and in bed again, she was so tired, she lay back and fell sound asleep.

THE NEXT MORNING, EVAN WAS THERE to see Natalia bright and early, with a serious expression on his face.

"Good morning, Natalia, how are you feeling today?" he asked, rocking backwards and forwards on his heels next to her bed where she sat cross-legged drinking a cup of coffee.

"I feel great," answered Natalia, setting her coffee cup down and standing up to hug Evan. "I am ready to get out of here and go home with my husband."

"You miss James," said Evan.

"Evan, I don't have any feelings towards James. I am very much in love with my husband, with you," said Natalia, leaning in to kiss Evan.

"What, Natalia, no," Evan interjected, grabbing Natalia's shoulders and holding her back from kissing him. "James is your husband."

Scrutinizing Evan's face for earnestness, Natalia asked, "Is that true? Really? James is my husband?"

"James is your husband."

"But then, what are you doing here, what, but, I…oh," stammered Natalia, spying the framed photo next to her bed of herself and

James hugging Anna, Allan, and Ben. Pink spread up Natalia's neck and into her cheeks.

"I'm sorry, Evan, I feel so confused. I, well, we aren't married? It was all a dream then."

The intensity of pounding in Natalia's head increased.

"Oh, Evan, stop looking so anxious! I know I suffered a blow to the head, but I am sure you heard the brain trauma was not severe. I'm going to be fine, maybe better even than before."

Evan sat down on the edge of the bed. "Yes, but what else did the doctor tell you?"

Natalia looked down at the bed.

"Natalia?"

"He said that my symptoms..." She stopped and took the notebook from her bedside table, reading out of it. "Dear Natalia, your symptoms are invisible now, but they are there. Even though you don't need the physical therapy anymore, you will continue to have problems with learning new information, with concentrating, and with your memory. Confusion is normal. You could experience chronic headaches, depression, or anxiety and have trouble sleeping."

Natalia put down the notebook and looked up at Evan expectantly.

"Do you remember the accident? It's okay if you don't," Evan rushed.

"No. I don't remember. The doctor said a car hit me in Zürich. What was I doing in Zürich?" asked Natalia.

"You were helping Mary work a charity event that she was putting on," replied Evan, taking her hand.

"That's right! I remember now." Natalia bounced to her knees on the bed. "I was putting on a charity event with Mary. We were there together. But James hit you and then Eva—" Natalia gasped. "Eva hit me! That must have happened before I was hit by the car!"

"What? Eva hit you? Wait. Slow down. James didn't hit me," answered Evan. "I wasn't even there. I was taking care of our kids."

"Yes, you hit James. You punched him in front of everyone at the charity event."

"Natalia. Please listen. I was taking care of your and my kids that night at your house. Do you remember that?"

"What? No. My parents were taking care of the kids…" Natalia looked at Evan for affirmation.

Evan shook his head.

"I don't want to talk anymore," said Natalia. She lay down on her bed and rolled away from Evan, closing her eyes. The dream had all been so real, she was having a hard time letting it go, especially as there were so many gaps in her memory from before the car hitting her. She was automatically filling any gaps with information from her dream.

"Listen, I want you to know I will be here for you, no matter what. Remember the doctor said it is normal that you are confused. Perhaps it's best if I stop visiting for a while and give you and James some space to work through this together. He is your husband. You still love him, don't you?"

"No. James doesn't love me. I could sense it from the moment he walked in the room when I awoke from the coma. I saw it in his eyes. And the way he just stood there, not reaching for me. He didn't even take my hand in his."

Natalia began to cry. She turned around and grabbed Evan's hand, pulling him toward her. Evan lay down next to Natalia and took her in his arms. She cried herself to sleep. Still he lay there holding her, listening to her even breathing, until the nurse came to take Natalia to her next therapy session.

In the following days Natalia's life fell into a predictable rhythm. She woke up and ate breakfast in stilted silence with James, who came to visit her very early before going to work. Afterwards she had physical therapy and yoga. Evan came to spend time with her mid-morning. She had lunch and a nap, after which she had a therapy session to strengthen her cognitive functioning. Her parents brought the children to see her in the afternoon. Natalia could shower on her own, brush her teeth, and find her way around the hospital. Every day she asked when she could go home to her children.

ONE MORNING EVAN, NOT JAMES, was there bright and early for a visit. "I have been working up the courage to talk to you about why you ended up in a coma for days now. I decided the best way to explain is in a letter," said Evan while rubbing the back of his neck.

"But I know how I ended up in coma, Evan. I was hit by a car," answered Natalia.

"There is more you need to know," replied Evan, handing Natalia the letter for her to read.

As Natalia unfolded the paper and began to read. Evan sat down next to her on the bed.

Dear Natalia,

You married James eleven years ago. You have three children together: Anna, 8, Allan, 4, and Ben, 2. You worked for many years in Zürich in consulting but quit three years ago to be at home full time. Recently you were considering going back to work. I am married to Eva, your good friend, and we have three girls together, Holly, 7, Lauren, 5, and Lindsay, 3.

You and I have become best friends over the years. We have spent many hours together with the children. You have been the best friend I could ever ask for. I do not know when I fell in love with you, but I know I have loved you for a long time now. No, nothing physical ever happened between us and I never told you I was in love with you.

Eva and James were having an affair. You caught them together at the hotel the night you were working the charity benefit with Mary and Mike, to see if you wanted to take the job they had offered you to work at Elegant Events. Seeing James and Eva kissing shocked you; you fled out of the front doors of the hotel and into the pathway of a car, which hit you. You were taken to this hospital and were in a coma for a number of days.

I know this is a lot to take in; it is especially unfair for someone suffering from brain trauma. But you need to know everything to move forward with your life. James and Eva are in love. But what is important is regardless we are all going to work together to take care of the children, all our children, and importantly, you.

We all love you. We want you to be able to come home. So my family and I, with your permission, are going to move in with you, James, Anna, Allan and Ben. I love you, Natalia, I want to take care of you. James and Eva still will have long hours to work at their very demanding jobs, but on Saturdays they will be home with you and the children. The rest of the time I will be there to take care of you and the children.

Yours,

Evan

Natalia dropped the letter onto the bed. "It's a dream," she said.

"No, Natalia, this is real what I wrote. All of it," he replied, taking a deep breath.

"I believe you," answered Natalia. "I mean you hitting James. It was in my dream. When I was in the coma I had the most extraordinary dream. I may not remember the weeks of my life leading up to the accident, but I remember every moment of my dream. I dreamed I was married to you and we had three children together, Nick, Nathan, and Annabelle. I owned an event planning business in Zürich. James was married to Eva. They had children of their own."

Tilting his head to one side, Evan asked, "Really? You dreamed you were married to me?"

Nodding her head, Natalia reached for Evan's hand. "Yes. While in the coma I dreamed that all of my recent wishes had come true. I had married you instead of James, I owned a thriving event planning business in Zürich, and I was confident, competent, and strong. I could afford any designer dress or handbag I possibly wanted. Mary and I ate and stayed at some of the most exclusive restaurants and hotels in Zürich during our work. I had a new and fabulous life."

Taking a fortifying breath and placing a hand to her heart, Natalia continued, "But my children were missing; of course they were missing; I had married you instead of James. We had beautiful children together in the dream, but my Anna, Allan, and Ben were gone. I kept asking, 'Where are my children?' First I asked the question aloud. Then the question cycled over and over again in my mind, like a drum pounding in rhythm with my heartbeat.

"Seeing my children when I awoke from my coma, from my dream, filled me with such intense joy. My brain injury, waking up hurting in this hospital, my confusion, all of it together couldn't lessen how lucky I felt to be with my kids again," said Natalia, wiping tears off her cheeks.

"I understand," answered Evan. "Whenever I think about if Eva and I should have married, especially since I found about the affair, I always come to the same conclusion. If I hadn't married Eva, I wouldn't have my children. And I wouldn't trade them for anything."

"Exactly. When I woke up I knew."

"What? What did you know?" asked Evan.

"We come into the world cherishing love above all else. We thirst for beauty, we are sensitive to wonder and joy. I think that is why we crave children. We are craving answers; we are searching for meaning in this life, to our existence. If we let them, our children, open us to wonder, they chase us to joy and push us to the limit of our capacities. They test our ability to love unconditionally. There isn't anything more important than loving children. Not just your own. Any children you have in your life."

"I feel that way too. You know I love your children like my own," said Evan, gazing into her eyes.

Wrapping her arms around Evan she said, "Oh, Evan, what are we going to do now? I literally feel like tiny bugs are crawling all over my skin at the thought of sharing a home with James again."

"I can be your happy ending," said Evan, bringing his lips to hers.

"No. No man is ever the happily ever after that women are looking for," answered Natalia, pushing him gently away.

"Thanks a lot!" answered Evan.

"Well, what boy grows up listening to stories where the action figure meets superwoman and that is how he lives happily ever after?" asked Natalia. "There is love, beauty, and wonder to experience. And there is so much to learn, so many ways to grow and stretch ourselves to feel we are adding value to the world. The action figure manages to get the girl along the way in some story-lines, but he always finds the courage to save the world in some way in all of them."

"Okay, okay, I get it," said Evan, grinning.

Natalia rested her head against Evan's chest, listening to his heartbeat, smelling his clean scent.

"Someday I will tell you more about the dream. When I have more energy, when we have unlimited time, maybe a bottle of wine to share. Of course we had our own story in the dream, but I also dreamed a lot about working at my business and about Mary. Oh!" exclaimed Natalia. "Who is taking care of my event planning business while I am in here?"

Evan rubbed Natalia's arm reassuringly. "I wrote that in the letter, Natalia. You have been working as a full-time mom for the past three years, you don't have your own business. Mary owns an event planning company in Zürich. You went to help her execute a charity event at a hotel in Zürich the evening of the accident. You were considering taking a part time job at Elegant Events. Perhaps that is why you dreamed what you did."

"Oh, so Mary owns the business?" asked Natalia. "She offered me a job to work for her?"

Evan nodded.

Natalia was quiet for a long time.

"I like my version better," laughed Natalia. "I would rather be her boss than Mary be mine. She's bossy enough as an employee; she's probably unbearable as a boss."

Evan smiled at her. "It's good to hear you laughing."

"I feel happy. Oh well. I don't have my own business. Oh, but James offered me a job as a partner at his consulting company," said Natalia, breaking into a big grin.

Evan cleared his throat, reaching up to rub the back of his neck.

"I really don't think that happened, Natalia."

"Well, I am pretty sure..." began Natalia. Stopping in mid-sentence, she looked at Evan.

"So you get to go home in a few days, are you excited?" asked Evan.

Natalia reached out and traced Evan's jaw line, then patted him on the chest. "You're changing the subject, Evan. He didn't offer me a partnership at his consultancy, did he?"

"Well, even if he had," began Evan uncertainly, "you have some work to do on your cognitive functioning and recovery before you would be able to handle that kind of work again. And would you really like to spend so many hours away from your kids right now? Especially considering how much they have missed you?"

"Oh," said Natalia, her smile faltering, her shoulders rounding forward. "Well, I want to be with my kids, but I want to work too. I want to be a happy mom and therefore I need something else in my life besides them. And I want to set an example for my daughter that women can work and be successful too."

"Let's talk to your neuropsychologist, okay? It sounds like going back to work is really important to you. So we can ask her how you can start working towards that goal. Maybe we could even call Mary, see if you could start soon working for her a morning a week and work up from there?"

"Oh, did you hear about Mary's engagement to Mike?" asked Natalia, trying to mask her disappointment that she had a long road of recovery ahead of her.

"Has Mary been in to see you since you awoke from the coma?"

"No. Not that I recall."

"Then how do you know that Mike proposed to Mary?" asked Evan.

"She told me at my office..." began Natalia. Shaking her head Natalia said, "Wait, but that was a dream, right? So how do I know Mary is engaged to Mike?"

"I have no idea," replied Evan with raised eyebrows. "Unless..."

"What?" asked Natalia, leaning forward,

"Unless Mary came to see you and told you and you forgot all about the visit. You were very confused when you first awoke from your coma," replied Evan while reaching up and smoothing the hair back from Natalia's face.

"Mary was in to see you once after you awoke and many times while you were in the coma. She talked to you for hours while you were under the surface. Quite a few times Mike came with her to see you too. She had a lot of events to plan and I didn't like how much time she was spending on her phone working on events here with you while you were in the coma. But I didn't say anything."

"I talked with Mary just yesterday. She called me and wanted to know how you were doing. She said she wanted to come and visit you, but that Mike had just broken off their engagement. She said she had lied to him and he found out," said Evan, shifting from foot to foot in agitation. "She doesn't know what she is going to do; she just recently made Mike an equal partner in her business. I told her I thought it best if she came to visit you once you were home again, since she is so upset right now and has so much to work out. I told her I thought you would understand."

"That can't be true. I convinced Mike to give Mary a chance to tell him the truth! I should call Mike. I could explain to him again. I can get him to understand," began Natalia, with tears running down her face, completely unaware of the tears in Evan's own eyes, of how hard the conversation was for him.

"It isn't possible, Natalia," Evan insisted. "You are still so confused. You need to be patient and be willing to work hard to recover before you can help others. You might end up doing more harm than good."

Natalia fell silent.

"So, are you okay with Eva and I moving in to help out, given that Eva and James have had an affair?" asked Evan.

"No. I don't know if that is a good idea."

"Think it over," said Evan," and I will see you tomorrow."

NATALIA HEARD ALLAN, BEN, AND ANNA. She opened her eyes with a smile on her face, joy pulsing to the tips of her toes. Anna and Allan came bounding into the room and jumped onto the bed, wrapping their arms around Natalia and shouting, "Mommy, we missed you!"

Ben hovered at the door, before running and climbing up on the bed next to Natalia as well, snuggling in close.

"I have missed you three so very much," said Natalia, pulling her children close.

"How are you feeling, sweetheart?" asked John, entering the room and approaching the bed. He gently smoothed the hair out of Natalia's eyes and kissed her cheek.

"Daddy! You came to see me," said Natalia smiling. "I have missed you so much."

"I visited you numerable times while you were in the coma, honey. You looked just like a sleeping angel," replied John. "I held your hand and talked to you for hours. When I wasn't here, either your mother, Evan, Mary, Mike, Eva or James were here by your side."

"Where is my beautiful daughter?" called out Bren a few minutes later. "There she is! Children, get down from there and give your mom space to breathe."

"No," shouted Natalia. The children looked up, startled. Natalia hugged her children closer to her and repeated firmly, "No. I want them up here next to me."

Turning to John, Bren commanded, "John, go take the kids for an ice cream. I need to talk to Natalia about her future plans when she goes home from the hospital."

"No. I want my children to stay here, with me. They just arrived," insisted Natalia.

"Okay. I will take the children for a snack," agreed John reluctantly, "and give you two a chance to talk."

"Now," began Bren, once the children were out of the room, "you will be able to go home soon, but your father and I need to go back to work or we will lose our jobs. We have already used up all our holiday and sick days. I explained this to James and he told me that he has devised a plan involving Eva and Evan moving in with you to help out. I told him that is just crazy, given the circumstances, and I will not allow it.

"If you had been working this wouldn't be such a dilemma. You would have a daycare for your children or a nanny to care for them. You would have paid sick leave from your job so you could recover. All we would need to hire is an excellent cleaning service. But since you don't have a job, there are no childcare arrangements to rely upon."

Natalia just stared at her mother for a moment, utterly transfixed. *Does she know how she sounds?* Although Natalia did have to admit her mother was right. If she had a job, she would have someone to take care of the children during the week. What would she do when she went home? She knew she wouldn't be fit enough to take care of them for some time. Natalia's pulse began to race, her head to pound. Glancing over, she noticed the bright yellow roses on her bedside table that Evan had brought her that morning. *Evan. Evan will help me,* thought Natalia, her ragged breath beginning to even.

"Mom," said Natalia, "I am thankful to you and Dad for coming and taking care of the kids while I have been in the hospital."

"Of course, honey," began Bren, breaking into a smile.

Interrupting her, Natalia said, "But it isn't my fault I was in an accident and I now need someone to care for my children and me. And if you are not going to be the one to help me when I get home, then I am not interested in your opinion of those who are trying to devise a plan to do so."

"Natalia, I explained that I will lose my job if I stay," said Bren.

"It is fine, Mom. Really, I think it is for the best. You criticize me in every conversation we have. You either disagree with my life choices or are disparaging my performance. Right now I just need to be around people who support me, who make me feel loved, and who value me for who I am," replied Natalia.

"Oh, Natalia," said Bren, her hands to her cheeks, "I do love you."

"Then start choosing your words more carefully," insisted Natalia.

Bren took a step toward her daughter, reaching out a hand, and then fell back as John walked in with the children.

"Hello, sweetheart, everything worked out?" asked John.

"You are leaving me," replied Natalia in a choked voice.

"No! You are more important to me than any job," said John, looking directly into her eyes. "I will stay and take care of you and the kids. Of course I will."

"That means a lot, Dad. Really. You love your job. I don't want to cause you to lose it. Evan is going to help out to begin with. We can see how that goes and I will call you if I need you. Okay?"

"Well, if you are sure," muttered John, rubbing his chin,

Natalia nodded, turning her attention back to her children and listening to them chatter about their activities and friends. It felt like a fraction of a moment and they were already leaving her to go home for dinner. Just like that Natalia's heart darkened. Alone in the hospital room, she wondered how many days she had left until she could go home to her children.

"HELLO LOVELY, HOW DID YOU SLEEP?" asked Evan, entering the room with a smile on his face. Evan stood in front of the bed, shifting from leg to leg. "So, did you give the idea of Eva, the kids, and I moving in to help you some thought?"

Natalia nodded silently.

Evan waited for her answer, and when she failed to give one, buried his hands in his pockets and took a deep breath before saying, "You never said anything was wrong with your marriage before the accident, Natalia. You said you hated him working so many hours, that the kids missed him. I was the one complaining so bitterly about my marriage. Perhaps you and James could work things out."

Natalia massaged her forehead in silence

"I think this is all far too much. It is too fast, too soon. I am going to go," said Evan, kissing her on the forehead.

"No!" shouted Natalia, grasping his arm. "Just wait. Let me think."

Evan perched on the edge of the bed, his foot jangling. Five minutes later he sighed.

"James was always working, he was never home. And even when he was at home, well, we just, started touching each other less," began Natalia, her face reddening. "We stopped giving each other a kiss or hug hello or goodbye. Lovers, they touch each other when they pass by one another in the hall, or while working together in the kitchen. They give each other a quick kiss, or touch each other's hair. They go to take the other's hand while walking. They put their hand on the lower back of their love at a cocktail party, that sort of thing. Or they even playfully push each other out of the way, but they touch," said Natalia with closed eyes. Opening them, she looked at Evan for understanding.

Evan nodded at her and she continued, "James worked so late and was so tired when he came home, he was rarely interested in the trivialities of my day. We stopped talking years ago. He stopped doing the little kinds of things for me, the tiny things that say I love you, like bringing me a cup of tea, or a glass of wine. I felt like he didn't see me anymore. I felt like my presence wasn't necessary, like I didn't bring any value to his life."

Evan drew Natalia into his arms.

"Why didn't you ever say anything?" he asked.

"How do you bring something like that up? It wasn't like we ever had one big fight. The hurt and recriminations built up so slowly, the distance between us grew year by year until we were no longer best friends, no longer lovers. I guess I just accepted some of the responsibility for it. He was a terrible friend to me for years and years. Yet I continued to try to do everything right, to be the perfect mother, create and maintain a beautiful home, be the most thoughtful friend, be the ideal hostess for his parties, keep my best possible figure so he would find me attractive, but none of it worked…." Natalia trailed off, lost in thought. Shaking herself, she turned and looked at Evan. "Last year I stopped acting loving too. For years and years I tried to be the perfect wife and I decided, well, that I could exhaust myself chasing after him, but he would always be just out of my reach. I couldn't catch him. He wasn't ever going to stop, turn, and look at me with love in his eyes. Did he ever? I can't remember."

"Oh, Natalia," sighed Evan.

"Don't feel sorry for me," said Natalia.

"Natalia, I think you are the loveliest woman on the planet. If I had only known, I would have stolen you away from that idiot faster than you can blink," exclaimed Evan.

Natalia lowered her chin, relaxing her shoulders. Taking a deep breath, she said without looking up, "What about Eva?'"

"What?" asked Evan.

"Don't you think Eva is the loveliest woman on the plant?'"

"I did," affirmed Evan. "Until I met you."

"She's your wife," said Natalia, punching a pillow. "You don't need to be here, Evan. I know you are angry with Eva because of the affair, but you could try to work things out. Think of your children. I can recover without your help. I can do this myself. Take care of Eva and your little ones. I can get better on my own."

"No you can't," said Evan. "You'll need help."

"Well, James will just have to do it then. He deserves having to help me, after what he did," said Natalia.

"I didn't want to give up on my marriage," insisted Evan. "I wanted to try and make it work. But I just couldn't. Obviously. Since we have been fighting for years. And Eva has been having an affair with James. Whether we end up together or not, Eva and I are over as lovers, but for the sake of my children I will work like hell to maintain a friendship with the woman," said Evan through gritted teeth, punching the pillow.

"Natalia, I have been in love with you for years now. Now I am free to acknowledge it. Our children deserve happy parents. Listen, I have to go pick up my kids, okay. Just, how do I make you understand?" Evan asked, standing up. "You might forget this conversation. I am going to write you a letter, okay?"

Taking a pen and the notebook from her table, Evan sat down and wrote for ten minutes. Handing Natalia the letter, he kissed her once again on the forehead and rushed from the room.

Natalia got up and stretched. She took the letter, but then lay down on the bed, closing her eyes for just a moment. She was so very tired.

HOURS LATER NATALIA AWAKENED to a darkened room. Switching on a light, she reached for the letter.

Dear Natalia,

Yes, I loved you before, but I love you now too. What does this mean? It means your very existence brings value to my life. It means that when you fully recover, whether you choose to be with me, or James, or go out in the world and fall in love with someone else, I will always have a place for you in my heart. Above all else, it means that I want the best for our children. We talked innumerable times about how our children came first in our lives, that we wanted to give them the gift of a beautiful childhood full of fond memories and love. I will work to give that gift to all of our children in the next year, while you recover.

I have some difficult emotions to work through against James and Eva, but in the end, I think it best for you, and critically, for your children and my own, that we all live together until you are well so I can take care of you all. Then, when the doctors are certain you can take on your life with full functioning, you will decide what you think is best for you and your family.

Do you want to go and work in consulting again? Work for Mary and Mike? Own your own business? I support you. Dream big, Natalia; chase your dreams with hard work. I will cheer you on every step of the way. After all, life is short and life is precious. Your accident and talking with you in the past few days have made me hyper aware that we need to chase after love, fall into wonder and stretch to help others in the time we are given.

Being able to take care of you, it is not what James deserves. It is what I deserve because I love you. Yes, it will be hard; I'm no idiot. But I want it to be me. Let it be me; let me show you how much I love you.

Yours,

Evan

Natalia lay down on her bed and cried. She cried out of happiness that someone loved her, regardless of her injury, or how she had permanently changed because of it. She cried because it would be hard, her road to recovery, and because she didn't want anyone to have to help her. She cried because her husband had betrayed her; he had fallen in love with not just another woman, but one of her good friends. She cried because she missed her children, and felt a loss at not being able to be there for them. She cried because it tired her to be so confused so much of the time. She cried for the months of memories she had lost. She cried at the loss of the business she had thought was her own, at the opportunity to go back to work in consulting as a senior partner that was an illusion. She cried until her pillow was drenched, and then she fell asleep.

When Natalia awoke the first thing she saw was the stack of books Evan had brought her from home. The middle book looked familiar. Pulling it out, she flipped randomly through it. She came to a page and read the passage highlighted in the middle of the page.

"Feeling sorry for yourself consumes energy that could be used to turn your life around." -Dr. Goulston

Natalia put down the book.

Well, I could have died and I didn't, she thought. *Time to move forward.* Picking up her notebook, she reread Evan's letters.

Dropping the notebook, Natalia took out her phone.

```
Hello James, Yes, Evan told me about us all
living together. Okay for now. I want my own
room. -Natalia

Hello Eva, I can't believe you slept with
James. Yes, I know you will be moving into my
house. Don't get too comfortable. -Natalia

Hello Mary, How are you? Please, please tell
Mike the truth. He loves you. He'll give you
another chance. Please, please go talk to
Mike; I really hope you can work things out.
-Love, Natalia

PS. I would like to accept your job offer.
The doctor said I could be ready in as little
as three months to start working part time.
```

Dear Evan, Sometimes we need to dream our way into a better reality. Let's start our life together. -Love, Natalia

ABOUT THE AUTHOR

Heather Lenz was born and raised in Boise, Idaho. After graduating with a degree in International Studies, she married her Swiss soul mate eight months after meeting him and moved to Switzerland. After completing an MBA, she worked for five years in marketing. She currently lives in Romanshorn, Switzerland, with her husband, daughter, and two sons. This is her first book.

www.heathernadinelenz.com

www.ingramcontent.com/pod-product-compliance
Lightning Source LLC
Chambersburg PA
CBHW022155170626
46807CB00005B/2217